BOOKS IN THE RENEGADE STAR UNIVERSE

Renegade Star Series:

Renegade Star

Renegade Atlas

Renegade Moon

Renegade Lost

Renegade Fleet

Renegade Earth

Renegade Dawn

Renegade Children

Renegade Union

Renegade Empire (April 2019)

Standalones:

Nameless: A Renegade Star Story

The Constable

The Constable Returns (April 2019)

The Orion Colony Series:

Orion Colony

Orion Uncharted

Orion Awakened

The Last Reaper Series:

The Last Reaper

Fear the Reaper

Blade of the Reaper (April 2019)

STAY UP TO DATE

Chaney posts updates, official art, previews, and other awesome stuff on his website. You can also follow him on Instagram, Facebook, and Twitter.

Search for **JN Chaney's Renegade Readers** on Facebook to join the group where readers can come together and share their lives and interests, especially regarding Chaney's books.

For updates about new releases, as well as exclusive promotions, sign up for the VIP mailing list. Head there now to receive a free copy of *The Other Side of Nowhere*.

https://www.subscribepage.com/organic

Enjoying the series? Help others discover the Variant Saga by leaving a review on Amazon.

THE LAST REAPER

BOOK 1 IN THE LAST REAPER SERIES

J.N. CHANEY

SCOTT MOON

CONTENTS

List of Acronyms	1
Chapter 1	3
Chapter 2	17
Chapter 3	31
Chapter 4	49
Chapter 5	59
Chapter 6	79
Chapter 7	93
Chapter 8	111
Chapter 9	123
Chapter 10	131
Chapter 11	153
Chapter 12	171
Chapter 13	177
Chapter 14	185
Chapter 15	195
Chapter 16	203
Chapter 17	213
Chapter 18	225
Chapter 19	235
Chapter 20	245
Chapter 21	253
Chapter 22	261
Chapter 23	273
Chapter 24	279
Chapter 25	287
Chapter 26	297
Chapter 27	309
Chapter 28	319
Chapter 29	331

Chapter 30   339
Chapter 31   353
Chapter 32   363

Get a Free Book   369
Books in the Renegade Star Universe   371
About The Authors   373

For all the Renegade Readers. You made this possible.
-J.N. Chaney

This book is dedicated to all the readers and writers at Keystroke Medium. Without your support and encouragement, I wouldn't be where I am today. Thank you!
-Scott Moon

LIST OF ACRONYMS

- **AI**—Artificial intelligence
- **AWOL**—Absent without leave
- **BMSP**—Bluesphere Maximum Security Prison —Ultramax IX
- **CD**—Climbdown Day
- **CIM**—Computerized Inmate Monitor
- **CV**—Curriculum Vitae
- **DM**—Dreadmax Marines (inmates on Dreadmax, often falsely imprisoned, who have prior military experience and protect people from gangs and cannibals)
- **Feg**—Fredrick Eugene Grady
- **HDK**—Highly Destructive Kinetic (weapon / rifle)
- **HDK 4**—Shortened (11 inch barrel--from the

trigger assembly) HDK commonly used by spec ops and law enforcement

- **HDK 4 Dominator**—Full length (16 inch barrel--from the trigger assembly) HDK with double high capacity magazines and a grenade launcher under the barrel)
- **HUD**—Heads up display
- **LAI**—Limited artificial intelligence
- **LED**—Light Emitting Diode
- **LZ**—Landing zone
- **MRE**—Meals Ready to Eat
- **NG**—Nightfall Gangsters
- **QRF**—Quick reaction force
- **RC**—Reaper Corps
- **RSG**—Red Skull Gangsters
- **SD** regulator—Slip drive regulator
- **UFS**—Union Fleet Ship
- **UPG**—Union Prison Guard
- **X-37**—Halek Cain's Reaper AI (limited)
- **YT**—Galdiz 49 rifle, sniper model. (YT is a randomly generated model number)

1

"GET BACK IN YOUR CELL, CONVICT," ordered the guard while jerking his thumb.

I didn't know the man's name, only that he was an ugly jackass who—at two-forty—outweighed me by twenty pounds. I liked to think I was lean and mean, just the type of death row inmate guards should respect.

But they didn't. Because they were assholes.

I hated assholes. And bullies. And guards. And anyone associated with the Union. My mood always sucked after a bad night with the restraint on my cybernetic left arm. No one wanted me running around with the ultimate shank.

Death row was seriously cramping my style. Living with electric disruption of my hardware was a tingly slice of hell.

The constant pulsing of the sub-dermal disruptor felt like a continual drip of lactic acid into my shoulder and upper back. One of my eyes was artificial, loaded with upgrades that had made me really good at my former job. Whenever I tried to use these features now, a computerized monitor would flood my bloodstream with nausea-inducing meds.

Super unpleasant. And because the Union restraint specialists were sadists, the effect always lasted an hour beyond the offense that triggered the pukefest.

Worse than anything they could do to me were the nightmares associated with why I had the prosthetic.

If my jackbooted babysitters understood what I was, they'd ask for a transfer—maybe sue the warden for putting them in mortal danger and causing all the stress that came with guarding the devil.

"The buzzer hasn't sounded," I said, aware this wasn't what the man wanted to hear from me.

It was pretty damn clear he didn't know what to do now. Clenching one fist on his stun baton didn't intimidate me, and he knew it. His taunts were lame, and I had stopped giving a fuck a long time ago. So he stood there stinking like cheap tobacco smoke, trying to slow his beating heart.

I resented him for his poor taste in cigars as much as anything else.

A vein pulsed in his neck. His eyes were too wide. He sweated like a whore in church.

"It's about to go off," he said, then looked over his shoulder toward the control station where the riot team waited, even though there weren't enough people in this wing of the Bluesphere Maximum Security Prison—Ultramax IX—to stage an uprising.

It was mostly just me.

"But it hasn't gone off," I countered.

"Why do you argue every time? Makes me look like a punk."

"And there's your answer," I said.

"You better check yourself," he told me. "Ever felt a stun baton across the bridge of your nose?"

"Not today, I haven't," I answered.

He sputtered nonsense, clearly out of insults.

The klaxon alarm overhead that I'd come to dread more than the bad food, shitty plumbing, and lack of Starbrand Cigars, blared with eardrum-damaging force.

I smiled sarcastically. "Happy?"

"Get back in your cell! Do it now!" he commanded.

"You're glad it's time, be honest," I said, goading the beefy man as I retreated into the small vacation home they kept telling me was a five-by-five cell with locked doors. "You don't really want a shot at the title. You're all talk, no walk."

He was relatively new at BMSP—Ultramax IX. Been there about a month. If he'd been one of the regular guards, we'd have more of a history. All we'd done so far was call each other names.

He pushed out his chest. "One of these days I'm gonna educate you."

"Zero fucks given," I said, staring him down. "Go back to your circle jerk."

The bars slammed shut. Why were there bars instead of stainless steel blast doors? Because the Union was cheap.

Never mind that Union spec ops—dark ops specifically —had made me who I was… right before they fucked me.

Their mistake. No one in the Reaper Corps had the foresight to offer a decent retirement option. Now I was too dangerous to release and too valuable to kill.

I hoped.

Not like BMSP death row was a vacation paradise. Probably better than being dead, but not by much. What was an honest killer like me gonna do?

I knew all about the guard's dialect, and could guess right where he'd grown up, give or take.

I was from the same sort of neighborhood. After I left, I learned that the local gangs had made my mother a widow, so I slipped off post for a few weeks to put the worst of them down. From there, presto—death row for one unman-ageable liability to the Union.

Kiss my ass. Train me as a killer specializing in infiltra-tion and assassination and what did they think I would do?

Please.

The guard stared at me like he expected something to happen.

"What?" I asked, cocking my brow.

"You know *what.* Plug in or I'll get ten of my friends

and do it for you," he said, trying his best to look intimidating.

"You'd need them." I was bored with this guy, so I picked up the earbud and put it in. It was actually just an antenna for nerve-ware. The ultra-soft construction wasn't for my comfort. The security experts of Ultramax IX were worried I'd find a way to weaponize a bead of silicon.

Like I'd do that.

"Happy?" I asked, ignoring the brief struggle between my Computerized Inmate Monitor, or CIM, and X-37, the Reaper nerve-ware the warden's doctors couldn't remove even if they had known about it.

"Ecstatic," he said, glaring. "Now go play with yourself. I'll be at Gisela's to see some girls."

"What's your name, guard?" I asked.

He wrinkled his lips at the question. "UPG 1592."

"Your parents must've hated you," I said.

"That's my badge number: Union Prison Guard 1592," he said, very seriously.

I stared until he realized I was mocking him. "I pieced that together, but thanks, 1592."

Snorting profanity, he turned his back on me and dragged his stun club along the bars of other prisoner cells while walking back to the control booth.

"You think I could take him, X?" I asked out loud.

"I am not here to stroke your ego," said X. The CIM inputs created sound via vibrations of my inner ear, a technique that could be used for compliance through pain. I had X-37 turn that feature off while convincing the CIM it was still shocking the shit out of me.

"What about him and the riot squad?" I asked, climbing into my bunk.

"My advice, Reaper Cain—don't push your luck," said X.

I leaned back and smiled, going straight into a structured daydream designed to keep me sane. The smell of tobacco smoke filled my nostrils as my fingers twisted an imaginary Starbrand cigar. Staring at the ceiling, I reminded myself who I was and why this place would never beat me.

My name is Halek Cain, formerly a Reaper in the Union dark ops. So what if I was on death row? Absolutely nothing would break my mind, least of all the guards or the inmates. I would find a way to beat them all, and I'd do it with a smile on my face.

The bastards should have killed me.

"INMATE CAIN, it is thirty-nine seconds past reveille." The CIM's cheap, slightly digitized voice was my constant companion, almost as annoying as the electric disruption of my cybernetics. The implant had one job—monitor my every move and mood. Behavior modification was something the warden added against senate approval.

I didn't blame the man. He was smart. Not ruthless enough to have me killed, but he did his best to be a prick.

The Reaper nerve-ware allowed the crude tech to do its thing, preferring to lurk in the digital shadows until needed, like I normally did during long infiltration missions.

Sometimes, I think X antagonizes the CIM, urging it to give me a hard time or generally make my life difficult. Maybe I'm anthropomorphizing both of the limited AIs. But maybe not. Stranger things have happened.

"Inmate Cain, it is now forty-nine seconds past reveille. Get out of bed and perform the required daily hygiene outlined in regulation 0450-a-1," said the CIM.

"What's in it for me?" I asked.

"Proper hygiene is good for your body, Inmate Cain. More importantly, rules are rules. Time to get up. I must harass you until you sit up, wash your face, brush your teeth, and have a bowel…"

"Yeah, yeah, yeah. I'm up," I groaned.

"You have a meeting with Warden James Esquire III at 0830 hours. Regulations require you to groom and present yourself at the bars at precisely 0815, Union Standard Time," continued the CIM in its tinny inflection.

"What's in it for me?" I asked again.

"Repetitive questions will only delay your routine," the CIM said.

The damn thing was learning.

I brushed my teeth with paste from an edgeless wall

dispenser using my finger. Toothbrushes were far too dangerous for someone like me to possess. Everything I needed oozed from holes in the wall—toothpaste, body soap, food, and water. Twice a day, I got to put some of these gifts down a hole that opened at precisely 0755 and 1755 hours.

"You wanna answer, X, since I'm working so hard to make myself presentable?" I asked. "What's the warden so fired up about that CIM can't talk about it?"

"You will be offered a chance to leave Ultramax IX for forty-nine standard hours plus transit time," replied X-37.

I froze with one toothpaste-y finger still in my mouth. "Wha—"

"The warden will explain what you must do." This was CIM again. The rhythm of its digitized speech distinguished it from my more refined Reaper nerve-ware.

Shaking my head, I finished my morning rituals. "He already explained the only thing I had to do in here is die."

COMMANDER BRIGGS LEANED against the warden's desk with his arms and ankles crossed.

If the disrespectful posture bothered the warden, I couldn't tell. This man had spent most of his adult life in special operations. He'd gone to the Naval Academy on a netball scholarship and was slightly taller than me. None of the guys I'd served with during my time in spec ops had been burdened with beach muscles or pumped up with steroids and bro-split workouts the way the warden seemed to be.

Guys like this were strong as hell and could run and fight all day with no need for relief, or drag a sled full of gear across a harsh, alien landscape.

Commander Briggs was no different. He had most of the same scars as me, but nothing obvious unless you knew where to look—slash marks on his hands, a burn behind his left ear mostly covered by his short hair, and something in his eyes that was every bit as real as the physical damage a life at war had caused him.

Scars could be informative when you understood what they cost, what they really meant. Shrapnel gifted me with a vertical groove through my left eyebrow that continued down my cheek. My sergeant had told me to keep my visor down, but I was never very good at taking advice.

Oops.

I knew better than to mess with anyone from spec ops. I'd been there done that before getting plucked for dark ops, where my training not only got harder but weirder. Long story.

Not many people made it through Reaper training. Fewer stayed in the field half as long as I did. There weren't many of us left.

"Warden," Briggs said without looking at the man whose office he had invaded.

"Yes, Commander?"

"Get out."

James Esquire III, Warden of Bluesphere Maximum Security Prison, left without a word. The wood-paneled door clunked shut and sealed in a way that made it very clear it wasn't made from wood.

"Kind of gloomy in here," I said, stalling while I looked around and took stock of what was in the room. I suspected there was at least one recording device and perhaps a quick reaction force waiting behind a hidden door. "Mind if we turn on some lights?"

Briggs punched a button on the desk, illuminating the room. "You're quick. I bet you know everything about this room from that one glance. And I'm guessing you already have at least part of an escape plan formed based on that information."

"It's not my escape you should be worried about, but what I'd do before I attempted it."

"Like kill me?" he asked, nonchalantly.

Shrugging, I selected a leather couch and flopped down. Stretched out, I felt almost human—determined to forget about my tiny cell for as long as possible. "I don't really know you, so don't piss your pants. Besides, the warden's as much a prisoner here as I am. No one can get out of this office without permission. There's a door behind that stuffed gazelle. Did you replace his security team with your own quick reaction force?"

"What makes you think that's where the door is? Just looks like some tasteless taxidermy and a wall to me."

"The gazelle is cheap. The warden's not gonna want his

goons knocking over the tiger or the bear. And you can see where it's been moved. Wear marks on the floor." I waved a hand at the grooves dismissively. "Probably actually attached to the sliding door. What are we doing here, Commander?"

Briggs took a short tour of the room, popping his knuckles then rolling his neck. If I didn't know better, I'd think he was looking forward to a fight.

"You're on death row. I never liked you when you were with spec ops and didn't hear good things about your career after that. So let's not pretend we're going to be buddies. I'm here to offer you special treatment in return for certain services you might render the Union."

"Great. I've always wanted to go on another suicide mission," I replied sarcastically.

He ignored that. "I've read all of your mission debriefs and can tell you this will probably be a walk in the park for you."

"You act like I'm going to do it. Don't make assumptions. Life is easy here. Maybe someday I'll be executed, but how is that different than dying out there with you?"

Briggs laughed. "You're not gonna work with me. I'll watch your every move, sure. You'll take orders from me. But the last place you will be is with me on the battlefield. I don't trust anybody who's been in dark ops more than a week, and Reapers are freaks."

"And yet here we are," I said, spreading my hands wide.

Briggs stood near the couch at a slight angle that gave

him the advantage if I abandoned my extremely comfortable slouch to attack him. He looked bigger and more pissed off than when I first saw him by the desk.

"Let me shuck it down to the cob for you. I have a mission that you're going on—like it or not. In return, you get special treatment. All you have to do is recover one VIP from a tough spot."

"Tell me again what you mean by special treatment."

"I won't have you executed tomorrow."

"Oh! *Tomorrow*. You know what, that might be a relief. Let's do it. I want to see if you have the authority to quash my appeal that's been in limbo for two years."

"Don't test me," warned the commander, lowering his voice.

"There's a catch. Something you're not telling me. Hostage rescue is a mission that spec ops trains for. You don't need me."

He shrugged. "The individual in question is a doctor lost on a humanitarian mission. He's connected—not the type of person my bosses are going to forget about."

"Stop bullshitting me, or we're done," I said.

"The humanitarian mission was on Dreadmax."

"Dreadmax? You want me to infiltrate the place the warden threatens to send me if I misbehave? The place worse than death row at BMSP? Put me back in my cell. I have an appointment at 1755 hours."

"Godsdammit, Cain! I'm giving you a chance for a pardon and you're making toilet jokes. Drop the tough guy act and listen. You have the best infiltration record in the Union. Orders of magnitude more successful than anyone else in spec ops or dark ops combined. Better yet, you are, how can I say it, accustomed to incarceration," Briggs said.

I couldn't take this bullshit anymore, so I stood up. He stepped back, probably seeing the look on my face and wondering how many people I'd shanked since being in prison. "This place isn't a mouse fart compared to Dreadmax. Here we have asshole guards, unreasonable curfews, and shitty food. That place is probably run by cannibals and crazies by now. Whoever your VIP is, he's dead or worse. But most of all, you're forgetting what kind of infiltration I did."

"You brought people out of Glandar, Roxo III, and Kanick's World," he insisted.

"Those were kidnappings, except Roxo. That was an assassination and I only brought the body out as proof of death," I corrected.

"Pretend it's a kidnapping. Keep the principal alive, and it's no different."

"Dreadmax isn't like going to a planet," I said, thinking of the legendary environment shields covering parts of the station's surface.

"We have full schematics and state-of-the-art surveillance you can use to plan your infiltration and exfiltration route," he offered, as if that would sway me.

I wasn't even thinking about taking this deal, and he

probably knew it. "Schematics from when? When it was a system defense platform?"

His embarrassed expression told me I was right. Their intelligence on Dreadmax was shit. I'd be going in blind and without support. No matter what he said about this being easy compared to my prior missions, this was a one-way trip. He probably wanted me to find this lost puppy so he could send in his own teams and leave me there to die.

"We have the original architectural plans and the maintenance records up to the point it was turned into a correctional facility."

"Dumping ground, you mean."

"There is limited power, gravity, and life-support, so I seriously doubt the criminals we dropped in there have made a lot of changes."

I took a few seconds. "Briggs, you're a total son-of-a-bitch. You've got to know all of your troops hate your guts. Hell, it takes a certain type of officer to knowingly send men off to die, and you're exactly the kind to do it without a second thought. Far as I know, you're trying to march me into a suicide run."

"Think what you want, but the whole point of a mission like this is extraction. If you die, then the mission fails," he said, unmoved by my casual insults. "Give me an answer or I'm sending you back to your cell."

2

THE WARDEN's office was nice. Threats about having me executed seemed abstract and distant compared to having to leave. I walked around the room until I found the liquor cabinet and opened it. Pulling out a bottle, I looked over my shoulder at Briggs. "You mind?" I asked.

He glared at me. "Stop fucking around. You went AWOL and killed seventeen people. There's a reason you're on death row. Frankly, talking to you makes me want to toss my lunch." The commander's eyes lingered on my prosthetic—a deadly tool when the nerve-ware wasn't being disrupted by BMSP safety protocols.

I twisted the cork out, grinding my teeth and resisting the urge to turn the bottle into a weapon. He had to realize I could beat him to death before his QRF made it through the door. "They were gangsters and they murdered my father and a bunch of other people I grew up with. Bastards, every last one of them, and they deserved what I gave them."

"Doesn't matter what they did. That's why we have a justice system. You had no right to go full vigilante. You did, however, have an obligation to stay with your unit and follow orders."

"Briggs, my unit conducted counterinsurgencies, kidnappings, and assassinations. You're gonna honestly stand there and tell me there's a difference?" I raised my brow as we locked eyes. "Don't be so naive."

"You know there is," he answered, overlooking my use of his name instead of his title. "Screwed up as the galaxy might be, and no matter how unfair you think it is, society operates on law and order. You killed—"

"I've killed a lot more than seventeen people and you know it. Some of them"—I spared him a glance—"I killed for you."

He shrugged. "During a state of war, but those were never personal. Even if you ignore the law, that's that difference."

I drank from the bottle. The amber liquid burned all the way down.

He continued. "I didn't come here to ask you. You're doing this mission, one way or another."

I looked at the bottle of allegedly expensive whiskey. "Someone needs to tell the warden he got robbed. This is horse piss."

Briggs didn't take the bait. I put the bottle down and faced him. "Did you read the part of my file where I don't respond well to authority figures?"

"That's why I never liked you. When you were in spec ops, the officers were always complaining about your shitty attitude."

"I'm not doing your mission. Go get your little lost sheep yourself."

He sighed, pausing a moment before finally shaking his head. "Wrong answer, Cain."

———

As BEATINGS WENT, the one I received after telling Commander Briggs off was one for the record books. There was a lot of profanity and cracks about his mother and certain animals. Maybe I taunted the guards a bit more than I should have, but I didn't think it was a stretch to assume they enjoyed the company of wild boars. I mean, it certainly would have explained a few things.

Curling into a ball in the corner of my cell where I was sometimes allowed to take a less than private shower did nothing to stop the bleeding or slow the swelling. Something heavier than mist but less dense than actual water came down from the ceiling and rinsed a layer of the blood and grime from my face and body. It was cold, so I was confident it wasn't urine this time.

Fucking guards.

I couldn't blame this on Briggs, no matter what kind of unfair asshole he was. Spec ops doesn't stoop to bullying. They'd have given me a chance to fight back. Code of honor and all that.

Regardless, I was a fucking mess right now and seriously wondered if a different answer would have saved me a beating. Hadn't had one like this in months.

Boot marks decorated my body. I held up my left arm and examined it, the worst of my pain originating there. The tread impressions were nearly perfect. I could track a man across a planet from prints like that.

Breathe, Cain. Forget about it. Figure out what you need to do.

As I lay there, my mind swam with options while I tried to work out what to do next. I was damn sure about two things: I was sick of this place, and Commander Briggs wasn't going to take no for an answer. Clearly.

Telling him to fornicate with a razor boar hadn't been smart. All I got was a serious ass-beating, and I would still have to do what they wanted.

Well, maybe I didn't have to, but they'd keep this up until I either agreed to it or died. One of those two options was preferable to the other. I just had to decide which.

What exactly had they lost on Dreadmax? Based on all of this, it sure didn't seem like some no-name doctor.

What I should've done was rest until they sent me one of their poorly educated, underpaid medics. I'd probably get some decent pain meds and stitches.

The problem was time. Whatever Briggs had in store

for me was going to happen soon. I needed to have his secrets figured out before then.

I'd heard of humanitarian missions to prisons. Some of my best conversations since arriving here had been with do-good volunteers. I wished I'd asked what kind of doctor this mysterious good Samaritan was supposed to be. For now, I assumed he was a medical doctor and that it was possible he went to the worst penitentiary in the galaxy to do good deeds.

Laughing hurt and I spent several minutes trying to stop. Everything Briggs said was half-truth. He wanted me to find someone, and that someone was important. What I needed to know was what Briggs planned to do with me when it was over.

Fuck it. Anyplace was better than here. I'd rather go on a mission to hell than spend one more night in this cell, which made me wonder why I'd refused.

I crawled to my bed and pulled the scratchy blanket over my battered form. Several revelations occurred at the moment I was slipping into unconsciousness. The doctor was probably actually a scientist who had been doing some illegal shit where no one thought it would matter.

Which basically made it a mission for someone in dark ops. Someone expendable. It might even be a mission for a Reaper.

"Inmate Cain, you are required to wake up. You've slept one minute and nineteen seconds past reveille. If you do not move from your bunk in five seconds, I will be forced to initiate a stimulus," said the voice of CIM in my ear.

By stimulus, he meant one hell of a shock delivered into my spine. Not lethal or even debilitating but very unpleasant. I'd had worse, like the time a pissed-off guard stepped on my face.

"Please acknowledge, Inmate Cain."

"Yeah, yeah. Wouldn't want to get in trouble with the man."

"Correct," replied the CIM.

"What do you think, X?"

"Please refrain from attempting contact with your X-37 Reaper AI," the CIM said.

Neither the CIM nor X-37 were true artificial intelligences. Their specs listed them as *limited* AIs. Within that broad designation, there was a world of variation. A CIM was like a more sophisticated ankle bracelet. X-37 was completely different. It helped me navigate strange worlds and murder people—a standard of usefulness the CIM could only dream of.

"Do you really want to risk contact?" X-37 said, his voice sounding distant and scratchy. As part of my cybernetic upgrades, he couldn't be removed, only quarantined. But Reaper implants like X-37 rarely came without a downside. Interaction with X brought certain consequences.

"Please check the earbud, Inmate Cain. I'm losing connectivity with BMSP servers," the CIM ordered.

The earbud was only an antenna. The actual hardware was wired someplace I'd never found.

I massaged the earbud. "What's on the schedule, X? I'm tired of CIM. Make him shut the fuck up."

X-37 made a quiet beep that indicated he was about to give me information. It was a weird glitch that I attributed to damage from an earlier mission.

"You are to remain in your cell for a visitor."

"Details?"

"None available at this time."

Another alert warned me I didn't have much time to shit and shower. I only wished I could shave, but that was something they did for me during medical checkups.

Thankfully, the military had taught me to be quick and efficient. As a result, I had some idle time before my visitor arrived.

"Are you daydreaming, Reaper Cain?" asked X-37.

"You got a problem with that?"

"Sometimes your heart rate increases. At other times, it decreases. It makes it difficult for me to anticipate your needs." A pause. "I don't have the capacity for imagination."

"Not really my problem," I muttered. "But thanks for interrupting."

"Insincerity and sarcasm detected," acknowledged the A.I.

THERE WERE things an inmate could do besides stare into space when there was nothing but time. I'd tried them all. When I was bored with dreams and old memories, I would perform physical and mental exercises or meditate. There wasn't time for the former at the moment, so I did some stretching and then sat cross-legged on my bed to calm myself.

"Your heart rate is forty-six beats per minute and your respiration steady," noted X-37.

"I didn't really need to know that, but thanks for the insight."

"You're welcome, Reaper Cain."

The paint inside Ultramax IX was tan, I thought. Or maybe it was just dirty. Didn't matter. I knew the look of every crack in the veneer. Underneath the paint was nothing but engineered concrete reinforced with steel—a simple design made to last.

This place was made to keep people like me locked away forever. A depressing thought, but there it was.

Good thing I was going on a field trip.

At the end of the hallway, far out of my view, one of the main doors opened. It had that sound of a heavy slab of metal slamming. Men were talking, but I couldn't make out the words.

Footsteps.

Another door.

Warning klaxons ringing overhead.

The door to death row.

If I were paranoid, I'd have assumed my visitor was taking his or *her*—let's be hopeful here—sweet time to make me feel a little more uncomfortable. Add a little dramatic effect for whatever show they were about to give me.

That would make them stupid, though, because no one knew the waiting game better than an inmate on this block.

"Inmate Cain, your heart rate is accelerating. Are you anticipating a confrontation?" asked CIM.

"That's none of your business, but sure. Why not? Why would I think I might be beaten or interrogated or put in isolation? Like that's ever happened," I mocked.

By the time I ended the conversation with my cybernetic monitor, I'd identified who was coming to see me. Made me proud, actually. It'd been a while since I'd identified a person by the sound of their footsteps.

Frederick Eugene Grady, one of my old spec op buddies, sent the guards back the way they'd come so we could have some privacy. He moved closer and talked to me through the bars.

"You can come in if you want," I said.

He laughed. "You never change, Hal. From what Briggs tells me, this is a waste of time anyway. I'm not sure why we bother to ask when we can just put a gun to your head."

I smirked. "You always were a smooth talker, Feg."

"You know I hate that name."

I shrugged. "Life's hard, then you die in a maximum-security prison—as the victim of a scientific experiment. Or, best of all, fighting for the Union, who doesn't give two—"

"You know you don't have a choice," he interrupted. "Take the mission or you'll get lethal injections tomorrow— and they'll be poorly administered. Sick bastards know how to make it pure torture. They saved you specifically for something like this. If you won't cooperate, why bother with such a huge pain in the ass?" Grady asked.

"Fuck off, Feg." I used his initials because he hated the nickname, which meant that was all we called him before dark ops recruited me from spec ops.

"Could you use my real name one time?"

"We're done," I said, firmly.

"Remember AIT? Those were good times," he said. "Back when we were soldiers for the Union with nothing but bad pay to complain about."

The room was too hot and I was tired of working out in the corner and staring at the ceiling after lights out. Talking to myself. Imagining life outside this cell. Dreaming of a chance to go on a mission.

"What's it gonna be, Hal?"

"I don't work for the Union anymore."

"That's not an answer," he said with a huff, exasperation filling his voice.

"It is."

SITTING on death row was one thing. Getting served notice was another. My seventeen-month-old appeal was thrust onto the fast-track—reviewed and denied about five seconds after I refused the suicide mission. Briggs woke a judge up with a secure gal-net link and put a rush on circumvention of every constitutionally guaranteed protection of my due process.

"Union prosecutors followed every law to the letter. But they know people and how to get things done," Briggs said, leaning against the back wall like neither of us were killers and I wasn't about to get tortured to death.

"How long, Doctor?" he asked.

"Not long now. I'm drawing up anti-anxiety meds to calm the patient before we begin." The doctor looked like a mad scientist. He only worked about three days a year and didn't shave or brush his teeth during his enforced sabbatical—or so it seemed.

"Inmate," Briggs corrected.

"I beg your pardon?"

"Halek Cain is an inmate condemned to death, not a patient," explained Briggs.

"Of course."

"Tell me I'm wrong, Hal," Briggs said.

I ignored him. Other things occupied my thoughts— restraints that were too tight, the exact layout of the rooms and hallways between my cell and the execution chamber, shitty food.

It was unfair as hell but no surprise. My last meal—

steak and potatoes—had tasted bland and I was pretty sure most of the guards had spit in it.

Or worse.

There wasn't a way to escape this. Once, about halfway here, I thought that if I could get past the cafeteria into the maintenance locker room…

"Hey, I've been thinking," I said, suddenly.

The death doctor stopped with one hand on the lethal injection switch. Briggs glared at me. The audience behind the one-way glass probably put down their wine glasses.

"I'll do it. Send me to Dreadmax. I'll find your stupid scientist."

Briggs almost looked disappointed, but I knew him well enough to understand he was pissed I forced him to take this all the way to the end of the line before giving in.

"Doctor," Briggs said.

"Sir?"

"Get out."

"I really can't do that," said the doc, shaking his head. "There are procedures. Concerns for the welfare of anyone about to be pardoned or otherwise take a plea bargain."

"If you don't get out, I'll snap your neck," Briggs replied in an emotionless tone.

That did the trick. The doctor scurried to the door. "Leaving now. Just don't pull out any of the intravenous tubes unless you have the training to do so."

"Out," repeated Briggs.

Moments later, I was alone with the spec ops commander.

He crossed his arms. "No more games. If you take this deal, I expect your professional best until we're done."

"As long as you don't ask me to kill anyone. This is a hostage rescue all the way."

"It's going to get rough. You may have to fight."

"That's different. I'll do what it takes to keep myself alive, but I'm not doing political assassinations or cleansing," I said.

"Fine," he agreed with a reluctant, albeit relieved tone. "Be a killer with a conscience. Whatever flies your ship, but finish the mission and do what we need. That's all anyone cares about."

"I'll get it done," I told him.

"Excellent," he said. "Then I guess I should say welcome to the team, you stubborn bastard."

3

GRADY RETURNED with two guys I didn't know. I assumed they were on his spec ops team, part of a security element. Probably badasses who specialized in mixed martial arts and who'd been hired to kill me if things went south.

I hadn't been popular among my peers, even when I was spec ops, but I thought most of them could empathize with my situation. Their masters could turn on them at any moment, the same way they had with me.

Maybe not the spec ops guys, but definitely anyone who'd seen something the folks upstairs didn't want other people to know.

All three of them were average height and build, unless you knew what to look for. Walking down the street, they'd look like normal guys. None of them had the over-muscled physiques of bodybuilders, but I had no doubt they were strong as hell and ready to throw down.

Grady's knuckles were covered with massive scars from all the fights he'd been in. He had another that ran from his upper lip down across his chin—not unlike the shrapnel wound ten years ago that nearly claimed the eye I was born with. We used to tell him he should grow out some facial hair and cover that ugly scar up, but he never did.

Death row wasn't like other prisons, or other parts of prisons. No one cat-called me or harassed my escorts. We didn't really know each other, and few of us had the energy for those types of shenanigans. We were doing our time and facing our end in our own way.

When the last prison gate slammed behind me, I realized this was actually happening. I was leaving this place, maybe for good, and it felt like waking from a long dream.

Grady and his two buddies escorted me quickly to a shuttle full of humorless soldiers. From there, we entered a slipspace tunnel. The pilot refused to fill me in on the flight plan, so I could only guess our destination.

Not that it really mattered. They handcuffed me to a table in a briefing room, forcing me to listen to the briefing we were about to have. I guess they knew me well enough to know I probably would have opted to crash in my room for the duration of the flight.

Briggs always entered a room the same way, fast and pissed off. He slammed down a pad on the huge table as other members of the team filled the room. These were officers and handlers, very important people who planned things so that other people could do the fighting and dying.

Grady moved to the back with a couple of other spec ops guys to listen and take notes.

"All right, Cain," began Briggs. "This briefing is for you. Everyone else knows the whats, whys, and wherefores. So we'll get down to the details you need to know and start getting you fitted for your gear. We'll be entering a slip tunnel soon, which will take us to the system in question. Don't ask. You don't need to know where it is."

"I know what system Dreadmax is located in," I commented.

The officers and intelligence types murmured and typed alarmed messages into their pads. One put a hand to his ear and hurriedly left the room like the sky had just fallen.

Briggs leaned toward the table and stared down at me where I was handcuffed in my chair. "Thanks. For that."

"No problem. When you play stupid games, you win stupid prizes. I didn't think that was a secret, or why would you have told me where I was going?"

What followed was an awkward silence. Maybe some of the officers were pissing their pants as their careers evaporated from what they already saw as a failure. Hard to say in a room like this, but one thing was certain: this mission was such that failure meant a lot of resignations, with enough blame to destroy lives.

And I was at the center of it.

None of them could imagine going in alone to

Dreadmax and bringing out a hostage or prisoner or what-ever this guy was. I'd been in dark ops long enough to know anything they told me needed to be taken with a grain of salt. And a shot of whiskey, if possible.

"Your mission is simple, or at least straightforward," began Briggs. "Doctor Paul Hastings was lost on Dreadmax during a humanitarian mission. You were selected due to your training and specializations. We will insert you with a small team who will provide overwatch and extraction once you have located and secured the target." Briggs flipped through several pages on his device to check details. Appar-ently, few of them were for my edification.

By team, Briggs meant the group of elite operators who would watch my every move without actually helping. I'd take all the risk and they'd do…whatever.

"This is a good deal for a retired spec ops guy like you," I said to Briggs. "Giving out orders and walking us through it like a middle grade teacher. Probably makes you long for the good ol' days."

My old friend Grady suppressed a smile. Other opera-tors laughed openly.

"I'm active duty," said Briggs, curling his lip in annoyance.

"Hard to say with a face like yours," I said with a shrug.

Briggs activated several screens. "Check yourself and pay attention. You won't be able to come back and ask me questions when shit goes sideways."

"Okay. How big is the quick reaction force if I find the

principal and can't rescue him unassisted? What if there are casualties? What's the rally point?" I asked, firing questions at him.

An officer who didn't name himself moved forward. "You're putting too much thought into this. You go straight in, grab the target, and come straight out. That's it. Don't get creative."

"Why don't him and his guys do that?" I said as I hooked my thumb toward Grady and his squad of elite soldiers.

They gave me half answers and straight-out lies. I knew there were two reasons I was going on this mission. One, they didn't care if I died, and two, there was going to be some killing involved. "Am I *bringing* Hastings out or *taking* him out?"

The unnamed officer went white as a sheet. "What the hell kind of question is that?"

A glance at Briggs, then Grady, confirmed my suspicions. Not everyone in this room understood what I was. The pretentious schmuck telling me not to get creative would probably shit his pants if he knew I was a Reaper.

Arguments broke out. Briggs glared like he wanted to throat punch me.

"Everyone settle," said Briggs, casting a glance around the room. "Cain knows he's expendable, and that's a big part of the reason for his selection. But I can't overstate the fact that his training and his track record in deep infiltration into hostile areas is unequaled."

"All true," I said, taking a paper cup and drinking its contents, which turned out to be water when I was hoping for coffee.

Briggs launched into his serious-as-hell commander's voice. "I also know you're too proud to do this half-assed and you'll go all the way to get him back. The fate of the Union depends on his recovery, and that's no shit this time. He has someplace to be. You'll get him in twenty-four hours or go back on death row. Grady and his team are good, but not even they have that for motivation."

"What happens after twenty-four hours?" I asked.

"People die. So don't be late." Briggs gave Grady a hand signal. "Get Cain kitted out. Make sure he's proficient. Jerking off in a prison cell probably hasn't done much for his combat efficiency."

"You'd be surprised," I said, right before I was escorted from the dimly lit room.

THE ARMORY on the ship said a lot about what type of vessel we were on. The UFS *Thunder* was far larger than I expected. I wondered if we were going to rescue a doctor or start a war. There were enough lockers to equip a company of soldiers. Fortunately, none of them were here now. We left our escort outside the door.

"I was getting worried," I said, walking around still handcuffed near my waist. After I counted the lockers and looked for various wear marks that might indicate the age of the ship, I faced Grady and his two tough guys.

He walked to a table in the center of the armory where the gear I'd be wearing was stacked. "About what?"

"I've got a better imagination than you, Grady. If I said I wasn't worried about getting stuck into some sort of experiment with a high mortality rate, I'd be lying."

"Get over here so I can explain this stuff."

I sauntered over, still deep in my assessment of this room. If I were to make an escape attempt, this place would be important one way or another. Whoever came after me would be armed from this room. There was a door to a powered-armor-equipping area and another to bots and drones.

"Why don't you just send these soldiers down to storm the place and clean up with your spec ops guys?"

The slow look he gave me confirmed my suspicion. That was probably an option.

"Holy shit, Grady. What type of people are we running with?"

Instead of answering, he pulled out an HDK 4 with a silencer. A moment later, he placed a pistol, also with a silencer, down and lined it up precisely with the first weapon. I had forgotten that about my old friend. He was compulsive.

"I bet you still have three t-shirts perfectly folded in your locker on top of your other inspection-ready uniforms."

"You got a problem with that?" he asked, furrowing his brow.

"No. What about body armor?" I separated the stack of gear into equally neat piles and lifted up a ballistic vest.

"Put it on so Sergeant Crank can check the fitting. It should be pretty close, because we have your exact height and weight measurements from your CIM," Grady said.

"How about we save some time and do it all at once?" When I'd geared up from head to toe, I turned around and spread my arms from Crank to check my work. There was a weird moment when I thought he might pat me down, but he checked all the straps and tie-downs with methodical professionalism instead.

"You're good to go. Looks like you stayed in better shape than the other assholes on death row," Crank said. Up close, he looked like he could probably deadlift two or three times his own weight despite his deceptively lean build. I made a quick note of his flexibility, because he seemed to have a hard time getting up and down.

Maybe that was from a recently completed workout or a nagging injury, but it didn't matter. If this guy came after me, I'd use the information accordingly. If he was the one coming to save me, I hoped he'd suck it up and get the job done.

"Happy?" Grady asked.

I wasn't happy because they knew they could do better. "You took the stuff straight off the rack. The HDK has to be ten years old."

"Where we are going, simple is better. Get in, get out—"

"Take me back to my cell on death row," I cut him off.

Grady cursed under his breath and looked at his feet before meeting my gaze. "Listen, Hal, I'm not trying to fuck you. Believe whatever you want about Briggs and the mission planners, but you and I fought together and I'm not hanging you out to dry."

"He fought for this gear," Sergeant Crank interjected.

"There were several people who thought you could do this without being armed," Grady continued. "It was a two-hour argument. I had to threaten to quit just to get you this much stuff. So stop breaking my balls. I'll be handling over-watch with my team, and believe it or not, I know how to run a QRF. This mission sucks, I'm not going to try and dress it up. But when was the last time you were on a mission that you felt good about from the beginning?"

"Touché." I spent some time playing with the guns: aiming, dry firing, taking them apart and putting them back together. The armor was what really pissed me off. It was dumb gear, no digital enhancements whatsoever. On the bright side, it was less likely they could track me remotely from the armor—or cut the power because it didn't have power.

"How close are you gonna be, Grady?" I asked.

"You'll have sub-dermal monitoring implants for track-ing. Comms will be extremely limited due to the environment shield holding Dreadmax together."

"Sounds like an ankle bracelet for a parolee," I said, scoffing.

He lifted his hands in an *oh well* gesture. "Pretty much."

"For the record, the stuff is junk. When this goes sideways, and you know it will, you can tell whoever is in charge of this fandango it failed because they didn't let me plan it."

"I already told him you'd say that."

THERE WERE a dozen cafeterias on a ship the size of the UFS *Thunder*, some larger than others. Grady and his two buddies took me to the smallest and stood guard while I ate. I waved a hand toward the prepackaged food. "Help yourself."

Grady crossed his arms and leaned back in his chair. "I wasn't sure how much you'd need."

"Are you going to just stare at me while I shovel this crap down?"

"Has to be better than what you ate on death row."

"Food is just food. Fuel for the machine. Give me a chocolate bar, and we'll talk."

Grady nodded toward one of the packets in the meal ready-to-eat. "You never know what you're going to get."

I skipped ahead and tore open the small package with my teeth. It was full of some chewy, fruit-flavored candy. I threw the entire handful into my mouth at once and mashed it, thinking it might grow on me.

"Any more details than they gave in the briefing?" I asked. "Does this guy have medical needs? Allergies?"

"Finish your food, and we'll hit the range," replied Grady, not really answering my questions. "Then we'll run through some training exercises, make sure you're still sharp."

"I'm good to go right now," I said, slapping both hands hard on the table and standing abruptly. A jolt of electricity shot through my left arm. For a hot second, I thought they'd left the prison restraint software active.

Grady and his men flinched and tightened their security. I pocketed some of the soft candies from the other MREs without letting them see it just to see if I could do it.

If they realized I had palmed the items, they didn't let on. Grady wanted me to sharpen my skills, so I was going to sharpen all of them. "Let's do this!"

"He's a fucking lunatic," said the third man who I didn't know yet. His name tape suggested he was called Maverick.

He looked like as much fun as a spec ops field manual.

Grady walked in front of me, and the other two followed. We didn't encounter any crew-members, which confirmed Briggs had more than just my old friend and his goons monitoring me right now. This was an elaborate operation, perfectly coordinated between spec ops and ship security. I had to be impressed.

"Quite a hike," I remarked, surveying my surroundings.

My left eye revealed evidence of deep, sonic cleaning. This corridor had been prepped well.

"It's a big ship," Grady said without looking back.

"Battleship?" It was a test question. I still wasn't sure how *friendly* my old *friend* was. Would he save me when the chips were down or leave me to fend for myself?

"Destroyer class. But you already knew that."

"How would I know that?" Looking back at Crank and Maverick, I gave them a winning smile. "I was in dark ops, not the Fleet."

Sergeant Crank didn't answer.

Grady stopped at the door and swiped the security card. "It's a VR range. Better than the real thing."

"Says you."

Inside, I realized it was not only a virtual reality facility, but a small, infrequently used one. Probably for fleet officers who only used it once or twice a year the day before mandatory qualifications.

Grady waved his hand at the practice weapons. I stepped forward and started with the HDK—short barrel, magazine fed from the bottom between the trigger assembly and shoulder stock, optics on top, flashlight below the barrel, and a personal favorite of mine. My escorts stood back and said nothing. They were probably impressed but never showed it. I drew a smiley face on one target with bullet holes just to make sure they were watching.

"Nice," Grady said. "You always were a fucking spaz."

"So what if you can shoot," Sergeant Crank said. "How is your conditioning?"

It was a dumb question. The guy should've known better. He'd been in spec ops long enough to know we worked out wherever we could, even if it was a cell. That was what kept us from going crazy.

What he was really doing was looking for a fight. First, we'd have some sort of macho gut check workout and, lo and behold, we'd wind up on the mat punching and choking each other.

He probably wouldn't poke this bear unless he was confident in his abilities. A quick glance at Grady and the other guy confirmed my suspicion. They were curious, probably had a betting pool going.

"I'll get by," I finally answered.

Crank popped his knuckles and furled his upper lip into a sneer. "Yeah? You been doing jumping jacks and push-ups?"

He was trying to piss me off. Yeah, sure I'd done the calisthenics, but I'd also been doing handstand push-ups and making every conceivable exercise as difficult as possible—from doing tons of reps superfast or super slow or in combination with other body-weight exercises.

He had to know this. That was what he would've been trying to do if he was taken prisoner and put in confinement. There were also meditation exercises and a number of other techniques to hold on to the sanity for as long as possible in the harshest environments imaginable.

"You want to throw down or what?" I asked, tossing a glance back at him.

"Yeah, Cain. That's just what I want. We've got a ranking system. How long an operator can keep me from choking them out. Grady lasted thirty-eight seconds."

"How long are you gonna last?" I asked.

Crank's eyes went wide, and he smiled in anticipation. "You gonna give me a fight, then? Some real competition?"

The stiffness I'd noticed earlier probably indicated he trained a lot, too much, like a black belt in jiu-jitsu trying to maintain rank. So he had some injuries, and also five hundred ways to put me down.

I walked onto the mat and kicked off my shoes. He snorted a curse.

"Aren't you going to bow to the mat?"

I faced him and started moving around to get loosened up. "Why don't you make me?"

"That's bullshit. You can disrespect me, but don't disrespect the dojo or the art," he demanded, giving me a hard look.

I've always had a healthy appreciation for practitioners of martial arts and other disciplines. But the mat is just a mat to me. I'd never been here before and I didn't know who ran the place. Maybe if I did, it would be different. There was no wise sensei or sifu demanding respect, just a couple of spec ops dudes squaring off for no good reason.

"Fine," he said when I didn't respond. Crank gave the

training area a short bow, but the moment he got on the mat, he rushed me with a flying superman punch.

I sidestepped without even raising my hands to block.

Landing on one foot but recovering quickly, he circled around to face me again. He dropped low and tried to take me down by pulling my knees out from under me like a galactic-class wrestler. I lowered my center of gravity and widened my stance, pushing down on his head and one shoulder to keep him away.

Takedown defense wasn't one of my best skills, but I stuffed his attempt easily.

I winked at Grady.

"Are you even breathing hard?" he asked, panting a little himself.

"Nope."

"He's got ten years on you, Crank. Step it up a notch," commented Grady, clearly enjoying the spectacle.

Crank tried the tactic again and I drove my knee into his face. Blood spurted across the mat. Without waiting for him to recover, I grabbed one of his arms and pulled him past me, then jumped onto his back to lock in a rear-naked-choke.

Eight seconds later, he was out cold.

Had he learned his lesson?

Of course not.

Pushing himself to his feet, he shook his head, trying to focus his eyes on something other than abject humiliation and defeat. Moments later, he snarled curses. "Again, you son-of-a-bitch."

We circled each other for a while, fists up and feet moving nimbly. I remained cautious. Just because I put him down once didn't mean he was a pushover.

"You think that was clever?" he asked. "All you did was raise the price you're gonna pay."

I dropped low and shot forward, grabbing his left knee and leveraging my weight into it. There was no way one leg could hold my entire body weight. He went down hard.

With no hesitation to celebrate, I scrambled on top of him and took the mount position. Getting my heels locked in and holding him in place took longer than I planned. He continued to fight, but I chipped away at his defenses until I had him in an arm bar.

He rapidly tapped his hand to submit, but I increased the pressure until he screamed.

Grady tried to pull me off a second later, but I stood on my own and walked away.

"That was a shit move, Hal," he said, his face a mask of fury. "You could've maimed him with that stunt."

"He'll be alright. I know when to stop, unlike him."

Grady held my gaze for a long time, his expression tense. "I think that's enough testing for one day. Let's get ready to do this mission before you disable the team who is supposed to come and help you."

Grady kicked everybody else out of the room after Crank and I were done beating the shit out of each other. I got hit by a bit of agoraphobia in the large training room, which wasn't large by a normal person's standards. As tough as I thought I was, spending so much time in isolation on death row had probably done permanent damage to my psyche.

"That was a fucking circus," I said.

He pulled a bench from the side of the room and sat on it, steepling his fingers together and looking at me thoughtfully. "It had to be done, and you know it. None of these guys have seen you work or trained with you."

"I'm glad you remember, at least."

He shrugged. "You're a freak of nature. Always were. I wasn't surprised they made you a Reaper."

"We have time for real training?"

He probably knew this was coming. Behind all the ass kicking and trick shooting were hours of practice. We moved onto the mat and went through combative drills, slowly at first, and then much faster. I pushed the pace until we started making mistakes and then backed down to a more reasonable level.

By the end, we were sweaty and laughing.

"I wish I knew what went wrong with you, Hal." It almost sounded like there was a hint of regret in his tone.

Not having an answer, I strode toward the door, pretending I could leave whenever I wanted. It kept me sane, but I knew it wasn't true.

Grady joined me and we went into the main room.

It didn't take much to see what was going to happen

next. The camaraderie we'd shared slipped from his expression the closer we got to the exit. In the main room, a squad of ship soldiers waited.

One of them stepped forward. "I'm Sergeant Myers. Turn around. My men are going to place you in restraints."

Grady started to say something.

The sergeant interrupted him. "This was discussed. Cain is still a criminal. He doesn't get to roam the ship. Look on the bright side, our brig is much nicer than death row."

4

GRADY and I walked across the gangway. His team wore heavier armor and carried more weapons than the recon gear they assigned me. Triple-weave carbon fiber protected my shins, forearms, and torso. Hoverboarders wore thicker helmets than what the Union thought I needed.

"You have secured comms with my team and medical sensors. I'll know if you get hurt and how bad," he explained as we walked.

I ignored Grady, more than a little annoyed he hadn't remembered my pregame ritual. In short, I liked to think things through without a lot of chitchat. There was too much subterfuge around this mission, not unusual in my line of work—or what had been my line of work—but fuck me running, this was ridiculous.

Something was wrong. Grady's nervousness betrayed the gravity of the situation. He wasn't just worried about a failed mission. If I didn't come back with this doctor, there would be consequences.

I needed to stop thinking of him as a friend. We hadn't operated together for a long time. People changed. Shit happened.

He kept talking and I kept ignoring him, preferring to look out at the hellhole they were about to push me through. Okay, they weren't actually going to push me. I'd jump. Hesitation was something I'd gotten over in basic training a long time ago.

Dreadmax had been a battle station before it was decommissioned and left dormant for two decades. Someone decided it wasn't a big enough failure in its original role and turned it into a prison for the worst of the worst. The problem was the overly grand design the Union hadn't been able to support at the time. They wanted a ship the size of a moon with the firepower of a few cruisers.

Fortunes were made long before the construction finished. Typical Union bureaucracy and pork-barrel politics had lined a lot of pockets.

Where did they go wrong with the design? They wanted to travel slip tunnels and dominate entire systems with one ship. It was so big, it was like a moon made of fat rings and bulky spires. But once the damn thing was nearly built, funding had gone dry. With only three-quarters of the facility built, the boys upstairs had decided it would make for a better prison than a space station.

"That's the reason we're going to drop you instead of attempt a landing," Grady said.

"I'm sorry, what?" I hadn't been listening, so I didn't know what he was talking about. The briefing had stated they would land, and I would deploy from the ship while they set up security. I'd known that was bullshit the minute they said it.

Grady, my old friend, would push me out and see if I survived the first ten seconds in Dreadmax. Then maybe he'd follow and mop up with Sergeant Crank and the others.

Most of the superstructure was steel, the cheapest they could find. It necessarily had shielding plates and some energy fields to maintain pockets of surface environment, but I could see huge strips of rust and several towers that had collapsed in disrepair. There were observation towers rising in several places and shorter buildings two or three stories tall that looked like dormitories or warehouses.

"Looks like a trillion-ton doughnut. Barely has a hole," I said.

"You have a way of minimizing everything. That's half your problem," stated Grady.

"My problem is I'm too good at sneaking into places and killing people."

The main ring, so thick it was hard to see all at once,

had streets of a sort, trenches with point-defense batteries that had been repurposed to blow the shit out of misbehaving inmates. Some of the point-defense turrets had been stripped and welded shut.

"Those used to be automated, back when there was a budget to run proper security on this place," Grady said.

"What if they decide to mutiny and take the place over? There's a shipyard right there on the horizon," I said, pointing. The structures below passed faster and faster as we decreased altitude. Dreadmax had a central spire with the main ring spinning around it. It almost looked like a sphere, or a moon, but that was an optical illusion. Matching speed with the ring wouldn't be hard for a good pilot and ours seemed to be one of the best.

He shook his head. "None of the ships work. They would have been better off scuttled in space. I was told by someone who knows someone who heard it from a guy that the shipyard is full of sentimental projects, ships named after people who invested enough money to get their name on the prow and demand they not be jettisoned into the void."

"They don't look that bad," I said. Moments later, we passed over the shipyard and I realized how wrong I was. If Dreadmax was in bad shape, the moored vessels were ten times worse. One actually cracked loose of its moorings and drifted away as we passed. It was like watching the bottom of the ocean and seeing a sea creature shake free of the sand.

Debris floated free where it shouldn't have existed in the first place. There were several hangars with blast doors that looked as though they hadn't been opened for a decade. I wondered when the last time they'd parked a super carrier in there was.

"The only important parts of Dreadmax are the power plant, gravity generators, and life support. If any one of those things goes down, it's over for the convicts," Grady said.

"And your doctor," I pointed out. "I have a pretty good idea one of them is going to fail in twenty-four hours."

Grady flushed red, indicating I'd guessed correctly.

"Nice. Thanks for holding back. That's something you should've told me during the brief. Maybe when we were planning this out."

"You didn't plan it," he reminded me.

"And that's part of the problem. Briggs says I'm here because I have the experience, but that only counts for killin', I guess. Doesn't matter that I've got more experience with extractions than every single one of you. What if I ran into trouble and requested a pickup time well after the entire place goes dark? And what the fuck happens to the people down there when it does? Shouldn't there be an evacuation mission?"

"Every person in that place was already sentenced to death at least once," Grady said.

"Like me. How cheery," I remarked.

"Don't be an asshole."

"You're not the one about to be pushed out of an airlock. I mean, I'll jump on my own. Anyone pushing me is gonna have broken fingers, but you know what I'm saying."

"Believe it or not, a lot of people are counting on you. Lives are at stake," he said.

"Sure. I'll bring back your doctor, or scientist, or whatever he is. You can take that to the bank."

"Just stick to the plan," he retorted. "We don't need any of your hotshot cowboy shit. Step one foot off the planned route and you're dead along with the principal."

"What the actual fuck, Grady? No plan ever works like that. The second I'm down, ten things will go wrong. If I'd planned this mission, there would have been allowances made for random shit."

"Like I said, you didn't—"

"Stop reminding me," I interrupted.

"You brought it up."

"Grady, why aren't you doing this mission with your team? Doesn't spec ops do search and rescue?"

He didn't respond, which was in itself an answer.

Grady's team wasn't expendable. More importantly, it wasn't the only team on this mission. They had already sent at least one group of unstoppable badasses. Who were probably dead. Or worse. Whatever that might be.

"Are you going to swoop in once I find him? Steal my glory? Leave me there on the ultimate death row?"

"I'm running your extraction team."

"But you're not the only spec ops unit on this operation," I said, pointedly. "You're just the only one I'm allowed to know about."

He adjusted his gear and checked his team as he answered me, a good way to avoid eye contact. "Stop breaking my balls, Hal."

"What fun would that be?" I slugged him in the shoulder. "We're friends, right?"

"Sure, Hal."

"Then, as a friend, would you mind shutting the fuck up and letting me get my head straight? If you're going to lie and hold shit back, I want to focus on what I need to do to survive this."

"You're a real son-of-a-bitch."

"Yeah, I've heard that." I took out one of Briggs' cigars, a lighter I lifted from another officer, and nursed it to life.

"Where'd you get that?" he asked, mouth slightly agape.

"Don't worry about it."

THE DROPSHIP TREMBLED as we passed through the atmosphere shield. Turbines twisted downward to keep us from crashing into Dreadmax. We were over a landing field bordered by one of the mechanical trenches.

"That's damn close, Andrews!" Grady shouted.

"Not my fault. The power must be running low for the shield to be so close to the surface. Might be better to just land and fly along this crap," Lieutenant Andrews said, a good-natured lilt in the tone of his voice.

"Not an option," said Grady, struggling to be heard over the noise.

"Roger that. We'll talk again when I slam into one of these watchtowers," muttered Andrews in response.

I heard everything they said. "I'm ready. I'll go now."

"Negative, Hal. You have thirty seconds before optimal deployment."

Leaning toward the hellhole, I took a breath and fell forward. A static line attached to my back immediately pulled the ripcord on my grav-chute. It took about twenty seconds to glide down.

Static garbled the sound of Grady's voice in my ear piece. "That was reckless. Don't fuck up now. I'm tired of cleaning up your messes."

The second my feet touched metal, I released from my gravity-parachute and sprinted toward the nearest cover. The backup guys watching me were probably losing their minds that I didn't pack up my chute, but why would I waste time on that?

The dropship turbines tilted backward again and my ride sped away. It didn't feel like they were coming back for me. Ever.

"Well, at least there's atmosphere. More than I expected really."

"There are better ways to test atmosphere than to deploy a parachute," X-37 said. Unlike Grady's garbled radio voice, X-37 sounded like part of me.

"Where am I, X?"

"You are one hundred meters from trench one forty-two. Would you like a more exact measurement, including centimeters and elevation?"

"Maybe later. Can I get down a level? I'd prefer to travel beneath the surface in case there is atmosphere lost through the degrading shields."

Several seconds passed, which was an unusual time lag for X-37. "I have quarantined the BMSP CIM for the duration of this mission. As to your question, traveling beneath the surface of Dreadmax is not part of your mission plan. Can you advise a reason to deviate?"

"Because deviation is fun. And I've already gone off the plan. We jumped early in case you didn't notice."

"This was noted. Can you explain?"

"Can you keep a secret?"

"Of course, but while the CIM is quarantined, I am unable to determine how much data it will gather passively. It will sync up with the mainframe on the UFS *Thunder* the moment we return."

This was interesting because I assumed the CIM would need to get all the way back to the Bluesphere Maximum Security Prison before spilling the digital beans.

"I don't trust Grady."

"Analysis shows this to be an appropriate precaution. I will look for access to the below deck area."

"What is it, X? You seem hesitant," I said suspiciously.

"My analysis suggests that there is a reason no mention of below decks was considered in the briefing."

5

PRISONS HAVE GANGS. Abandoned space stations populated by convicted murderers have the worst gangs imaginable. And crazies. I hadn't gone a kilometer before spotting dozens of watchers. Shadowy faces peered out from windows and alleyways and ventilation shafts.

Moving quickly, I stopped at the corners of buildings and checked my back trail to be sure I wasn't being followed. The place was quiet and dark. The star field was intense, with no competition from artificial lighting. The moon and the nearby planet were somewhere on the other side of Dreadmax now, throwing a weird glow up from the horizon of the main ring.

"Can't go this way. You'll die," said the slightly distorted voice of a child through a public address speaker.

I looked around, blood running cold as I struggled to

remember how long this place had been a prison. Twenty years?

"X, how long has this place been open for business?"

"I'm not sure 'open for business' is the phrase you're looking for. Would you like me to consult my database of human languages?"

"We've been through this before, X. Just answer the question."

"Twenty years, three months, five days, seventeen hours, and three minutes."

"I'm assuming it's a coed facility."

"Why wouldn't it be? Are you concerned about the children watching us on the surveillance cameras?"

I reminded myself that X-37 didn't have extrasensory abilities. He was making inferences from my behavior and my sensory data.

"I bet none of them were convicted of capital crimes."

"There is a zero percent chance anyone born on Dreadmax has had due process," remarked X.

I moved to the next position, wondering why the child spies seemed so interested in my welfare.

"Didn't you hear me, mister?" asked the child.

"Why are you following me?" I asked.

"You're funny. We're not following you. We're watching you."

This confirmed a couple of things. One, there was some sort of active surveillance system in place. Two, it was controlled by children, which meant adults couldn't get into the control room or didn't care about video surveillance.

"Please sweep your eyes across the landscape," X-37 ordered.

"Sure thing, X. Anything for you."

"Sarcasm detected. There are three cameras aimed at your current location. By outward appearances, they are inoperative. No LED power indicators seen. However, analysis of the situation suggests they are, in fact, fully functional. The public address system is operating adequately," X-37 announced.

"Figured that one out all by myself." Steam burst out a vent, explaining some of the rust I saw during the flyover and warning me of the lack of maintenance on this place. That type of inefficiency shouldn't exist on a trillion-ton battle ring—even if it was decommissioned.

Moving, listening, and searching along narrow walkways at the bottom of metal trenches, I picked up other noises that were more dangerous—like gunshots in the distance.

"Someone thinks they can take down the dropship with small arms fire," I said, not expecting a comment from X-37.

"That would be a false assumption," replied the child's voice instead.

"Hey, kid. Come out where I can see you."

Several voices laughed through the PA. It sounded

weird because the air pressure inside the environment shield was wonky as hell.

"We're not stupid. It's safe in the tower. Crazies can't get in. The RSG don't care about us and the Nightfall Gangsters don't come this far."

"What's an RSG?" I crept under a surprisingly sophisticated cluster of cameras, PA speakers, and listening devices.

"Red Skull Gangsters, dummy," came the indignant response.

"I should have seen that coming," I muttered.

"Hey, mister. We're serious. You can't fucking go this way. Slab is having a big party."

"Slab?"

"He puts people on a slab. Cuts them up and eats their fingers."

"Your mother tell you that?"

Several children laughed nearby. They weren't just watching via camera feed, they had creepers.

I moved into an extremely narrow passage probably not meant for humans. There were rails along the floor and walls where I imagined maintenance bots could travel. It took a lot of twisting and squatting low to get through, but I came out in a new trench and heard what the watchers were talking about.

A quick scan of the area fed X-37 details I couldn't pick up from such a quick peek.

"There's an armed guard at each corner and a rover," X-37 said.

"Got an eye on him." I looked around for a camera but couldn't find one. "Seems like all the cameras in this area are disabled."

"Perhaps you should heed the advice of the child in the tower," X-37 cautioned.

"Let's call them kids or watchers. Just humor me on this," I said.

"I always do."

I wish my Reaper AI could highjack the Dreadmax security systems, but if wishes were fishes, then beggars would eat. And I'd be on my own ship heading out of the system.

"Update me only when needed. I want to go silent for a while and concentrate," I whispered before I crossed the street and ran in a low crouch through shadows cast by a massive three-story building ahead of me. It looked like a repair facility for large ships, a dry dock that could handle up to a destroyer class. The building had a main hangar and several smaller hangars. The building attached to it rose up three stories but probably went below decks as well.

It was probably as large as the entire BMSP facility.

I passed near the sentries on the way and noted their weapons. I wasn't sure how prison gangs could be carrying better weapons than I was, but I thought I'd ask Grady in a strongly worded complaint as soon as I saw him again.

"Contact imminent," X-37 said.

A wheeled vehicle with a chassis magnet holding it

down in case of gravity loss sped around the corner, something obviously wrong with the motor.

"Okay, maybe now isn't a good time to put you to sleep. What the hell is wrong with that thing?"

"It seems the locals have removed the electric motor in favor of an internal combustion engine."

I sprinted away from the party. "Whatever. It's loud as fuck and it stinks."

"I'll take your word for it."

"Trust me, X, I wouldn't lie to you."

The car screeched to a stop near the entrance of my hiding place. One shouted while another shone a flashlight in my direction. I pressed my back to the wall and held my breath until they moved on.

Loud music boomed from Slab's building. The sound of a crowd cheering and stomping feet was unmistakable.

"Doesn't sound like a prison," I remarked.

"There are no guards who don't work for the gangs. The residents of Dreadmax probably understand it is a matter of time before all systems fail," X-37 replied.

"What about the kids? Is there a normal part of this place where people have settled down and learned how to survive with a modicum of civility?" I wondered.

"Doubtful," X-37 said.

"Hey, kid? Are you listening?" I felt like a dork for calling out, but I needed to know. They were a good resource if they controlled the surveillance system and were willing to answer some questions. Maybe they'd even provide real time intelligence.

I checked my gear, hunkered down, and pulled the mission tablet from a slim backpack attached to my recon gear. The Reaper AI could give me information, but I wanted to look at the map.

"This sucks, X. We need to be on the other side of Slab's building or inside it."

"That is only an estimate of where the doctor will be, based on his last known location and observation of the locals," X-37 said.

"You mean gangs and crazies. Let's not sugar coat this goat fornication." I packed up and moved out. Staying in one place more than a minute or two felt dangerous.

The station was turning toward the planet, which was between us and the sun for a while longer.

"Darkness is good," X-37 reminded me.

"Sure." What bothered me were sounds. Screaming, shouting, and random gunfire or improvised explosive devices.

"Who the fuck would they be torturing on this place?"

"Anyone they want," came the matter-of-fact reply.

"Thanks for that, X."

"OVERWATCH ONE TO CAIN. RESPOND." Grady sounded annoyed.

"I heard you the first time. The RSGs have more than one heavily armed patrol in this area," I whispered, then dashed into a building.

"What's an RSG?"

"Hold on. I need to clear some rooms."

Not wanting to get shot in the doorway, I moved quickly through then slowed down just enough to provide a stable shooting platform while walking heel to toe. The standard HKD 4 short rifle came with red dot sights, infrared targeting options if I had the right helmet to go with it, and fifty round magazines. The bullets were small, but fast and accurate.

All things equal, I wished I had a shotgun for rooms this size. The HKD was decent for a lot of jobs and master of none. Not the worst choice in the armory.

I kept it at low ready, down six inches from my plane of vision so I didn't miss seeing someone crouched. There were three rooms in this structure, each with doorways rather than closable doors. I sidestepped without slowing, viewing a larger and larger section of the room I was about to clear, then went through.

By the numbers. No mistakes. No rushing to failure.

"Clear, no Red Skull Gangsters in this crib."

Grady grunted acknowledgment. "Glad to hear it. That's what RSG means? Where'd you learn that?"

"Some kids from the neighborhood told me."

"Bullshit."

"Do me a favor, Grady, and pull some strings. This

place needs evacuated no matter what happens with my mission. Make some calls. Get something going on that."

"That's not my job and it sure as hell isn't yours," he said, but I could tell he was talking to his team and pointing at screens in his command center. He'd probably at least send up a request.

"There's some sort of shindig going on in maintenance hangar 1847 Zulu. Lot of noise. Music. Gunfire. Everything you might expect in a maximum-security prison."

My old friend keyed up without talking. Sounds of a busy command center came through my earpiece.

"I could use visual confirmation there are children on Dreadmax. All of the inmates should have been sterilized before being sent there," Grady said.

"Well, that didn't fucking happen. Or someone put these kids here. I'll make sure to ask first chance I get."

"Send me a picture. Just one. I can't justify compromising the mission for your personal photo album," Grady said as he typed on his forearm keypad.

I knew the sound. I'd seen him do it often before I left spec ops.

"I haven't put eyes on them yet."

"What?"

"Audio comms only with the kids."

"Godsdamnit, Hal. You had me all worked up."

One tap of my helmet lowered the volume until I could barely hear him, especially as I moved closer to the maintenance hangar and the hellish party this Slab person was throwing.

"The clock is ticking, Cain. Find the principal."

"That might not be possible. If he ran into the RSG, he's probably in that building with about a thousand murderous thugs guarding him."

"Can't be that many."

"Sounds like everyone the Union's convicted in the last year," I said, slipping dangerously close to one of the spotlight vehicles. Motherfuckers were loaded for bear. Galdiz 49 heavy rifles, one YT sniper model, body armor. Fucking spotlights. Fucking motorcars with battery packs for magnetic road locks.

"We're doing a high-altitude flyover to confirm or deny your reports," Grady said.

"You should have done that before you pushed me through the hatch."

"No one pushed you," he reminded me.

A new vehicle, an armored car with a crew-served machine gun, rolled around the corner with its headlights off. I had a gut feeling these guys had received training before earning their life sentences.

Methodically, the crew of the new vehicle used their spotlight to sweep the trenches and walkways. The light stopped on my position, even though I doubted they could see where I was hiding.

The heavy machine gun opened fire, cutting holes in

the walls around me. I dropped to my stomach and crawled for a bot tunnel.

"X, can you help me out here?"

"Certainly. The tunnel you are entering is a dead end. There will be a filter welded in place."

"Thanks. For. That."

None of the bullets reached me and the gun crew apparently didn't want to leave their vehicle, lucky for me. Twenty minutes later, I backed out of the worthless tube and dropped into a pile of debris created by the sustained machine gun fire.

"Cain for Overwatch," I said quietly.

"Go for Overwatch," Grady said.

"What kind of gang members have light armored vehicles with crew-served machine guns?"

He answered somberly, "Don't worry about that now. We confirmed there is something going on in the hangar building. They've pulled in all of their patrols and barricaded the doors. Smaller groups of people are locking themselves in wherever there are doors or gates."

"Why would they do that?"

"Because there is a swarm of foot traffic flooding into the area. They're... running," he answered, hesitantly.

"Running?"

"Yeah, but the way they do it, they look like animals."

Crazies. Perfect.

"Shelter in place," Grady shouted. "I'm not shitting

you. Our scans show the assholes are fucking freaks. Probably cannibals."

"Good thing I'm perfectly safe under this power conduit. Who would look here?"

"Find someplace better. They'll see you."

"Too late." I strapped down my HKD and pulled my pistol. There wasn't room for much else.

The ground shook as the horde charged around the corner. Thousands of men and women in rags leaped over trenches, walkways, and small structures like the power conduit. It hummed with energy. Thin, poorly fitted metal covered the wiring within. Rust colored the edges.

Dreadmax had a lot of rust—not something normally seen on a space-capable vessel.

"X-37, when did I have my last tetanus shot?"

"Three standard months ago. The warden ordered it. You told him to screw off, but his medical staff gave it to you anyway."

"Right. How could I forget?"

One of the crazies jumped onto the power box, slamming down both feet with unnecessary force.

"Run the pack. Run the pack. It's dinner time!" The man jumped away, racing to join another group of unwashed, insane humanity.

"This too shall pass," X-37 whispered as five more, then ten, then a hundred screaming lunatics ran over my position.

"Hilarious. You missed your calling. You've got jokes," I murmured.

"Overwatch to Cain, are you still there?"

"Yep. No thanks to you."

"We're moving out of radio contact. Will be back around in nine minutes. The swarm is coming back the way they came..."

Static ended his broadcast.

Looking at the first of the crazies to come back this direction, I suddenly felt very exposed. My hiding place had been perfect when they were traveling in one direction, but now I was basically squatting against a wall where they would see me easily.

I scooted back, stood up, and ran for the first service trench leading away from the maintenance hangar. The people inside had fires going and surprisingly decent music. It looked cozy.

"Grady won't like this route. It's an even greater deviation from the original plan," X-37 pointed out.

"The original plan was shit."

———

"FOR THE RECORD, I've seen enough of the crazies. Let's find the doctor and get the hell off this hunk of junk," I muttered after two hours of escape and evasion brought me back into visual range of the maintenance hangar building.

"What about the children in the surveillance tower?" questioned X-37.

"Well, X, they haven't exactly been helpful. But I'll see what I can do."

This time, I was on the correct side to begin searching for my target.

Not that it mattered.

The RSG were out in force harassing another class of inmates, those not affiliated with a gang and not yet turned into screaming cannibal freaks.

"You'll need to secure a complete evacuation of the facility to be sure there are no innocents left behind when the gravity generator fails," X-37 said.

"You think that's what's going to crash?"

"It will go down shortly after the power fails, and before you ask, atmosphere will be lost almost instantaneously. If you're still here, I recommend being inside the superstructure. Two or three levels down to be safe. People there will be able to survive indefinitely."

"Might be better to get shot into the void. We haven't seen any evidence of the doctor and I don't have a way to develop an informant. I have to go into the RSG building," I said as I stashed my HKD and survival gear underneath an abandoned vehicle.

My pistol and my knife stayed on my hip for now. Later, I'd have to hide them where they were easy to reach.

"Of course," said X-37.

"What would I do without you, X?" I asked, not expecting a response.

Light finally spilled onto the surface of Dreadmax, reflected from the nearby planet. It looked habitable, but I knew it wasn't. Made for a nice view to contrast with the deteriorating surface of the space station though.

"Why aren't these people living within the ring?" I wondered.

"It's full of crazies," answered X-37. "It was overrun soon after security forces pulled out and started dropping inmates with single-use life pods."

"And you're just now telling me this? How many crazies can there be down there?"

"Level V is the hydroponics facility. Even at full population, there's more than enough food to sustain ten thousand human adults indefinitely. Unless they ruined it. In the future, I'd advise you to ask better questions."

It wasn't the first time X-37 had given me this advice.

Two-story row houses that looked like ammunition boxes lined several of the protected trenches leading toward the maintenance hangar. Metal walkways crisscrossed the space above the alley-like streets, some falling down or otherwise promising to be structurally unsound. Men and women, and more than a few children, stepped out on their ground-level porches and waited for RSG tax collectors.

Grabbing a poncho from a man who looked too scared to resist, I blended with a group of people being taken inside the RSG stronghold.

"Haven't seen you before, friend," a man said.

"Just passing through."

He laughed and looked around at the thugs who had *encouraged* the work party. "At least they're not sending us on a scavenging party. I hate going down to the greenhouse. My brother-in-law likes it, but he's better at pilfering shit than I am. Always comes back with some extra food. First time I tried that, I'd get my hands cut off."

I studied him without being obvious. He'd clearly been on a starvation diet for a long time and may or may not have enjoyed the benefits of running water and plumbing. "What are you in for?"

He looks at me strangely. "Beg your pardon?"

"Dreadmax is a maximum-security prison," I said, intending to elaborate but losing the words. I was wondering if he was young enough to have been born here, but I was pretty sure he was in his thirties. Hard living had made him look older than he was.

"I colonized the wrong planet. Next thing you know, I'm doing maintenance for gangsters and hiding my daughters under the cistern. What about you? Are you a hardened killer?"

I didn't bother with an answer. As soon as I could, I moved away from these people and slipped into a series of hallways inside the main building. The rest of them were being put to work in the hangar repairing machines on some kind of assembly line. Some of the parts belonged to wheeled vehicles and others seemed to have been salvaged from the shipyard some distance around the ring.

There was a grim sort of economy with the place. Offices and smaller workshops overlooked the ground floor from the second and third levels. I spotted heavily muscled freaks with tattoos and piercings leaning over to watch their workforce. They seemed to be hungover and pissed off at life.

Every door to the place had at least two guards that appeared sober and well-armed. They had military weapons, but also some very nasty black-market variations that violated most galactic treaties.

The tortured screams from the night before made a lot more sense now.

I slipped into a hallway that ran the perimeter of the massive building, then ducked into a stairwell when I spotted two hard-asses approaching at a fast walk. They were talking to each other, swearing and laughing. They might have been convicts, but I wouldn't have doubted if they'd had some military training. Or maybe they were cops, former guards who went bad or got left here.

"Overwatch for Cain, how copy?"

"I copy fine, but now isn't a good time. I'm looking for the doctor."

"It's about time. What can we do to help?"

"How's that evacuation plan coming? The longer I'm down here, the more innocent civilians I'm encountering.

They have a class system to get things done, like food collection and basic maintenance."

"Don't worry about the evacuation. I've sent a request up the chain and used all the hot-topic words politicians need to hear to authorize anything," Grady said. "I'd be skeptical if I hadn't seen some of these people in the daylight. No kids yet, but I'm willing to believe you."

"You're an asshole. Why don't you come down here and see for yourself?"

"You're always talking about how this would be going if you had planned the mission. Well, my proposal had been to go in with spec ops and clear this whole area until we found the principal and pulled him out. So don't lecture me."

I ducked into a supply closet as an old man carried buckets of water toward what smelled like some type of alcohol distillery at the end of this passage. He never looked up from his feet.

I opened the door a crack. "Like I said, Grady, this isn't a great place for me to talk. I'm deep in hostile territory without weapons or a quick reaction force to pull me out of the fire when it gets hot."

"What happened to your weapons?" he asked.

"Don't worry about my guns. They have better stuff to kill people with. Ever been shot with an acid thrower?"

"No, Hal. That's illegal. What's next, weapons of mass destruction? Nerve gas? Execution camps?" Grady asked.

"That's nice coming from someone who knows how

many people are going to die when the power plant takes a shit."

There was a long pause before I heard Commander Briggs break in on a remote line. "That's enough of that talk, Cain. Do your job. Let me worry about collateral damage."

"I met a guy who said he colonized the wrong planet and got relocated to Dreadmax. I thought this place was for murderers and traitors, not rogue colonists."

No one answered.

"That went well," X-37 said.

"Whatever." I picked up the pace, heading toward the sound of loud music and drunken laughter.

"What exactly are you doing?" X-37 asked.

"If the doctor is valuable to the Union, he might be valuable to whoever's running this place. Slab or whatever his name is. Remind me to tell them he's got a stupid name if we run into him."

"I can't see how taunting the man will help you complete the mission," replied X-37.

I arrived at a balcony on the third level overlooking another large hangar. There was a walkway circumventing this level with several private suites that were probably not for inmates in the beginning. It was the cleanest, most heavily guarded section of the building so far.

High above, there were dim LED lights, but many were out. The result was a harsh gloom that reminded me what type of facility this was.

Gathering up cleaning supplies, I turned myself into a janitor and pressed on. What was the worst that could happen?

A pair of guards stopped me, one with his left palm held forward and right hand holding the rifle he had on a sling. His partner didn't say anything, only watched me.

They were solid, true professionals.

"Jonesy already cleaned this level. Who the hell are you?" asked one.

"I'm the lucky bastard that gets to clean up the doctor. Can you guys stop making him shit himself?" I replied.

"Yeah, that," the lead guard said.

"Lucky guess," X-37 whispered in my ear.

I'd assumed the screams were from the VIP's torture session. I knew from experience what happened when your body couldn't take any more abuse.

6

AFTER THE GUARDS let me in, I spotted the good doctor immediately. The sole occupant of what had been an officer's suite was tied to a chair and only half conscious. He was balding, slightly overweight, and covered in dried blood.

I took a bucket of water, a shop towel, and cleaned him up like a bedridden invalid who'd been sitting in his own filth for too long. Nothing could take away the stink, but he slipped out of his daze and watched me with increasing interest.

"You're not one of them," he said, speech slurred like a drunk.

"It doesn't matter who I am. Are you Doctor Hastings?"

Tears leaked from his eyes as he nodded vigorously.

"I'll be right back."

The hard part of the ruse was maintaining the lazy, disinterested shuffle of a defeated man. My acting skills were a bit rusty. And I was angry.

The stoic guard ignored me, preferring to watch the hallway like he would shoot the next person he saw. The other one looked me up and down, made a disgusted face, and waved me toward the exit.

I drew my silenced pistol and shot them both dead—catching the bodies as they fell.

"I'm assuming you assholes were really bad people who deserved this."

They were speechless of course.

"If it makes you feel any better, I'm probably not far behind you," I said to their corpses.

I dragged them into another room and closed the door. There was blood, but luckily, I was the best janitor on Dreadmax. *Got blood smears? Call Halek Cain and make the body disappear today!*

Drying my hands on the stolen poncho, I returned to the interrogation room.

Doctor Hastings had moved away from his chair while I was gone. He was standing with his arms crossed, hugging himself as he looked through the window to the main hangar below. It was like a private booth at a stadium and it made me wonder what the Union officers who originally ran this place had talked about while watching their minions.

"This wasn't always a prison," he said.

"Step back from the window," I ordered.

He looked at me, then complied, moving away. "I'm not an idiot. The glass slants outward from the bottom of the windowsill, suggesting there is considerable glare when viewed from the outside. I doubt anyone down there could see us, even if they were looking," he said, unperturbed.

The party was ramping up again. Music thumped the walls. A caravan of vehicles with Red Skull Gangsters hanging off every side rail and bumper rolled into a large bay door at one end. Engines without mufflers revved. Air horns blasted a juvenile call and response that quickly got on my nerves.

Each truck had a cage in the back.

Doctor Hastings went pale. "I was hoping she got away."

Several pieces of the puzzle fell into place. "What are you doing here, Doctor?"

He faced away from me when I asked the question, wiping something from his eyes as he moved toward the door like he might run for it. I had to give him credit, he was playing it pretty cool for an amateur.

"I wouldn't do that," I warned. "I mean, how did it work for you last time?"

"I haven't tried to escape. They have my daughter. She tried, continues to try to get away, but they always catch her and three other young women. It's part of some inscrutable gang law they have. One girl escapes, and they bring back three extras for the cages. Nothing makes Slab and his Red Skull thugs happier than a drunken killing spree."

"You didn't answer my question."

"Research. I was here on a research project."

I crowded into his personal space and brushed imaginary dirt from his battered jumpsuit. It was one of the original prison uniforms. Someone had scrawled his name on the tag, misspelling it: H-a-y-s-t-i-n-g-z.

"How many attempts have there been to rescue you?"

"I don't know," he sputtered. "Just you and your team, I suppose."

"You don't know because I'm the first person to get this far. Think about that for a second. You should be realizing that I'll be the last. If you want out of here, you're coming with me and you're going to do everything I say."

"I can't live without my daughter. There's no reason to rescue me if you don't help her escape too."

"She's not part of my mission," I replied.

"There must have been some kind of mistake. The Union cares more about her than me. Call someone for new orders. They won't let us leave Dreadmax without her."

"Why?" I asked.

"She's my daughter. Please rescue her," he pleaded.

"What are you doing here, Doctor Hastings?" I asked, repeating the question.

"Please, sir. Don't make me go against the Union."

Ignoring his oddly dispassionate plea, I spoke so softly

he had to lean forward to hear me. "I need information to do my job. *Answer* the question."

He shook his head and backed away. "I can't abandon my work. Just leave me here."

The RSG music continued to shake the floor. Bass thumped a driving beat that filled the entire facility.

"That hurts my feelings, X. He's more scared of the Union than me," I said.

Doctor Hastings perked up when he realized what I'd just said and what it meant. "You are talking to a nerve-ware AI. Are you a Reaper? I thought they were all dead."

"You would think that. The fact that you even know what a Reaper is means something. What are you doing here, Doctor, and why do they have a destroyer with three companies of soldiers and multiple teams of spec ops commandos ready to storm the place?"

Looking at his feet for several seconds before he answered, he exhaled forcefully.

"About a year ago, I realized the Union had quietly taken over my daughter's boarding school. I made inquiries to civilian and military officials I've worked with over the years. They had their theories and reassured me this just something that happened in the Union. I knew, however, that they were holding my daughter hostage."

"Sounds terrible," I said, nonplussed.

"The situation grated on me for a few weeks before I made my first mistake. I'm not a soldier or a spy or what-ever you are. My world is about research, using the scientific method to test theories—Occam's Razor. You know it?"

"All things being equal, the simplest explanation is most likely correct," I said.

"Exactly. One morning, I awoke with the firm conviction the Union wanted something from me that I wasn't providing them. All that was needed was information."

"You confronted the Union?"

"I set up an appointment and had a meeting. By the time I returned to my laboratory I'd been reassigned to… a place I can't talk about. It wasn't all bad. The facility and the brilliant minds I worked with were a dream come true for a scientist like me."

"But they put your daughter on Dreadmax to keep you in line."

"I didn't know that until later. We talked every day by video conference," he said, acting more like the man I assumed he was. The memory refreshed him. "Something went wrong and now the Red Skull Gangsters have her."

"The secret laboratory must be near Dreadmax if they were able to have a video conference in real time," X-37 commented in my head.

"She's a wonderful young woman," Hastings continued.

"I'm sure she is. If I can grab her, I will, but I can't do that while I'm arguing with you. We're leaving and you're doing whatever the fuck I say without hesitation. Understood?"

He nodded.

"I need to grab some things, then we'll call for extraction."

"Weapons, I assume."

"You're a smart guy, Doc. And observant. You wouldn't happen to be a medical doctor with trauma experience?"

"I have advanced medical degrees, but most of my work is in other areas."

"PhDs?"

"Several."

"Good to know. I'm sure they'll be useful when we meet the cannibals."

We moved out, fast enough that I had to drag the doctor onward more than once. On the way, I spotted a hopper full of surprisingly clean, perfectly folded jumpsuits. I found one of the smaller sizes, rolled it so tight it nearly disappeared, and shoved it into a side pocket.

"Why don't we just find a side door and use the maintenance trenches to reach your weapons and armor?" Hastings asked.

"Well, because I'm not shitty at my job. I checked for side doors, windows, and access hatches before I made my approach. It's called reconnaissance, useful when planning a rescue."

The building was full of activity—not just guards now, but anybody they'd been able to motivate with threats of violence and brandished weapons. Not everyone was here for the party. Some worked like slaves—fixing machines, cleaning up bloodstains, dancing for drunken assholes with guns.

"There must other exits," Hastings asserted, looking over his shoulder nervously at the sound of a door slamming.

The lights went out, plunging the corridor into darkness until red emergency panels called the original crew to battle stations. I doubted Slab and his thugs understood what battle stations meant, but they'd pushed the button.

"There are doors, but they open into areas with a lot of folks I'd rather not meet," I said.

We moved into a new section. Hallways and doors were now metal walkways and staircases. The grating above us shook from the sound of running feet. A group rushed down one of the ladder-like staircases.

"That's our cue to head the other direction," I announced.

"We can't go back the way we came," Hastings said, starting to panic. "Are we being attacked? Are they sending in Union soldiers?"

"Someone hit the alert button, but that doesn't really mean anything. They probably think it's a fire alarm and use it to wake everyone up. Thank whatever gods you pray to that the music is so loud."

"We have to do something! Let's wait here for the soldiers."

"Chill, Doc. Take a breath. The cavalry isn't coming."

I'd seen this before. He'd get more worked up each time

we encountered a problem. There wasn't time to reassure him.

"Let's move," I ordered.

"I can't. I mean, *we* can't," he clarified at my look." It's too dangerous."

I grabbed the collar of his jumpsuit with one hand and poked him in the ribs with my pistol. "I can't afford to waste a bullet on you and I don't want to carry you, but there will come a time when you're better dead than left here to be compromised," I informed him.

None of that was part of my briefing, but I made certain assumptions. The look on his face confirmed his research was illegal as hell, the type of thing that got a person silenced rather than expose the entire operation.

His reaction meant something. I filed it away for later consideration.

"I'm not arguing with you. I just don't think this is a good idea," he responded, hastily.

I dug the pistol into his rib cage and pushed him in the direction I wanted him to go, toward a stairway. I heard people coming down from two levels above and hoped we could outdistance them.

It took several steps before I got the doctor to move on his own. This really would've been easier with a team. I needed two people to manage Hastings and at least one to cover our back trail. If I was a real Reaper, I would've had authority to impress dark ops agents or spec ops soldiers into service, which would've been useful about now.

We reached the main level and ran across the launch deck. The main hangar was full of people. Some were looking for us and others were partying. A few seem to be doing both. The sound of loud music, slamming metal doors, and occasional gunfire filled the room.

"What are they shooting at?" he asked, nervously.

"I have no idea. There's been a lot of random gunfire since I arrived." I pulled him behind a transport vehicle without wheels or an engine. Similar vehicles lined one side of the massive room, still leaving space for the enslaved construction workers, and beyond them, hundreds of GSD gangsters and their thralls.

I could smell the homemade alcohol and some kind of synthetic tobacco or marijuana.

"That's not even a live band," Dr. Hastings said in candid horror.

"Yeah, that's bullshit. I'm filing a complaint. Come on, let's go."

As usual, the man tried to go the wrong direction, but this time, I realized it was for a different reason. He headed for the cages and a young woman I assumed was his daughter.

So far, the search parties hadn't noticed us among the regular denizens of Dreadmax. That was bound to change. I was running out of both time and patience with Hastings. If he wasn't the principal, I'd leave him here.

"Hastings, get your ass behind one of these trucks and hide. I told you I'd get her if I could. You're not helping."

He ducked behind one of the parked, non-functional heavy transport vehicles. There were missing pieces that suggested these were often salvaged to service other vehicles.

"Stay there. Don't move. If I have to come rescue you, I can't do anything for your daughter."

"I understand. Thank you. Please don't let them hurt her."

"I'm gonna hurt you if you don't shut up," I grunted.

"You're very abrasive for a rescuer."

"Wait until you really piss me off. Which will happen if you move one fucking inch from here."

Eyes downcast, the poncho I had stolen pulled up to cover my scars and cybernetic augmentation, I slipped through the workers and pretended to load pallets as I watched the drunken celebration on the other side of the maintenance hangar.

This wasn't someplace I wanted to be. The more time that passed, the more time the real guards had to get organized. There could be checkpoints with pictures from the building's surveillance cameras soon.

"Hey you, what the fuck are you doing? Those pallets have already been loaded," a foreman said. Behind him, guards worked their way through the crowd examining people.

Three more of the heavy patrol vehicles entered via the bay doors, each with a man on the crew-served machine gun. The work crews shrank backward, clearly afraid the guns being turned on them.

"I'm used to prisons where we have to make shanks out of toothbrushes. These assholes have military hardware," I muttered as I retreated from the angry foreman. "I could use some help, X."

"My only recommendation is to leave. You can't help the girl. You can, of course, disregard this advice if your purpose is to commit suicide," X-37 answered dispassionately.

"You know me better than that, X."

By the time I reached the doctor, there were at least a dozen more guards searching the work crews. They were either being thorough or had guessed how I evaded them.

"We're leaving. If you want me to help your daughter, you'll do everything you can to get to safety. Until that happens, there's nothing I can do for her. I really don't want to knock you out and carry you, so let's fucking go."

He gave in, but not before he started crying and blubbering that we had to save her. The Union would do this, the Union would do that… He just wouldn't shut up.

"STAY CLOSE. Run when I run, get down when I get down," I said, striding toward the bay door the trucks had come through. "This is going to get dicey."

"Okay, okay. Are you sure we can't just grab Elise and run for it? Please."

I didn't bother to answer. The professional guards I'd seen on the upper levels moved through the crowd with submachine guns and shotguns. They were searching zone after zone. Maybe they knew what I looked like and maybe they didn't, but if they were half as good as I thought they were, I wouldn't be able to withstand close scrutiny.

The poncho disguise was lame and wouldn't last much longer. Regardless of whether or not they had a viable description, every one of them had seen Hastings.

Picking up the pace, I bumped the foreman who had yelled at me earlier. He fell to one knee and cursed.

"What the fuck is your problem? Didn't you hear me the first time? I saw you try to ditch me!" He strode forward, fists clenched for a fight.

He shoved Doctor Hastings out of his way and got in front of me. I hit him three times in the space of a second: left jab to his temple, right cross to his chin, and a left forearm strike across his neck and the brachial nerve. The final strike had all my weight behind it as I twisted at the waist and lunged forward.

The foreman collapsed.

I grabbed Hastings. "Run for the bay door!"

Twisting on the balls of my feet, I shot the closest guard and took his submachine gun. Throwing down the silenced pistol, I transitioned to the new weapon and opened fire on two more guards.

The crowd surged one way and the guards the other. I fired on the nearest heavy machine gun car and it fired back. I dropped to the floor even as I finished my attack and rolled sideways, hoping I hadn't made a huge miscalculation.

There wasn't time to evaluate the carnage that ensued. Workers and partiers alike panicked, stampeding toward the exits. I saw Hastings get swept up in the tide and carried outside of the building.

I hadn't planned it that way but could make it work. Looking on the bright side, the principal was free of the building and hidden in the crowd.

Staying as low as possible, I made my way to the undrivable vehicles and scrambled beneath the largest. Bullets slammed into it as I came up on the other side and ran along the wall until I found one of the bay doors.

Outside, chaos ruled. Hundreds of people were fleeing the carnage, but what caused the problems were scores of family members running to see what was happening. Panicked parents and screaming children added to the confusion.

7

I FOUND HASTINGS SOON, not far from where the tide had picked him up.

The scene became more than just panicked families and teary reunions. The sound of gunfire and the sight of the walking wounded also provoked a group of men coming from another worksite. I was shouldering the doctor into a narrow side trench when I first saw them. More and more of the men and women came together and marched toward the armed gang members.

"Now's our chance," I said, rushing through a series of twists and turns to reach the derelict vehicle where I had hidden my gear. The submachine gun was cool, but I didn't have much ammunition left. The sooner I reacquainted myself with the HDK and my body armor, the better.

Shots rang out, but I couldn't see who fired them. I

dropped the body armor over my head and adjusted the straps.

People sprinted away from the sound of gunfire. One of the heavy machine gun vehicles raced past. I put on the rest of my gear and went for a better look. Doctor Hastings continued to ask questions and I continued to ignore him, only having to push him back once or twice.

Another vehicle raced past in the other direction.

"What's happening?" Hastings demanded.

"They're looking for us."

"Why are they shooting at everyone?" The alarm in Hastings's voice grated on my nerves.

I hated working with civilians and amateurs.

"They're not shooting at everyone," I said, rolling my eyes.

"They're shooting at a lot of people. Oh, gods! They just drove over that man!"

Looking at Hastings as tears ran down his filthy face, I wondered two things. Why had I wasted my time cleaning him up, and could he keep it together for the rest of this escape. I knew one thing—he'd keep bothering me about his daughter until I did something.

I was also fucking furious at the sight of the display cages. Vigilantism had always been my downfall. I'd nearly been washed out in the early days of my training for trying to do the right thing when it was counter to the mission.

Some things never changed. I had no illusions that my

moral code would withstand close scrutiny, but I didn't like bullies.

"Follow me." I took Hastings to a walk-in supply locker and shoved him through the doorway. The frame was heavy and it had enough power to have lights inside, which I hoped would keep Hastings from losing his nerve and doing something stupid.

The surface of Dreadmax was as large as a city. At times, I thought of it as a darkly exotic metropolis rather than the exterior of a space station with an environment shield over it. What looked like doors to buildings were really hatchways to the interior. The surface was uneven and had a skyline a lot like a caged city, but it had originally been a series of maintenance trenches, point-defense batteries, and docking bays.

"One second. I want to make sure this doesn't access the lower levels."

"Is that a problem?" Hastings asked.

"Where do you think the crazies come from?"

He swallowed hard.

"Looks good. One way in, one way out. I'll be right back," I said.

"Wait! What do you want me to do here?"

"Close the door. Wait for me. Don't leave, no matter what."

"What are you doing?"

"I'm going after the kid."

"She's not a kid, she's my daughter. And if you call her that, you'll have problems."

"Fucking great," I replied.

Leaving my principal here violated every standard operating procedure and protocol of the Reaper Corps. I wanted to tell Grady what I was doing just to drive him bat shit crazy.

"What do you think, X?" I asked.

"You have a seventy-eight-point two percent chance of failing given your recent bad decisions," it replied.

"If I didn't make bad decisions, I wouldn't be me."

"You wouldn't be here either," X-37 countered.

"True."

I ran with a group of panicking civilians, nearly reaching the depopulated maintenance hangar before the mob surged another direction. Crazies had heard the noise, apparently, and groups of twenty or thirty were braving the daylight to run people down.

The RSG treated them like everyone else in the crowd —shooting anyone who got in their way, firebombing places they thought people were hiding, and dragging new thralls away from their families to put in cages while crazies preferred stealing older, weaker civilians they could pull into access hatches and disappear with.

"I wish they wouldn't start fires," I muttered, not really caring if X-37 had a comment.

"It violates logic. Oxygen is a perishable commodity on

Dreadmax, even though it may seem abundant," answered X.

Slipping away from the crowd was easy.

I ducked through one of the open bay doors and slipped into the shadows to get a feel for the odds against me. Things had to be better in the gang stronghold than on the street.

"It looks like we got lucky, X," I said. "None of the pros are here. Just the second-string guards."

The assholes were drunk and high. Two of them argued over a beer keg that had been fashioned from a gas tank, while another group opened a cage to drag out one of the girls.

"This would be a hell of a lot easier if that was the kid we're here for," I said.

X-37 made a clicking sound I thought was meant as chastisement. "Her name is Elise. Doctor Hastings warned you not to call her a kid," he reminded.

I walked toward the cage and the rape-in-progress of the girl who wasn't Elise, or the kid, or whatever.

Two of the men saw me at the last second, which surprised me, because I didn't think they were that alert.

"Find your own—"

I threw back the poncho and raised the submachine gun, squeezing the trigger the moment I had my first target lined up. The weapon wasn't silenced.

All three men fell as the thunder of the weapon echoed

in three short bursts through the massive maintenance facility.

Tossing it aside when it was empty, I grabbed the HDK from the tactical sling over my shoulder and readied it.

Nearby, the jerkoffs fighting over the booze stared at me dumbly. I shot two of them before they started moving, and the rest went down just as easily.

"Shall I keep a tally of your kills?" asked X-37 nonchalantly.

"I'm just getting warmed up, X. Don't worry about it. There won't be a judicial review of this mission."

An eerie silence fell over the area. I had never been one for superstition, but this felt portentous. Glancing up at the windows where I rescued the doctor, I realized he'd been right. It was impossible to see inside from here.

Whatever. So he was right about one thing. That didn't mean he wasn't a lying snake.

Running to the cage, I slid aside the crossbar that couldn't be reached from the inside and swung open the tiny door. I had pulled people out of prison camps before, and most of the time, they were surprisingly hard to get moving. Depending on how long they'd been captive, they could be fearful of taking that first step to freedom.

Elise was different. She bounded to the floor of the hangar then ran to the next cage—somehow appearing less disheveled than her father.

Slab's goons had inexpertly bleached her naturally dark hair and trimmed her utility jumpsuit to fit their brutish fantasies. Someone had blackened her eyes a few days ago. The split lip and finger marks on her neck were newer.

Undernourished but full of youthful rage, she was clearly acting out a plan she'd worked on a thousand times in her head.

"We don't have time for that," I said.

"You go to hell!"

"Fine." I sprinted to one cage after another. "But the real guards are on their way back by now."

She ignored me.

"You could say thanks."

The look she gave me could have melted ice. "I don't know you. And if you think I'm going anywhere with you, you've got another thing coming."

"Your father sent me," I said as I spotted a pair of the elite guards returning. Before Elise could respond, I yanked her into one of the maintenance bays.

"What the hell?" She twisted to break free, but I pulled her right arm over her left and bear-hugged her so she couldn't move.

"Listen, kid. I don't care what you do as long as you don't get me caught. I was sent here to rescue your father, not you. If you can keep him motivated, then I've got a use for you. If you are going to be a spoiled brat, I'll just leave you here."

She yanked free the moment I relaxed my grip. "You don't know me. What gives you the right to call me a spoiled brat? I'm pissed off, okay? Why don't you try being in a cage for a week?"

I stepped to the doorway and looked for the elite RSG guards. "What's your story?"

"None of your business," she snapped, rubbing her wrist. "Can we go now?"

"Only if you want to get caught."

She shifted uneasily, and started pacing, clearly afraid of going back in the cage. There was an animal desperation in her eyes that I hadn't seen in very many people her age. I thought she was fifteen or sixteen, but it was hard to tell. She'd been roughed up pretty good.

She pulled a strand of hair to conceal the worst of her facial bruises and tugged up the collar of her jumpsuit to hide the damage they'd done to her neck. The velcro still worked, but there was nothing to do about the way her captors had turned the legs of her pants into short-shorts and the top into a sleeveless half shirt.

"Put this on." I tossed her the tightly rolled jumpsuit I'd grabbed after Hastings told me about her.

"What's this?" she demanded.

"I don't want you to catch cold."

She aimed her middle finger at me, narrowing her gaze like she would stab me if she had a knife… but she slipped into the never-been-worn jumpsuit, appearing more self-conscious in the new garment than in her old stripper costume.

"There are rules. When I run, you run —"

"Yeah, I get it. Don't lecture me. I'm not an idiot. You're obviously some sort of hotshot commando and I'm just a kid you're trying to rescue so you can get my dad to do things. Story of my life."

"All right, then let's try this out. Time to go. Now!"

We ran across the hangar and slid behind a pile of loot the RSG had collected over the past several days. Most of it was food or salvage that looked reasonably useful.

"What your story?" I asked a second time.

She looked around the corner for pursuit, then scanned the area above us. For an untrained teenager, she was doing well. Her survival instincts might actually be useful. All things being equal, I still wanted a team of well-armed and well-trained commandos as my QRF.

"I didn't like what my father was doing. Hated it. So I ran away. These cock-holsters caught me."

"You know what, I'm not sure why I believe you, but I think we're starting off on the right foot."

"We're not going to be friends. Don't try to show me how cool you are or that you want to listen to my drama. What the fuck's wrong with your arm? Is your eye fake?"

"Don't worry about me. Let's try this for your story. Some Union thugs moved you someplace relatively nice, and next thing you know, you're in a lockdown facility on Dreadmax. Something went wrong, and you tried to escape. More than once."

"You *would* know all that. They probably had you spying on me before they took me from school."

I counted the guards and tracked their movement. "There's going to be a chance for us to dart out the bay doors, assuming they don't close them."

"Okay," she said.

"We have some things in common."

"I doubt it."

"If you knew my history with the Union, you might be less skeptical. But I think you're right, we're not going to be friends. Partners, maybe. We both want to get your father off this place for our own reasons."

"I ran away because I thought it would decrease the Union's influence on him," she said.

"Time to go," I said, cutting her off. "You first, I'll fall behind you. If you hear gunfire, run faster."

The hangar bay felt larger and more exposed each time I crossed it. We reached the street and continued into a narrow trench without safety lights. Elise had no trouble keeping up. Maybe she was a spoiled rich girl, but she could run like the wind.

We laughed breathlessly when we reached our cover and were sure no one was after us this time.

"Okay, I'll tell you the other part." She struggled to catch her breath. "I also wanted to piss him off."

"Maybe we'll be friends after all," I said. "I'm really good at pissing people off."

"I believe it," she said, slating a glance at me.

"No need to get nasty, kid. Pay attention. There are a lot of dangerous people out here besides the RSG."

"I'm not a kid," she chastised.

"Maybe I'm just trying to piss you off."

"Whatever. Don't be a dick."

"Does your father know you talk like that?"

"Yeah, he hates it. Called him a pussy once and he stroked out. I thought he was going to need an ambulance." She laughed.

Something exploded near the RSG stronghold.

"Let's find your pissed-off dad and get away from this place before the power fails."

She didn't have a witty comeback for that last nugget of information.

Fires burned throughout the short Dreadmax night. The way it orbited the planet and its own rotation seemed to fast forward time. It was like we'd spent a lifetime on this rusty hunk of junk already. Elise continued to be pissed off and moody at the same time as only teenagers could. But she moved well and kept her mouth shut.

This wasn't her first time on the run. I wanted to ask her if she'd been a runner before getting locked up on Dreadmax. Now wasn't the time. With darkness upon us, the crazies were out in force. The RSG search parties had lost direction, but they were still mobile and dangerous.

I found several supply lockers just like the one I had left Doctor Hastings inside of that had been opened and firebombed.

"What? Why do you make that face every time we find one of these?" Elise asked.

"I'm not making a face."

"You are."

"I'm a Reaper, trained by dark ops. Professional as fuck," I exclaimed.

She leaned back against the wall where we were resting and bumped the back of her head against it several times. "Does everyone in this place have delusions of grandeur? There aren't any more Reapers. My father always told me they weren't real in the first place."

I shrugged. "Maybe there aren't."

"What does that mean? You tell me you're one thing, then tell me that thing doesn't exist? I liked it better when you were an arrogant son-of-a-bitch. Don't get moody on me. I'm the teenager, it's my right. Do whatever adult super commandos do."

"You don't seem like a teenager," I said as I peeked around the corner to look for a moving band of crazies. "Except for that crazy outfit."

"They put me in this!"

"Uh-huh."

She rolled her eyes.

I sobered. "You're an old soul, Elise. Stop carrying the weight of the world and be a kid."

"You grow up quick in my family. What's up with all these firebombed structures? Why do you get tense when you see one?" She moved away from the wall, mimicking my watchfulness.

"They're too lazy to clear buildings, so they just throw rocket fuel in there. Someplace on this decommissioned battle moon, there's probably a lot of unused fuel. I have it on good authority that they stopped landing and taking off here a long time ago and chose to just drop people in life pods. So the fuel tanks are probably full at some of the hangars," I said, taking hold of her arm and guiding her into the next passage.

She complied more willingly than the first time I tried this move, somehow understanding that I wasn't trying to push her around but only guide her toward safety. When she pulled her arm free, it was with much less attitude than before.

"I hope you know what you're doing," she said as she moved along a metal wall three times her height.

I caught her glancing up at some of the walkways, but neither of us heard footsteps.

"Keep moving. We're almost there."

"Are you really a Reaper?" she asked the next time we stopped.

"I was."

"That doesn't make any sense. Union assassins don't retire, I imagine."

"Strictly speaking, I wasn't an assassin."

"Have you killed anybody for the Union? Outside of a battle?"

"I have." The words came out flat, either due to my tiredness or due to my guilt at having said them.

Some of her teenage meanness came through. "Then you're an assassin."

"I also kidnapped people and blew things up."

"Like a terrorist."

"Terrorists are imprecise. I never accepted collateral damage as part of my missions. Neither did any of the other Reapers."

"So you only kill people who deserve it. That's convenient." She moved ahead of me and checked the next intersection like a pro. Her sweep of the trench opening into this area was quick but thorough and she stayed back as far as she could to avoid unnecessary exposure while still seeing what she needed to see. Maybe she'd learned the tactics gaming online.

"Why don't we forget this conversation ever happened," I said, moving in front of her to take the lead.

"You could just silence me. Isn't that what people like you do?"

"Yeah, kid. Don't push your luck. There's probably a reason they sent me on this mission instead of a spec ops team."

She didn't have anything to say after that.

Two of the larger, louder vehicles without machine guns drove into the street we were crossing and spotted us immediately. The drivers revved their engines and squealed their tires as they pursued us. I heard the magnetic gravity boxes click on.

This made the vehicles faster, so long as Dreadmax didn't lose gravity.

A few of the RSG thugs opened fire, missing us by several meters. I didn't think they had the training to fire from a moving vehicle, but all they needed was one lucky shot.

Elise screamed, causing me to hesitate and look for blood. There wasn't time to actually stop. She pulled away from me, cursing like a Soldier.

"I guess you're okay," I said. "Take that trench and head for the third gun turret on the horizon. If you get to it, you went too far." I stopped behind a support beam and fired at the lead vehicle. The driver never touched the brakes despite several direct hits on the window.

I hadn't really expected that to do much, but I had to try.

In the same breath, I sprinted after Elise. We ran into a passage that was far too narrow for the vehicles. I looked back but couldn't see what they were doing. By the time we reached the next turn, I knew they were chasing us on foot, shouting challenges and threats but also communicating with each other.

These weren't part of the military trained guards I had seen on the top level of the RSG stronghold, but they worked together fairly well. The pack instincts came to life at the sight of prey.

I looked up, hoping Grady was about to unleash hell on these assholes.

I didn't have a lot of toys in my mission bag, but I had swiped one claymore from Sergeant Crank. Once I'd let Elise get pretty far ahead, I stopped and affixed the explosive device to a wall, making sure it faced toward the enemy.

If I'd had a tripwire or time to set one up, this would be perfect.

Bullets ricocheted near me. I moved back as far as I could with the detonation plunger, hoping the wires didn't get tangled on one of the jagged edges in the narrow passage.

Two of the RSG dogs ran past the device. The bulk of the group came close behind them, also stopping to shoot from time to time despite their friends being in the line of fire. Weapon safety wasn't their strong point.

I hit the plunger, blowing five or six of the gang members into bloody chunks, then raised the HDK to dispatch the other two. One got so close, I felt the blast of his weapon's muzzle as I sidestepped and shot him in the throat.

"Okay, X. You can keep track of my kills, since we're about to go off the rails on this mission."

"About to, sir?"

There wasn't time to be sure I killed the men. I ran to catch up with Elise and found her crossing the last open area before we reached her father's hiding place.

Dreadmax continued to turn. The distant sun came up on the horizon, too bright to look at and too sharp to paint an even glow over the surface. Harsh shadows reached and twisted like something from a drug-induced nightmare.

Grady's dropship flew at me with the sun behind it.

"Cain for overwatch, I'm being pursued by hostiles. A little help, please."

What I expected was the roar of an auto cannon or a cluster of rockets. Instead, I saw Grady drop to the surface and charge forward with his HDK pulled tight to his shoulder and his attention on the people he was about to kill. The ship initiated cover fire, shredding the walls around my pursuers and taking out anybody who had made it through my claymore trap and wasn't deterred by the men I'd already slaughtered.

"Keep moving!" Grady shouted. "I'm right behind you."

"Where the fuck is your team?"

"Not authorized. It was a snap decision. Don't make me regret it."

I heard him grunt a curse about the time I reached the supply closet where Elise waited, wide-eyed and breathing hard.

"They shot your friend!"

"Not my friend. He'll be fine." I opened the hatch to the supply closet and saw the doctor waiting, sweating terror through his skin as he crouched near the back of the small room. He had the look of somebody who had been in complete darkness for too long.

"I kept the lights off. I didn't know what to do. There

were so many of them." He wasn't a small man, but he looked small right now, crouching defensively.

"Get your dad, kid."

Elise ran to her father and embraced him while I went back to check on Grady. My old friend came hobbling toward me with a big smile on his face.

"You're in a pretty good mood for somebody with a gunshot wound."

He kept the smile as he clenched his teeth against the pain, tossing me a first aid kit. "Help a brother out, will you."

After checking for further pursuit, I peeled away a section of his thigh armor and found one of the bullets had penetrated. It wasn't deep, but the bruise around the wound would be debilitating for most people. Stopping the blood was easy, but he was going to be slowed down for a while.

8

"Not bad, Hal. You got the principal plus one," Grady said as we moved into a new area and hunkered down to see which way the RSG and the crazies moved. There were a lot of both despite the sun illuminating the surface of Dreadmax with a harsh white light.

"We need to get to a pickup site," I said.

"I have the ship coming back around. Once we confirm you have the principal, we have clearance to pick you up. I told you this would be an easy mission," Grady said.

I noticed Elise and the doctor were watching him carefully. She kept her mouth shut, almost like this was too good to be true.

The girl had good instincts.

I shook my head. "It's too hot for an LZ here. They

have heavy machine guns on vehicles, and I saw at least one crate of surface-to-air rockets in their stronghold."

There was also a theory I wanted to test.

"Dammit, Hal. We're done. This mission is over. You have the principal and his daughter. The dropship can withstand small arms fire, you know that. You don't have to make up some story about rockets."

"I saw the rockets," Elise said. "Before he came, they used to shoot them off like fireworks. They're a bunch of psychopaths."

Grady clenched his teeth and hobbled to the edge of our hiding place to look for threats.

"The plan they gave during the briefing designated a shuttle bay for deployment and pickup," I said. "That's where we're going. Their spec ops team can get help from Soldier security if they need to."

"I should've known better. Nothing is ever easy with you," Grady said. "That's five kilometers from here. On a good day, any place other than here, that wouldn't be too bad, even with this scratch on my leg. But we're on the clock here, in case you forgot. And there's a lot of bad guys roaming the streets."

"You got that part right," I said.

"What did you do to piss them off?" Grady asked.

"Well, for starters, I stole their prize doctor, who seems so valuable, even if they don't really know who he is. I also killed a bunch of them." I paused to let that sink in. "I'll take point, you can act as the rearguard if you can keep up. I don't know about the doctor, but the kid is fast."

"I'm not a kid," Elise declared.

"She's not a kid," her father agreed a half second later.

I ignored them both and so did Grady.

"Mission Control isn't going to like this," he commented. "I doubt my decision to help you has earned me any points. Briggs and his bosses about shit kittens when you jumped early."

"Good. Serves them right. They should have let me plan this operation. What have you done to get the innocents evacuated?"

"I was told it's handled," he said with a shrug.

"You're such a dick. You know that's bullshit."

"They're sending a maintenance team to repair whatever is failing, give them more time to sort out the consequences of Dreadmax going offline with innocents on board."

His claim was almost believable. If I had to rescue a large number of people from this place, the first thing I'd do was buy some time. So maybe my old friend wasn't totally full of crap. But there was something he wasn't telling me. The guy looked guilty.

"Time to go," I said. "The Hastings family knows the drill. My way or no way."

"Not going to work, Hal. We need to secure this area for an immediate pick-up. Mission control is very adamant about this point."

"Elise, grab your old man and let's go," I said.

"Okay." She pulled her father to his feet and urged him into a fast walk.

I covered them. Grady brought up the rear, but we hadn't been heading away from the current landing zone for ten seconds when the dropship came around, hovered, and opened fire.

"Stay with me!" I grabbed Elise and the doctor, changing course and running for cover.

"What are they shooting at?" Hastings asked.

"Don't worry about it." I pushed my principals deeper into an alternate path that was going to require a lot of elevated walkway crossings and climbing over debris.

Grady caught up to us. "I told you we have to follow orders. Of course they're going to shoot if they think we've gone rogue!"

Pivoting on my heels, I punched him on the side of his helmet, staggering him without causing real damage.

"Fuck, Hal! You're such a pain in my ass. Let's go back and get on that ship!"

From somewhere above us, a trio of rockets fired into the Dreadmax sky, missing their target and exploding several seconds later on the interior of the environment shield.

"I told you they have surface-to-air rockets," I said, pulling him close for some private words. "That strafing run looked like more than warning shots. I understand they might shoot at me, but it looked like you were in their crosshairs too."

"Don't be a paranoid jerkoff. That's always been your problem."

I ducked out of our hiding spot, looking for RSG thugs, crazy-ass cannibals, and Union gunships. It looked clear, but I knew that wouldn't last.

"We're going to talk about this," I said to Grady, then pointed to Elise, who seemed like the only person on this team with her head right.

We moved out. After several quick and dangerous crossings of metal walkways, I found what I was looking for.

"This is a stairway to below decks. Do you think this is a good idea?" Grady asked, still red-faced from our argument and running on an injured leg.

The doctor and his daughter went pale and watched us wide-eyed. I saw her trying to formulate words but cut her off.

"This is the peak time for crazies above decks. The sun is going down again and they'll be up looking for dinner. According to the schematics, there are long, straight tubes where they run heavy equipment on rails. Since they probably don't have any trains working, it should be the quickest, safest way for us to get to the pickup location," I explained.

"If we're gonna do this, then let's get to it," Grady said, leaning against the wall and aiming his HDK back the way we came. "I'm right behind you."

We hadn't gone very far in the five-meter-tall tube, when Elise came up to my side. "I don't like it down here."

"Me neither. It stinks." What I didn't mention was the evidence of crazies. This passage was one of their super-highways, apparently. The rails were raised slightly, leaving a depression on both sides of the support beams. I saw little shanties and tents made from various materials. They looked vacant, but there was no way to tell for certain, and I didn't have time to clear them out.

Every hundred meters along what was essentially an industrial-strength subway tunnel, there were side doors. I saw ventilation shafts and drainage grates. It was still hard for me to wrap my head around the possibility of flooding or the occasional venting of steam. I knew what it was—coolants from the titanic power plants on the lowest decks.

Whenever I found one of the steam-spouting pipes, I also found serious rust and degradation of the structural integrity.

Doctor Hastings saw what I was looking at during one of our rest breaks. "The venting of moisture isn't just from the cooling tubes. It's part of the agricultural and oxygen production areas. The hydroponics level causes this, I think. It's probably very humid on that level and I doubt they're doing quality control checks."

"That's at least four levels down from here," I said.

"You really do know the schematics of this place," he said.

"I need to go topside to make sure this is taking us where I think it is."

"You're not leaving us down here," Elise said.

"I agree with the girl for once," Grady added.

There wasn't much use arguing, so I climbed the ladder, did my security scan of the rooftop the access hatch opened onto, and stepped out. The others hurried after me and breathed deeply as though the air was better out here.

Maybe it was a little bit better. But probably not.

"Oh shit!" Elise squeaked.

I looked up in time to see a rocket streaking over Dreadmax. The dropship Grady and I had come on banked hard to avoid being struck. Two other rockets launched from different positions.

"A bunch of gang members can't take down a union dropship," Grady said. "It just doesn't happen like that."

My gut tightened and I felt sick.

Two rockets missed, but the third clipped one of the short wing-like structures that held one of the turbines used for landing. The dropship twisted, fought against the gravity generators of the Dreadmax, and faltered as the turbines screamed.

There were four turbines. Pilots claimed they could land with two, which I never believed. Of course, landing and flying were actually two separate maneuvers.

The dropship started a slow spin, canted too far to one side, then flipped over and broke apart as it went down. Another rocket struck it, exploding the main fuselage.

Bodies were flung out of the wreckage. Some plummeted toward the station while others spiraled toward the void. I waited for them to hit the environment shield and come down.

Beside me, the doctor spoke somberly. "I imagine they'll die either way, but the shield has become more and more porous. Some of the areas that are supposed to have a protected environment are very hazardous."

"You're not an expert on Dreadmax," Grady said, frustrated. "Stick to what you know."

I watched as the bodies went past where the environment shield should be. "Shouldn't this atmosphere bubble be venting if there is a hole?"

"If your friend would let me explain —" Hastings started.

"Let's get the hell out of here," Grady said, heading for the ladder to the subway. "My team knew how to eject from a crashing ship. I want to get this over with so I can look for survivors."

"Did you see anyone ejecting?" I asked.

He didn't answer, choosing instead to push ahead at a faster pace.

I was more than a little annoyed with the guy. There was a reason I was on point and he was the rearguard. All I needed him to do was make sure the doctor and his daughter didn't fall behind or wander off course. Now he was just being moody, stumbling down the ladder-like spiral staircase without paying attention like he should.

"Elise, you're going to have to bring up the rear while I catch up with Grady. Can you handle it?"

"Sure, Cain. As long as my father listens to me," she said.

"I don't see how this can be that complicated for the rest of our escape," muttered Dr. Hastings. "Maybe I should bring up the rear of our column. Is that a dangerous thing? I don't want to risk my daughter again."

"Elise knows what she's doing. She's got better instincts than you do. She'll bring up the rear. Grady and I will go ahead to have a look." I hurried down a stairwell enclosed by metal grating and found Grady looking grim. "What's wrong?"

"Do the crazies ever have weapons?" he asked.

I edged ahead of him and scanned the tunnel with my infrared eye. Grady knew what I was doing. He had a list of my full specs. He also knew some of the other gifts the Reaper Corps gave me before throwing me in prison.

A cluster of crazies worked their way down the temporary dwellings alongside the tracks in the subway. They grunted and cursed in a bastardized language I couldn't understand but weren't as loud and reckless as those I'd seen above decks hunting for people to eat.

These were a different class, and they were armed with crude firearms. One had a tactical shotgun with the barrel and stock sawed-off and wrapped in some kind of tape. Another had a pipe that was basically a zip gun, something I'd seen on a smaller scale in various prisons. It wasn't accurate and it would probably explode the first time he used it, but it would launch a slug that would punch through walls if the charge was powerful enough.

I counted seven of these new enemies. "They look like hunters, might be the warrior caste of the crazies. We should let them pass."

"Agreed," Grady said, "but we are really running out of time. I'm not sure what will happen when we make it to the landing bay."

I wanted to interrogate him about the fiasco with the dropship and demand a good reason why they fired on us, because while I wanted to believe they were merely trying to stop us from going a certain direction, I wouldn't doubt a more sinister motive.

The motley crew of warriors took their sweet time but eventually passed. I motioned for Elise and her father to follow me and for Grady to bring up the rear.

"No flashlights. No noise."

They nodded agreement.

I moved farther ahead than normal, hoping to detect problems before they happened. There were more and more tents and haphazard lean-tos underneath and beside the rails of the subway, impossible to clear as well as I wanted to.

We were almost to the next surface hatch when I heard Elise shout at her father.

"Get back from him!"

I turned and saw one of the underground warriors

stand up from a pile of blankets. It looked like there was another person or two in there and I didn't want to know what he'd been doing.

All that mattered was that the desperate-looking man had a hatchet in one hand and a shotgun in the other.

I aimed as the humanlike warrior pointed his shotgun and screamed a battle cry.

He fired and rushed forward with the hatchet at the same time I pulled the trigger. From further back, Grady also fired, striking the barbaric warrior in the knees. My rounds impacted the chest twice and then the head once.

The result was a crazy death dance.

Rushing forward, I paid attention to every possible opening to make sure it wasn't another threat. There were still tents on the edges of the tunnel, but also distant walkways in ventilation openings. Everything looked like a possible point of attack now.

The man we'd shot was human, but so bent over and unkempt that he looked like an animal—who carried a shotgun and a hatchet to his final battle.

I realized Elise was crying and swearing profusely at her father. When I turned, I saw he'd been shot in the chest.

"Grady, hold security while I do first aid."

Elise tried to help but only got in the way. I shoved her aside as I ripped off the top half of the doctor's jumpsuit and applied pressure bandages.

"I can help!" Elise screamed, clawing at my arm.

"Calm down, he's lost a lot of blood but has a decent chance of surviving. There's nothing more you can do."

"There is!" She lowered the volume but not the intensity of her words. "Tell him, Father. Tell him what I can do to save you."

Gently but firmly moving Elise back, I squatted over my patient. "Yeah, Doc. Tell me what she can do."

Silence. I could feel Grady trying to listen from where he was providing overwatch.

"I'm a Reaper, Doc. I have ways of making you talk."

He swallowed. Tears ran down his face and his voice was barely audible. "I used technology from the Lex project to cure Elise when she was a very sick little girl. There were never any side effects, so I assumed the treatment hadn't worked on her."

"It worked, Father. You know it did. I can transfuse my blood to you so you don't die."

"Let's just hold off on the highly experimental, dangerous-as-fuck field medicine. If he's really going to die, I'll give you a crack at him."

All the color left Doctor Hasting's face and I realized he was as afraid of his daughter's blood as he was of his own death.

9

"ONE STRAIGHT ANSWER, Grady, that's all I'm asking for."

My old friend was in pain. I understood what it felt like to nurse a gunshot wound. The penetrating trauma was a misery all its own, but the bruise resulting from his armor's attempt to stop the bullet from entering his leg could be bone deep. He needed to get back to the ship, have his wound treated, and take some rest.

"How the hell would I know about rockets on Dread-max?" he demanded. "Think about it. I didn't believe you until it was too late. Why would I do that on purpose?"

I looked at Elise sitting with her father, comforting him despite whatever anger she might have for the man. Returning my attention to Grady, I planned out a strategy for the interrogation—phase one, slightly confrontational, was done. It was time to shift gears and see if we were still friends.

"I'm sorry, Grady," I said, softening my tone just enough to be believable. "It's been a rough ten hours. I hate these ticking clock missions. Does something to my blood pressure, makes me cranky. I'm glad you're my overwatch and I guarantee no one else would've dropped down to slug it out with these crazies."

"Don't fucking mention it. When I dropped, I was expecting a quick grab and go with a little gunfire to tell stories about later." He shifted positions, extending his wounded leg to relieve some tension. "Maybe get me laid or some free drinks. You know how I love to talk—" Pain choked off his last sentence.

"We are in it together now." I briefly considered putting a hand on his shoulder, but he'd have seen through it in an instant.

He shifted his bodyweight, searching for relief. "Yeah, unfortunately."

I checked to make sure Elise was still paying attention to her dad, then leaned close to Grady. "You know we don't have a chance if we keep running into armies of gun-toting gang members. I've seen rebels overthrow governments with less firepower than these guys have. There's no way they left that kind of armaments at the prison when they pulled out."

"I don't know all the details," he insisted. "You mentioned something about a guy that got put here because he colonized the wrong planet. Maybe some of those people came down with weapons and other stuff. Maybe there's been black market trading going on here for years. Who knows? The point is, it's a giant shit sandwich, and we're gonna eat it crust to crust."

Grady and I settled into a semi-formalized staring contest that passed for conversation among spec ops members. Doctor Hastings interrupted, making an appeal to get moving.

"Can we please go before I pass out? I feel like my chest has been ripped open and all my ribs broken," he said.

I checked his wound. The pressure bandage was holding and there wasn't any blood seeping through. The entry wound had been small once I cleaned it up, possibly shrapnel instead of an actual bullet. I'd been wrong before, but his injury was a lot less life-threatening than it had seemed at first.

Which was good, because we had a long way to go.

"You'll be alright," I concluded.

"He was shot, dickface," Elise said, piercing me with a look.

"Watch your language, sweetie. The man doesn't know how to talk to people is all." The doctor realized he'd over-stepped, his words fading halfway through the statement.

"Whatever," said Elise. "I've got to pee. I'll be right back." She walked off and around the corner, leaving us alone.

I felt around the doc's torso for signs of internal

bleeding and found nothing. "You're right," I continued, looking at Hastings. "I only know how to make people beg for mercy and tell me their secrets."

"We don't want to miss our ride," Grady broke in.

"I'm sorry," Hastings said, ignoring Grady. "The stress of this horrible misadventure is getting to me. Please, just get my daughter and me to Union officials."

I spoke to the doctor in a low voice as I gave him some pain medication. "Trust me, Doc. No one wants to get off this rock more than me."

"I would say you are wrong about that," he replied seriously. "My daughter and I aren't used to this type of lifestyle. Please don't let her act fool you. She's still just a girl."

"She thinks she's tough," I said, watching for her to come back from her bathroom break around the corner.

"I'm sure she is, but not like you and Lieutenant Grady. She hasn't been trained or exposed to the way the galaxy is. It's long past time for us to leave. I'm not looking forward to what the Union will do to us, but that's not your problem." His words had that emotionless tone I'd noticed earlier.

"I'm not interested in saving you and your daughter just so that she can be made a slave or worse," I said, watching his reaction.

The doctor shifted uncomfortably, and not from the wounds. "Like I said, Mr. Cain, it isn't your problem."

"We'll go when the time is right. I figured out their schedule. Pay careful attention to the next RSG patrol you see. There will be fewer of them and they'll be less vigilant.

The novelty of the chaos is wearing off. As long as we steer clear of Slab's better trained soldiers, we'll be fine."

"That's good to know," the doctor said, distracted. He was clearly getting nervous that Elise was taking so long to come back.

I was betting he didn't have any idea of his daughter's grooming rituals. He was her father but hadn't really been her father. Boarding school didn't count.

"Be thankful you haven't met Slab face-to-face. When you do, it will be a terrible experience," he said.

"Listen very carefully, Doc. I used to be a Reaper. They put me on death row and brought me out *just* for this mission. On the off-chance I succeed, I *might* be a free man, or at the very least reinstated. What do you think this does for my motivation?"

"Well, I imagine it would make you very motivated. But that's not the right answer, is it? This is a trick question," he said.

"Very good, Doc. I've been prepared to die for a long time, but that doesn't mean I'm suicidal or reckless. What it does mean is that there are certain causes that are important to me, and I'm not afraid to give up the ghost if it means succeeding."

"I don't see where you're going with this."

"I want to know what you're doing here and how it involves your daughter. No bullshit. If the only reason the Union wants your kid is to use her as leverage to force your good behavior, I might be able to allow that, even though I don't like it. If it's something more sinister, then we're going to have a problem."

"We had three successful test subjects in the Lex Project. Three out of several hundred. They're gone—I had nothing to do with their escape, but the Union doesn't believe me. They want them back. That's more than I should have told you, and they'd probably kill me if they find out I said so much."

"You know where they are," I said, studying his expression.

He looked away. "What do you want from me?"

"I want to know what type of man you are. Are you trying to protect them? How far are you willing to go?"

He didn't answer. It looked like the doctor was going to vomit or pass out, maybe both.

Elise returned a few seconds later, hand on her hip and looking annoyed. "What are you two going on about?"

Grady whistled, drawing our attention to his post near the perimeter of the little alcove. "I think it's time."

I leaned in close to Hastings. "We're not done, Doc."

"No, I imagine we're not," he muttered.

I wished I had more time to interrogate him. He didn't understand how much trouble he was in. What he shared with me was more than enough to earn him a visit from a Reaper, if there were any left.

Would I kill him if Grady gave me the order? Probably not. Sure, he was pretentious and overbearing, not to mention weak, but those were hardly capital crimes. He also had a daughter and I wasn't in the mood to destroy a family.

Grady and I came together for a quick tactical conference before heading back into the subway passage. I caught him looking at the doctor and suspected he knew a lot more than he was telling me.

The only sensible course of action was to pretend I didn't know what I knew. We'd have our own showdown before long. I only hoped it didn't require one of us to die.

10

"No, you can't help me," I said, cursing that I had ever thought the kid had skills.

"You need a second set of eyes. You're getting tired. That means you're going to make a mistake," Elise said. "It makes more sense for my father to stay close to Grady, and me with you. If something happens, and we get split up, we both have protection."

"It's not about you, kid. In fact, a lot of people would rather I leave you behind. You don't even matter."

"Are you trying to hurt my feelings? That was just rude," she said, planting a hand on one hip.

"If you're not going back, then pay attention. What was in that side passage?"

She crossed her arms and gave me that annoyed look that was so universal to teenagers no matter what system they hailed from. "A pile of junk. Some boxes people are probably living in and a pushcart. Probably not any guns, because they have a big fireman's axe propped up like the sight of it would scare somebody off."

That was actually way better than I thought she'd do, but I was not about to tell her that.

"How many people were watching us from that pile of boxes and trash?"

She glanced over her shoulder, doubting herself for the first time during this conversation. "I… didn't see anyone."

"Two people. One under the blankets. Another further back in the shadows."

"There's no way you saw that," she said, uncrossing her arms and taking a step forward defiantly.

I pointed to my left eye. "I've got Reaper enhancements."

"Whatever. You're not a Reaper." When I didn't say anything, she straightened. "Wait, are you really?"

I heard engines revving and men shouting. The corridor had long curves that followed the ring of the space station.

"Grady, give me an update," I hissed.

Grady rushed forward with the doctor in tow. "We've got about a dozen RSG tough guys hot on our heels. One gun-car, two troop transports packed to overflowing, and a flatbed with a cage. They're driving on the tracks; looks like the vehicles were designed that way," he said. "I dropped back far enough to hear some arguing. They're not happy to be down here. I think the phrase 'let's just kill 'em and leave before the crazies get us' might have been said fifty times."

"The leader told them to take us dead or alive," Hastings said.

"Yeah, Doc. I was summarizing. They also said they wanted your daughter back in the cage. Or did you forget about that? They said if they go back to Slab without her, they'd all wish the crazies were eating them alive."

"How could I forget that?" the doctor asked.

I interrupted, not wanting to get drawn into a time-wasting argument. "Let's tighten up and start looking for a way back to the surface or a side tunnel not full of sleeping crazies."

"Good call," Grady said, massaging his leg and looking back toward the sound of the combustion engines without mufflers. "Don't wait for me. I'll catch up."

Half a kilometer later, I realized the passage was blocked, buried in rubble. We were now facing a T-intersection.

"How could there be a collapse without collateral damage?" Elise asked.

I pointed toward one of the skid-steers with magnetic wheels and an oversized shovel. "Nothing collapsed. Someone piled all this crap here for a reason."

"Which way do we go?"

"I'd like to go to the right, because I think that's a more direct route but—" I paused, not sure of what I was seeing in infrared and wishing I had confirmation. There was a sound coming from that direction I didn't like but couldn't identify.

Elise heard it and backed away.

I held up a hand to quiet everyone. It was light at first, but slowly grew with each passing moment.

Takka takka takka.

Takka takka takka.

Takka takka...

A mass of bodies surged toward us, causing everyone to spring back.

We'd found a major population center for the crazies. I also realized someone had been trying to block that tunnel.

"Grady, we need to double-time our asses out of here!" I barked.

The spec ops officer shoved the doctor ahead of him in the only direction left to us.

Elise and I passed them, racing forward to look for the next goat fornication we were bound to encounter.

"How much farther?" Elyse asked, a note of fear creeping into her voice.

The RSG caravan rounded the corner somewhat laboriously on the tracks, but immediately started firing weapons in both directions. The heavy machine gun roared to life, sending a stream of death into the charging cannibals.

Elise started laughing crazily.

"I'd love to know what's so funny," I said, not finding anything remotely humorous.

"It wouldn't make sense. Hard to explain," she said, her voice almost rambling, she was talking so quickly. "I was just wondering what else these freaks ate beside each other for there to be so many of them, you know? It's just so ridiculous that there are so many of them and they're all so insane."

"And that's funny?" I asked.

"I-I don't know. I'm a little stressed, alright? Is that what you want to hear?" she exclaimed, her voice rising several decibels and heading for shrill.

"Shh," I warned. "Stop here. Keep your eyes open the way we're headed. Grady and your father can't keep up this pace."

Men on the lead RSG vehicle opened fire with rifles, pistols, shotguns, and at least one crossbow. The bolt looked like a laser beam flashing past my infrared vision.

If I left my principal and the others behind, escape wouldn't be difficult. I could run much faster in the lowlight than they could, and I wasn't worried about breaking my leg when I fell due to the carbon fiber sheeting around my bones.

I wanted to shoot back but didn't want to give them an easier target. Maybe a crossbow that didn't have a muzzle flash wasn't such a bad idea.

"Grady, how is your leg?"

He and the doctor stopped briefly when they reached my position.

"Hurts like a son of a bitch, but I'll manage. Something's different about this area. It's cleaner," he noted, looking around.

"We're getting clear of the area controlled by cannibals. Sooner or later, we have to reach the vehicle these tracks were made for," I said. "Catch up to Elise and keep going no matter what."

"You don't have explosives," Grady said.

"I don't need much, just that right there from your vest. Taking out these rails will slow them down."

He handed over two small bundles of plastic explosives from the left side of his kit. I reached into his right leg pocket and pulled out the detonators that needed to be attached to make the breaching charges go off.

I took off, letting the others continue on without me while I set the charges.

Working quickly, I found a seam in the rails and strategically packed the breaching charges underneath it. I wasn't sure how much it would take to dislodge the tracks or whether it would be enough to prevent the vehicles from continuing, so I put it all in one place and adjusted the fuse.

It was a simple setup designed to operate in almost any environment.

It felt good to run flat out, and soon I'd caught up with the rest of my group.

Then I hit the switch.

The explosion boomed, flashing over fifty meters behind us and throwing shadows on the ceiling.

The RSG trucks plowed onward, grinding their wheels across the support beams for the rails. My demolition work wasn't going to stop them, but it slowed them down.

Men from the lead vehicle fired in frustration. Grady was struck a second time, right in the middle of his back armor. A round pierced his backpack easily but was stopped by the carbon weave panel underneath.

"You're just a lucky bastard today," I said, helping him up and urging him forward.

"I really thought getting kicked around was your job," he groaned.

"Come on!" I dragged him forward, forcing him to pick up the pace. "Elise, have you ever fired a gun?"

"Hell no!" Grady said through clenched teeth. "You're not giving the kid my weapons."

"It can't be that hard," Elise said.

I took Grady's pistol and handed it to the girl, who looked younger than ever with it in her hands. She dropped it, swore like a soldier, and snatched it back up.

"That's for if Grady and I die. There aren't enough rounds in it to waste right now."

Grady pulled away from me, showing Elise how to switch on the safety and where to hide it in her Dreadmax jumpsuit. "Don't drop it again."

She rolled her eyes like he'd said something unreasonable.

"Get your father moving. Grady, can you make it, or do you need my help? I'm the only one strong enough for you to lean on and still run."

"Fuck off. I'm good to go."

"You look it," Elise sneered, turning away from us to grab her father's arm and push him faster.

THE RSG THUGS KEPT COMING, stopping to fire blindly every chance they got. Maybe they thought they could see us, but I had doubts they could hear us. The vehicles were too loud, made even more so by the way they slammed over the support structures to the rails. Muzzle flashes revealed their progress in the gloom.

Grady moved like a champ despite his injuries. Doctor Hastings struggled, rarely looking up, and sweating so much I started to worry about finding drinkable water. Ten days of rest and recuperation wouldn't hurt the man either.

"Damn, Grady, do you have some good drugs you want to share with the rest of us?" He was tough, but I couldn't reconcile what I was seeing. It was like the first day of Reaper selection when we all pushed our bodies beyond what humans were meant to endure.

Doctor Hastings answered before my old friend could lie to me. "I think he's one of the soldiers who received the genetic modifications from one of our sister projects. I was told they were doing field trials."

"Try not to speculate on shit you know nothing about, Doc," Grady said, checking his gear and avoiding eye contact. "If that were true, it would be classified."

I waved a hand for them to shut the hell up. "At this point, I couldn't care less why you're keeping up with me, so long as you don't suddenly quit and get us all killed. Anything that helps us survive is a good thing. Did anyone see the access stairs to the surface?"

"I saw them," Grady said.

"Of course you did, tough guy," Elise drawled mockingly. "There were five since we first started getting chased by the trucks, which sound like they're getting closer if you ask me. Maybe we should go."

She had to know as well as the rest of us that her father needed a break. He wasn't just the principal, he was the weakest link. Which was how it usually went with these types of missions. If he wasn't the weakest link, he wouldn't need to be rescued.

I stared at the scientist for a second too long, thinking about the differences between my past life and what was happening now. I was actually trying to save this man, not just kidnap or kill him.

"X, help me out," I muttered.

"According to your recent sensory experience and my record of the Dreadmax schematics, we are approaching the surface and a personnel loading area," X-37 said.

"A train station," I remarked.

"Just so," said X.

Elise stared at me. "Oh my gods, you really *are* a Reaper. You're talking to a nerve-ware AI."

"You have a fan, it seems," X-37 said dryly. "While I can only gather data through your senses, it seems I am more attuned to them than you are."

I didn't wait for X to explain. "Time to go. Right now. Something's happening."

Elise clapped her hands. "You're a freaking *Reaper*!"

"Don't worry about it. Move," I ordered.

She shook her head in denial and awe. Apparently, the half-dozen times I'd told her what I was simply hadn't been enough. She just needed to see me speak to my nerveware.

Grady gathered her and the doctor and started moving at a fast walk. He adjusted his gear and checked his weapon on the move. I followed but spent most of my attention looking for anything I might have missed.

The RSG trucks seemed to be matching our pace. Their rearguard continued to fire at what sounded like a growing horde of lower-level crazies. Men with tattoos and excessive body piercings sprinted ahead of the first vehicle, entering my view and firing their weapons at the same time.

"You're too far to hit anything on the move," I grumbled, dropping to my stomach and holding a prone position as I squeezed the trigger. One, two, three of them pitched backward from my first volley. The others spread out.

"Hal!" Grady shouted.

I rolled to my feet and caught up quickly. There were two of the tight staircases twisting down from the surface between me and the rest of my team who were struggling onward. A group of RSG foot soldiers clambered down the metal steps.

"Keep going!"

"Wasn't planning on stopping!" Grady shouted back, then disappeared into the gloom. His image became ghost-like in infrared. The silhouettes of the doctor and his daughter were brighter—because they were hot from running.

My old friend had not only started healing much faster than possible, he was adapting to the pace like a professional athlete. All of these observations came in a second and I didn't bother to sort them out. Hastings claimed to have worked on the Lex Project, something the Union tried to keep secret, even from the Reaper Corps—which was stupid because we weren't easily denied when that kind of topic caught our interest.

The only side passage close enough to reach was full of debris, the obvious detritus of an underground camp.

Jumping off the tracks and sprinting across the uneven area between the tracks and the walls, I slung my rifle and jumped onto the small ladder. Bullets ricocheted all around me, screaming into the darkness after impact.

I ran into the side tunnel, stepping on bedrolls, an improvised stove, and what was probably someone's face, but I couldn't be sure.

Hands grabbed at me, turning my clothing and nearly pulling my rifle off the magnetic sling. I extended the blade concealed in my augmented left arm and slashed someone across the throat, then stabbed another who tried to drag me down.

Others jumped onto my back. I fell to my knees and right hand, shoving forward, kicking when I could, and stabbing as often as possible. I impaled one man who was too large to push past and pushed him forward like a snowplow.

"Get the hell off of me! Find someone else to eat!"

My words startled them. I used their hesitation to break free and run into the darkness. Before long, I was outpacing them with my infrared-capable left eye showing me where to step. Even with the Reaper technology, it was almost too dark to continue.

Twenty or thirty meters behind me now, the first RSG entered this narrow tunnel and gunned down the squatters I had disrupted. Their screams barely sounded human, but I wondered if I had offended them with the cannibalism crack.

"What do you think, X?"

"About what, sir?"

"Are the crazies even human?"

"They are, sir. If you are attempting to dehumanize them to ease your guilt, I advise against it. That will have long-term consequences for your psychological health."

"Damn, X. It was just a question. I was getting ready to say you seem more human than they are."

"That would be a false assumption. I am a limited artificial intelligence, restricted by the amount of hardware and software your body can hold."

A spray of bullets peppered the wall near me, causing me to trip and fall. I hit the ground hard, cursing as I made an unmanly sound. It was hard for me to break bones, but this type of injury still hurt like the devil.

"That felt great."

"Sarcasm detected."

"For the record, X, I don't need to dehumanize my victims to kill them. Everyone dies. They just die a lot sooner when they try to eat me."

"Shall I note that in your mission log?"

I scrambled forward, briefly considering the pros and cons of returning fire. Crawling seemed a better option. When I reached an intersection, I took the first left and struggled to my feet.

"Good choice," X-37 said. "Schematics show this will take you away from your pursuers."

"How do I get back to Hastings and the kid?"

"You will be unable to reach Doctor Hastings, his daughter, or Lieutenant Grady."

"Give me some good news."

"These side tunnels are well-maintained. There is a high probability you will encounter civilians."

"Thanks, but the locals haven't exactly been much use so far."

"After careful analysis of past events and your current

desire to remain among the living, my recommendation is to ask for help. Nicely."

"Thanks, X. I'll keep that in mind. Will you please just help me navigate my way through this shit hole?"

"Why certainly, Reaper Cain. It would be my pleasure."

The passageway turned three more times before I felt like I'd lost my pursuers. Slowing to a walk, I found my water tube, pulled it forward, and took a long drink.

"Your injuries require attention."

On any other day, I'd have a catchy rejoinder, but I was just too tired. Every muscle, joint, and bone in my body ached. I climbed the next two access ladders and looked for the dropship. Grady was no longer running overwatch from the vehicle and I thought it was as likely to gun me down as pick me up.

But if it was still orbiting Dreadmax, then it was still looking for the Hastings family. I had no illusions the Union would go out of its way to rescue the rest of us. Elise was possibly an exception. If she was an unwitting experiment, then someone would want to study her at least.

My own experience with being a prototype had left a bad taste in my mouth. We'd all been extremely motivated to fight for the Union when we joined the Reaper Corps. It occurred to me as I descended one of the ladders back to the sub-level passage that if there was a reason we had been disbanded, it was probably a good one.

A voice spoke from a speaker box at the bottom of the ladder. "Hey, mister."

Habit forced me to check the area around me for threats even as I answered. If this was the same kid who'd been watching me on the camera before, he probably thought I was extremely paranoid.

"What's up, kid? Can you find me a way out of here?"

"Name's Bug. What you want out of here for? I don't see no crazies or gangs. You could get to the farms from here or to the shipyard, and I ain't talking about the Red Skull Gangster crib. That hangar won't ever do nothing but collect loot."

"Why would I want to go to the shipyard?"

"People are nice there. All they do is work on stuff. Gangs don't bother them 'cause they check on the gravity generators. Kind of keep things working. My sister and a couple of my cousins went to them. Haven't heard no bad stories, so they must be all right," Bug said.

"Can you tell me what's up ahead or how to get out of here?"

"You didn't say 'please.' My mom and dad used to say that was important. Always say 'please' and 'thank you.' And don't eat people or touch open wires."

The boy on the other side of the speaker box was eating noisily, probably chips or crackers... or bugs? The picture jumped into my brain and couldn't be unseen.

"It's been nice talking to you. Have places to be."

"Yeah, yeah. You look busy now that your friends left you. Why do you talk to yourself?"

"Long story. What are you eating?"

"Orange crackers. They're supposed to taste like cheese, but I don't really know what that means. Very popular. Watching you is a special event. I broke open my stash."

The passage grew quiet, forcing me to accept how vast Dreadmax was and how easy it would be to get lost forever. "Help me out, Bug."

Crunch. Crunch. Crunch. "Sure thing, mister. Just keep going the direction you're facing. We'll watch for you at the next camera junction. Won't be able to see you in all of these hallways, but wherever there's a door, there is a talk box and a security. My friends agree you should go to the hangar."

"Friends."

"Bugs like me."

"Why not the farms? Maybe I could get something to eat."

"No one ever comes back from the farms. And they don't really have crackers."

"I thought you said no one ever comes back from the farms. How do you know they don't have orange crackers?" I asked, moving and watching for the next thing that would kill me.

"I go wherever I want. I'm a Bug."

"Interesting. Do you see my friends?"

"Sometimes. But they're far away. Must not like you. Take the next right, the third surface ladder will take you near the hangar. That's the way you should go."

"What'd you think, X?"

"The child's suggestion matches the available schematics. What do you have to lose?"

"Thanks, X."

"Hey, mister, are you talking to us or yourself?"

"Do you have cameras and intercoms among the hangar people you think are awesome?"

"Yeah, but they don't like us to talk so much. Since they're nice and don't tear up our stuff, we try to be polite. Say 'please' and 'thank you' and mostly shut up."

"Would you tell me what my friends are doing from time to time?"

"Sure thing, mister. That sounds like fun. Shut up, asshole!" the boy yelled at someone on his end of the commlink. "I'm fucking talking to the mister! My oranges! Stupid shitbag."

"Sounds like trouble in Bug land."

"You don't know the half of it, mister. I found those crackers myself. Bobby thinks he can take what he wants because he's bigger. I'll fucking shank him in his sleep... yeah, I'm talking to you, Bobby!"

The voice on the box faded as I ran into the darkness. I took Bug's advice as he argued with his friends and found my way to the dry docks and hangars I'd seen during our approach to Dreadmax.

The facilities looked entirely different from the deck. None of them looked flight-worthy, but the people worked on them tirelessly. Day and night and mostly in secret, they were doing the impossible business of salvaging even a single ship able to leave this place.

Mingling with the workers, I scouted the area before sitting on a crate to rest. An electric current, barely noticeable, pulsed from my augmented arm, through my shoulder, and toward my spine. The static in my vision was more noticeable. Every bone in my body ached from the stress I'd put on them over the last few hours.

Dark thoughts occurred to me during the rare moments of rest. This was how I'd be forever. No one from the Union was going to fix my Reaper hardware. The chance of upgrading was little more than a fantasy I'd used to keep me sane during long days and nights in the BSMP.

Fighting for survival pushed minor miseries into the background. I should have been thankful, but I was just exhausted and not feeling like giving a fuck.

"Are you certain you actually need this much rest, Reaper Cain?"

"Can you show a little compassion, X?"

"Not without an upgrade."

"Don't freak me out, X."

"Apologies, Reaper Cain. What are you implying?"

"I was just thinking about the impossibility of getting my gear upgraded, and then you say the same thing. Feels like you're reading my mind."

"Impossible, sir. That is merely your perception of coincidence."

"Uh-huh. Dishonesty detected," I said.

"That's my line, Reaper Cain." Something clicked where X-37 stimulated the cochlea of my inner ear to communicate with me. "The scientists who developed Reaper tech spent several years striving for and evaluating the possibility of an AI or limited AI with the ability to read the hosts' thoughts and found it to be impossible. Eventually, they abandoned pursuit of this goal after realizing that if achieved, it would do more harm than good."

"I'm going to believe you for now."

"Very good, Reaper Cain. Just remember all such occurrences are random. As a human, you interpret coincidence as cause."

"I'm sorry I started this conversation."

"Shall I mark it for later discussion?"

"No. I'll remember. Now shut the hell up. I need to make some decisions."

I found one of the gravity generators and saw there was a full-time crew monitoring it. One of them had a pistol, but none of them were guards. The RSG could wipe them out in an hour if they wanted to. I wasn't sure what prevented the crazies from overrunning the place with raw numbers.

"Can I help you, stranger?" one of the engineers asked, wiping his greasy hands on his coveralls like he would shake my hand. "Name's Peter."

I kept my distance but tried not to scare him. "Where's your security element?"

He backed away, not afraid, but definitely cautious. It

seemed like most of the people here had their capacity for fear burned away.

"You're not with the Dreadmax soldiers? I thought you looked different. They were talking about getting real uniforms a while back, but I still think they just look like someone drew a silhouette of the station on their shoulder patches."

"Dreadmax soldiers?"

"Some of them were actual soldiers, or soldiers of some type. Seems like they were just drawn together by common experience at first, but they patrol now. Help keep our hangar safe. No one wants the gravity generators or power to fail."

"Interesting."

"The DM escort us when we have to go offsite to work on something. Real lifesavers."

"Where are they now?"

He shrugged. "Do you mind if I ask who you are, stranger?"

"Halek Cain. I'm new."

"Figured that much. As long as you don't interfere with our work or mess with the children, you're welcome among us. You have to pull your weight, though. Whatever skills you have will be appreciated."

"Doubtful," X-37 whispered.

"I hear you, Peter. Don't worry about me. I'm not staying long. Do any of these ships work?"

"Just the smaller ones, like the *Jellybird*. Don't go near

them. That will get you shot. We've only got so many smugglers to bring supplies."

I stared across the hangar, spotting the functional ships immediately now that I knew they existed. A lot of work had been spent making them appear inoperable. There was a decent chance Peter was living in a dreamworld and none of them worked, but I filed the information for later.

"How many people can one of those functional ships carry? Do they have slip drives?"

"I'm not sure I should talk about that."

"Don't worry. I'm not a pilot," I lied.

"Oh, well, I don't see the harm in telling you the rest. The smuggler ships can't get more than a few of us off this place, so we were told not to think about it or talk about it. Better if no one starts fighting over them. As for the slip drive regulators, they can't be retrofitted to the freighters. I'm not sure why. I'm just a glorified mechanic."

"Thanks, Peter."

"Hey, Cain. Stay away from the *Jellybird* and the *Hopper*. Seriously. The DM will shoot you before you make it halfway."

"No worries, Peter. You be safe."

He nodded and went back to work.

11

I FOUND a water tap and drank until I thought I'd drown. Food was something else, nearly impossible to find even with the acceptance of the hangar engineers and their families. The few people I encountered looked like they were on a starvation diet and it didn't feel right to take anything from them, so I didn't ask.

Aside from Peter the mechanic, they weren't a very talkative group. I didn't blame them for keeping their distance. My body was smeared with gods knew what. Field bandages couldn't be hidden with this cheap gear. My Reaper armor had tourniquets and pressure bandages internal to the armor—press a button and, voila, I could fight for a few more minutes or days before I bled out.

The shit Briggs had authorized for this mission was ancient, something straight out of a museum.

The outskirts of the shipyards were a lot like the neighborhood around the RSG stronghold, full of quiet, desperate people that were afraid of strangers. I saw a squad of Dreadmax soldiers from a distance. They moved like pros and watched each other's backs. I wondered if they were convicted murders or political prisoners.

Not that it mattered.

The Union put them here and probably wanted them to die when the station failed.

"Can I ask you a question, X?"

"Yes."

"What is the difference between the Dreadmax soldiers and the Red Skull Gangsters?"

"Everything," X-37 said.

"Thanks. That was really helpful."

"If I had to choose one personality attribute to differentiate them, it would be the ability to think long term. The RSG live only for immediate survival. Each of them want to be as high on the food chain as possible. The DM are more organized. They do what they know. It is likely that some of them went over to the gangs. The value of our conclusions are limited by the sample size of our not very scientific observations."

"You're right, X. As long as they stay out of my way, we should be fine."

"Perhaps they could help us."

"Not worth the risk. Not yet."

"Noted. Perhaps you should check in with Bug."

"Sure thing, X. Just let me watch the normal people for a while longer."

Kids climbed over pipes someone had welded into a jungle gym and painted bright colors. Nearly everything else in the place was gray metal or black grease. Fathers, uncles, and older brothers worked on a dissembled forklift taken apart nearby. They were acting like they wanted nothing to do with the women gathered around their own project, but it was clearly a competition of some sort while the children ran around screaming like they were playing cannibals and gangbangers.

"It's time to go, Reaper Cain," X-37 said.

Thoughts of the children and their families stayed with me as I put as much distance between myself and the ship-yards as possible. Bug was probably right. The people there would help me, maybe keep me as long as I could pull my weight.

But they were builders and I was a destroyer.

"Are you in one of your moods?" X-37 asked.

"Are you chastising me?"

"One of my key functions is to regulate your hormones and monitor your vitals. Your heart rate and respiration suggest you're unhappy."

"I'm only human, X."

"You're a Reaper."

"I was a Reaper. Now I'm just some jerk-off running from the inevitable."

"My recommendation is to focus on one thing at a time.

The people of Dreadmax may need to fend for themselves."

"They're all gonna die, X. Now or when the next level of Dreadmax fails. Or when they try to take one of those ships out of the system."

"You can't do anything about that now. What you can do is evade the Red Skull Gangsters and the Nightfall Gangsters moving into this area, in case you weren't paying attention. Which you weren't," X-37 said.

The first thug I saw was an NG, dressed more like a lower level crazy than one of the rival gang, the RSG. He wore a battered jumpsuit with furs sewn into it. Pieces of metal protected his chest, one of his arms, and his shins.

"Where did he get furs, X?"

"Let's assume he's been to the agricultural level and that there are still animals. More likely what you're seeing are rat pelts. Or—"

"Scalps."

"What manner of clothing the Nightfall Gangster wears is irrelevant."

"You're not wrong," I said, studying more important details like the surprisingly elegant rifle that was longer than the man was tall. He was wearing a mask that concealed everything about his face except for his crazy, doped-up or drunk eyes.

"You stop for the Nightfall Gang. We kill you if you don't," he barked.

Snapping my HDK into place, I fired as part of the

same movement. I was fast, even for a Reaper. The optical enhancements of my cybernetic left eye—even at seventy-percent functionality—gave me greater depth perception with or without the infrared function activated. I was a damn good shot because I didn't hesitate to go for the kill.

The NG dropped out of view, wailing an undulating cry as he circled behind metal boxes and pipes covering the top deck.

"Play that back, X. I thought I plugged him in the chest."

"Correct. He won't live long."

Dozens of other NG answered his call. From another direction, I heard vehicles and the slightly more under-standable curses of the Red Skull Gangsters.

"You are being surrounded," X-37 said.

"But at least I'm running out of ammunition and starving."

"Sarcasm detected. If you continue twenty-five meters, there is a hatch the schematics suggest will lead you out of this predicament. Temporarily, at least."

"Thanks, X." I ran for it, realizing again how alone and under-equipped I was.

The hatch led to a system of rooms rather than a passage like I had hoped.

"I don't have time to predict whether or not you will find resistance in these rooms," X 37 said.

"And I don't have time to clear them. This is what we call panicked flight. It's surprisingly liberating." I ran through several rooms, only stopping when I realized I was passing a break room.

"Is that refrigerator running?"

"It is, but I don't recommend—"

Yanking it open, I saw several sealed plastic tubs. The contents were one uniform color. "I don't see an expiration date."

"If you are actually in a break room or kitchen, and the refrigeration has been on continuously, you can probably survive eating whatever is in that container. If this is part of a medical laboratory, on the other hand, I strongly advise not taking the risk," X-37 said.

I glanced around the room and decided it was a break room or lounge, despite looking a lot like a generic room with no ovens, microwaves, or dishwashers. It had sinks and metal tables, and there were several coffee cups that had been cast aside long ago.

"It's a kitchen."

"Confirmation unavailable."

"It's definitely a kitchen." I popped open one of the plastic tubs and poured the contents into my mouth. There wasn't a lot of texture or flavor, so I didn't bother chewing.

"How was it? My sensors indicate your stomach is convulsing."

"Tastes like chicken, or chicken Jell-O maybe." I opened the second container and downed it. "Ah, that was nasty. Let's go."

"You're not going to take the last one with you for later?"

"Ha, ha, very funny."

One room led to another and I eventually found another hatch taking me back to the top deck. Which was good, because I didn't want to go below on my own. There had to be a reason most of the people on Dreadmax existed on the top deck when its environment was the most likely part of the station to fail.

I opened the door a crack and peeked through. Even without my advanced optics, I could see there was trouble. In one direction, RSGs were fighting with NGs. In another, there was a large group of the latter screaming and yelling as they searched everything they could rip open to look inside of.

The access trenches in this area were both narrow and deep. This kept the RSG vehicles and their gun crews away but didn't help me escape. I could hear them patrolling the perimeter, wasting bullets and smashing into things. Two of the vehicles boomed music so loud, it distorted. One crew enjoyed booming bass and nearly wordless rhymes, while the other broadcast distorted synth guitars and screamed a lot.

"What are my chances of fighting through this?"

X-37 made several humming and clicking noises. "That's a stupid question. I refuse to answer it on principle."

"Here goes nothing." I headed into the rusty wasteland

of the Dreadmax top deck, crawling behind clusters of pipes, stripped construction vehicles, and the shells of point-defense turrets.

The Dreadmax gangs strutted through the area looking for a fight, while the vehicles slow-rolled wider streets on the perimeter.

I couldn't stop thinking about the hard-working ship-wrights and their families. What did they think of the chaos all around them, or did they even notice the gangs were hunting for someone? Sound didn't travel the same as it did on a planet and the fast and frequent transition from day to night was disorienting.

Moving with all my Reaper skill, I left their little civilization farther and farther behind. The futility of their efforts wasn't my problem.

There was obviously fuel for small vehicles and fire-bombs, but I couldn't imagine they'd be able to make any of the larger starships work. There was no way to test them, and the moment they tried to leave the system, they'd be shot to shit.

It warmed my heart that the Union didn't realize the extent of the operation, even if it was futile. Not everyone on this hellish place had given up.

"How far to the pickup point?"

X-37 took his time answering. "You are six point three kilometers from your destination. Farther than when you started."

"Story of my life. I'm going to have to run. There isn't

time for stealth."

"That's my assessment. There are inherent dangers to that course of action. I'll give you a thirty-two percent chance of success."

"Tell me what I need to do to boost those odds."

"I've plotted a course to likely locations where you can communicate with Bug. With my access to the original schematics and his real-time intelligence, I give you a nearly seventy-five percent chance to arrive at the pickup location in time for extraction. Is there anything else you would like? Something to complicate the situation and make my life difficult?"

"It's not just about you, X."

"Of course not. I don't actually care. It's beyond my capacity."

Panting as I ran across a walkway, I talked to my nerve-ware AI and looked for the next attack. Reapers learned to multitask or die. "What's the chance they get one of the starships working?"

"Insufficient data."

"Bullshit. Give me your best guess."

"I'm not built to guess."

"You guess all the time."

"If I were capable of taking offense, I'd be deeply insulted at that false assertion. You are approaching a talk box. As for your question, I have not seen anything that indicates they will be successful. Only the Union can save them."

"Please never say that again, X."

"Of course. How impolite of me."

A quick scan of the doorway next to the speaker box revealed only shadows, the smell of rust, and the stink of urine. "This place is all class. Cain for Bug, how copy?"

The kid was laughing when he answered. "Sorry, that just seemed funny. You're so serious. Your name's Cain? I guess that's cool. Probably better than Bug."

"Are you drunk?"

"Water's safer that way. Don't want to get sick."

"How old are you?"

"Fifteen. What's it to you?"

He was probably twelve, if that, but I supposed it didn't matter on Dreadmax. Not when the place was going to lose power, atmosphere, and gravity soon.

"You'd probably get drunk too, if you knew Climbdown Day was coming."

I ducked into a doorway and watched my back trail to be sure I wasn't being followed. The chances were slim, but that was how I'd stayed alive this long—by managing my paranoia.

"What's Climbdown Day?"

"That's when the sky falls and we all have to go down to the farms or die. It'll be bad. Slab and his gangsters think they have enough guns, but even if they win, the place will be stinking with dead bodies when the battle is over. Nasty. Not really sure I want to be part of that."

"It seems the inhabitants of Dreadmax are aware of their impending doom," X-37 said.

It made sense. Half the people were partying like there was no tomorrow and the other half were looking for ways to survive.

"Hey, Mister Cain, you're moving into the Nightfall Gangsters' neighborhood," Bug said.

Of course I was. "Thanks for the reminder. I was getting complacent."

"No you weren't, Cain. I can tell because you're not dead."

"Bug seems to have better situational awareness than you do right now," X-37 said.

"No comment." Movement caught my eye on one of the building tops. For whatever reason, neither the RSG nor the NG liked going on roofs. Probably afraid they'd get sucked into the void if they got too high. Or fall to their death, which I totally understood. Heights were never my favorite thing.

"Are you seeing what I'm seeing, X?"

"That appears to be a Union spec ops team, but I don't recognize any of their infrared markers and they weren't mentioned in the briefing," X-37 said.

"I was afraid you'd say that."

"There's a problem with the course I plotted," X-37 admitted while I was still watching the spec ops team.

"Give me the bad news. We don't have time to sugar-coat it. I mean, stop coddling me."

"Sarcasm detected. There is only one way to cross without exposing yourself—a trench identified as Tango 35, a narrow metal footbridge originally made for small drones to cross on rails."

"So exactly the same as the last five I've crossed."

"No. This one has collapsed. Only a cable remains. There's a note in the schematics. Apparently, it was scheduled for repair when the last survey was done."

I dropped away from my observation post and followed the course my Reaper nerve-ware AI had chosen. There was probably a reason there were no gang members or other threats in my immediate vicinity. The way was nearly impassable. If I'd had the doctor with me, we would have had to take an alternate route.

"This isn't a maintenance trench," I said when I reached the edge. The cable was so long that it drooped almost a full meter in the middle.

"I never said it was. This is an exhaust vent for the engines, rarely used, even when it was fully operational because the fuel requirements for moving something this big were far beyond their technology at the time it was built. On the bright side, if you're able to crawl to the other side, you will have avoided ninety-nine percent of your pursuers. Very few will be willing to risk this crossing."

"That sounds fantastic," I said sarcastically. "Can you tell if Grady was able to get the doctor and his daughter on the train. Will this put me closer to them?"

"Without accessing the security network, I can only

postulate on the sensory information you provide and my knowledge of their intentions."

"Cut to the chase, X."

"This will place you much closer to their estimated position."

"Then let's get to it." I moved boldly to the edge and gripped the cable with both hands. Next, I weaved my ankles around the cable and started pushing and pulling my way across. Blood rushed to my head. Lactic acid built up from my fingertips to my armpits. I wasn't even halfway when my legs started to shake. My augmented arm was strong but limited by what the rest of me could endure.

Watching where I was going or where I came from was nearly impossible, but I snatched a glance here and there, fully expecting to see a firing line of RSG soldiers betting how long it would take to shoot me off the cable. Below me, darkness and damnation.

Something, possibly the rotational force of the ring that was the main section of Dreadmax, caused the cable to sway side to side. I traveled ten or fifteen meters one direction then swung back the other way, all the while holding on for dear life.

"Talk to me, X. I need something to distract me." Going faster would be a bad idea and I knew it. I was too far from the other side to make it on sheer determination.

"Pace yourself," X-37 said. "Dreadmax originally served as a mobile dry-dock and foundry for three carriers that each had their own wing of smaller vessels. In addition to this, there were several squadrons of frigates, corvettes, and fighter wings."

"Must have cost… a shit ton… of credits."

"Fortunes were made long before the construction of this battle station was completed."

I looked down, unable to see any variance to the blackness. As far as I could tell, this trench went all the way to the core of the station, bypassing hundreds of levels. Just when I'd given up on seeing where I'd fall if I slipped, a bead of light went up the side of the abyss and disappeared into a wall.

"What the hell was that?"

"Speed lift. There is a notation that teenagers sometimes died riding in them. Something called a dare? The schematics show they deliver small items to and from the spine that supports the rings. Is that the sort of detail you're interested in?"

"I prefer information that will keep me alive, like maybe how much farther I have to go to reach the other side of this pit."

X-37 hesitated. "I'm not sure that information would be helpful."

Pain cut through my right hand and the muscles of my forearms. I hugged the cable to my body to give my grip a rest. This felt pretty good for about five seconds, and then became more work than it was worth. When I re-grabbed the cable, I missed with one hand and nearly fell.

The pressure shifted to my legs was unbelievable. One more screw-up like that and I was done.

I heard gang members shouting from the edge of the trench.

"It appears you have been spotted," X-37 said.

"How much farther?"

"Twenty-five meters, at an incline."

Cursing and grunting through the pain, I looked at nothing but the cable. It was rough and covered with rust, and it was the only thing I needed to stay alive for one more second, then the next, and all the way to the other side.

When I finally reached my destination, I didn't have the strength to pull myself onto the ledge. I could barely breathe and my vision was full of spots. X-37 seemed to be yelling at me, but I didn't care. Sounds were far away, unimportant, irrelevant to my throbbing hands and labored breathing. But it wasn't just my hands. I had muscle cramps in every muscle from my feet to my neck.

With slow, deliberate movements, I flung one hand up to the railing and seized it. Hanging there for what felt like an eternity, I thought about Doctor Hastings and his daughter, wondering what would happen to them if I fell to my death.

And then I was up on the landing, finally piecing together the reasons X-37 was shouting at me. The RSG thugs were shooting at me. Bullets punched through the thinner parts of the metal structure and ricocheted off others.

"Why exactly am I sitting here?"

"That is a question I've been asking you for some time now; twenty-seven seconds to be precise."

I rolled to my feet and ran in a crouch that was pure torture. My quads and lower back were on fire and I wished one of the bullets would hit me and make it stop.

"Reapers never quit," X-37 said.

"Not helpful. Save the pep talks for someone who gives a fuck."

TIME PASSED SLOWLY as I removed my gloves and cleaned the broken blisters on my hand with alcohol wipes from my first aid kit. "Damn, I'm a mess."

"You'll thank me later for prompting you to take care of that."

"Sure, X. Thanks. I think I should go back and cut the cable," I said, packing away my first aid kit. It was nearly empty and looking ragged.

"My analysis suggests this is a waste of time and will likely get you killed."

That was the best thing about X-37, complete honesty when the chips were down.

"If you can increase your pace, you will be able to reach the railhead, where I believe Grady, the doctor, and the girl will have disembarked. From the visual and auditory input you have provided, combined with inferences to their last recorded direction of travel, I pieced together evidence they most likely found a working train car and hitched a ride on it."

"Fantastic. I'm so glad they had an easy time of it." X-37 saw what I saw, basically, but always did more with it.

"Sarcasm detected."

When I spotted the train, I forgot about my own misery and all the times I'd thought of giving up. Grady had located a personnel transport, a tube-like train car that moved faster than the industrial flatbeds I'd seen up to this point. I checked my back trail one last time, then jogged toward what I hoped would be a happy reunion.

"You see there, X, that's how it's done," I said. "You tell me where to go, and I go. It's like we're a team or something. Kicking ass and taking names."

My mood improved the farther I moved from the cable crossing.

"I will archive a transcript of this mission for future study. I'm sure that many young and impressionable recruits will be fascinated. Especially the part where you ate the dark gray gelatin out of the medical locker."

"That was a kitchen, and the gray Jell-O was delicious."

"It's been said that acceptance is the first step to recovery. However, it's probably best not to know what is working its way through your digestive system at this point."

I was still hungry, but I didn't need to tell my Reaper AI that.

12

LONG BEFORE I became part of the Reaper Corps, I was taught to move cautiously, even when I was in a hurry. Patience and aggression could be first cousins, two sides of the same coin when needed. Sneak in, flip the switch, and kill everyone who resisted. It was a staple of the Reaper Corps during the last war with the Sarkonians. They made us shock troops for that engagement.

"I'm not sure why Grady hasn't tried to contact me. I understand that he doesn't have his ship, but we should be within line of sight communications by now."

"He could be sheltering in place, trying to establish contact with Commander Briggs. Most of the threats we've encountered are on the other side of the primary trench. I expect he followed his training regardless of how safe things looked," X-37 said.

"Maybe," I said as I crept forward. "I'd like to know where the mystery spec ops team is right now. Tell me what you found on them."

"I performed a check of the briefing minutes and found no mention of an unnamed scheme. Perhaps these were men left behind."

"I don't think so, X. Even from a distance, they seemed like a well-equipped unit with a sense of purpose." I crept along my back trail, hoping to catch these new players red-handed.

A voice spoke from a walkway I had thought was clear when I moved beneath it.

"You talk too much, Cain. Lazy habit. Of course, you're old school. Just another broken-down has been. Someone who hasn't learned to direct HUD menus with hand and eye movements."

I slid behind the pipe and looked up, seeing a large-framed soldier squatting down almost casually. Without my infrared eye, I wouldn't be able to see much, because he was in the shadows with the building behind him. Only an amateur would allow himself to be silhouetted against the stars.

"Where's your team?" I asked.

"Wouldn't you like to know." He jumped and landing right where I would've been standing if I hadn't flung myself out of the way.

His armored boots slammed onto the deck a split second before he dropped his elbow on my shoulder.

I twisted to minimize the impact and retreated, tripping over myself and firing my HDK with one hand. It was such an amateur-ish move, I was actually embarrassed.

He came at me like a pro, moving smoothly in a shooting stance with both hands on his weapon now, firing short bursts that tore through my light recon armor.

"Fuck, he's fast!"

X-37 didn't have a chance to respond.

"Just don't quit, Cain. That'll ruin my image of the last Reaper."

"Who the hell are you?"

"I'm the guy they made to replace you and the rest of the Reapers."

X-37 pushed information and advice at me in tactical mode, but even that was too slow. I reloaded and pulled the trigger at the same time the stranger slammed in a new magazine and fired. I struggled to my feet and retreated around the corner.

With my attacker barely a stride behind me, this was little more than a stall tactic.

"You're moving toward a ledge!" X-37 shouted, ringing my ears with several loud tones. When nerve-ware hit the max volume button, it rattled my teeth.

The spec ops man laughed as he transitioned from his rifle to a handgun, much faster than a reload. I wasn't sure how many times his bullets hit me, but I knew I'd struck his body armor multiple times and his helmet at least once despite how fast he moved.

I retreated until my back was to a railing. Behind me, the deck dropped away to a landing pad ringed with construction equipment and buildings of all shapes and sizes.

"Stop!" I shouted, hoping to stall with negotiation.

"Hah! I'll bite. What's your game, Reaper?"

"Who the fuck are you, really?"

"Captain Marley Callus. Now die!" He front-kicked me off the ledge.

"Five meters," X-37 said fatalistically.

My back slammed onto the deck.

Lights out. Game over.

THE SOUND of the super soldier's boots striking the deck woke me up.

It was about the only piece of luck I had. My HDK rifle was gone. The auto blade in my Reaper arm refused to extend. I desperately felt around for an alternative weapon and came up empty. "Are you fucking kidding me?"

I rolled onto my side just in time to vomit up the grey ooze I had consumed from the mystery fridge. The spec ops soldier ran at me, kicking me square in the ass and launching me forward, where I slid on my face before I could get my hands in front of me.

"That seemed unnecessarily personal," X-37 said.

hate it when you get into observer mode."

The soldier came at me again, inspiring me to scramble to my feet and run several steps before my legs gave out. Dreadmax was spinning more than usual. I started out falling on my face but somehow landed on my side like a power drunk.

My attacker stopped to laugh, then yelled something at his team, who were watching from the landing. "I told you Reapers were nothing."

I grabbed the deck with both hands and pulled, scrabbling my feet behind me like a fish out of water. From a certain height, the landing area looked smooth, like a picture of military order. From my vantage point, it was a tangle of industrial rivets, tracks for railcars, and openings.

I came to a metal grate.

"That's for drainage in the event of a fire with the need to deploy water and other anti-combustion chemicals," X-37 said. "It dumps into the sewers."

"Don't care."

The soldier's feet pounded across the deck. "Oh no you don't!"

I shoved myself through the gap and fell blind.

13

EMERGING from the pipe into stagnant water wasn't my finest moment, especially since I had gone face first with my own vomit liberally smeared down the front of my gear.

"Don't open your mouth," X-37 said.

For an artificial intelligence designed to make me the most efficient killer and infiltration specialist in the galaxy, X-37 had some weird hang-ups. Why should it care about whether or not I gagged on the sludge splashing all around me? I was more worried about water snakes or whatever might live in this slop.

I saw the room in layers of shadow that even my cybernetic optics couldn't sort out. When I stood up, I was almost waist deep. A filmy layer that looked like the skin of some rotting alien beast covered everything. The smell drove my stomach into new convulsions.

Turning right, turning left, I looked for the cause of a splashing sound. "What was that?"

"I have no data on what might or might not be in the sewer." X-37 seemed distracted.

"All right. This isn't so bad. Probably just rats. More scared of me than I am of them." I did a circuit of the room to be sure there were no real dangers and put my imagination in timeout. None of the spec ops soldiers, including the main asshole who thought he was such a bad ass, had elected to follow me this way.

I bent at the waist and put my hands on my knees, not sure if I needed to puke or scream. My bones ached, probably from flexing against the carbon fiber sheath that had kept me from being crippled ten times during this shit mission.

"X, I have water leaking into everything."

"You'll survive."

"Well, no shit, X. But that doesn't mean I want sludge down my shorts."

"At least you didn't open your mouth until you emerged."

"Good point. What is that smell?"

"Take a guess, or better yet, don't worry about it. My suggestion is to get moving as soon as possible."

Once I'd climbed out of the sewer, I tried to remove all my weapons and clean them. The compact first aid pack and gun-cleaning kit were waterproof. The problem was I didn't have any weapons.

The arm blade eventually responded to some tender loving care with the gun-cleaning kit, thunking out a little slower than usual but locking into place without a major problem. I left it extended until I was certain the housing was dry, then retracted it as I marched through an unlit section of Dreadmax.

No one had been through this area in a long time. Even before the station became a maximum-security prison, it probably was mostly maintained by bots and drones.

"Take the next ladder. There is a transportation tube above this section."

"I'm about done with trains and train tracks," I muttered as I poked my head over the top of the ladder and looked around.

"It's the best, and cheapest, way to move anything on a station this large."

"Thanks for that extremely valuable information, X." I climbed out of the pipe, moved away from the opening, and sat against the wall. "How long have we been separated from the principal?"

"Four point five hours. Six hours remain before the mission clock expires."

"That can't be right."

"Don't argue with me, Reaper Cain. You've been hit on the head several times. Trust me, I'm here to help."

"Then help." It felt like a dick thing to say, but I wasn't in the mood to say 'please' or 'thank you' or explain exactly what I expected the limited AI to do.

The tracks were narrower than what I'd encountered before getting separated from my team—probably one of the personnel lines that had moved crewman, pilots, and soldiers to every part of the battle station before everything went sideways.

There were actual lights in places—dim but functioning. I found a set of locked escalators and ran up to the next sub-level. "How far down am I, X?"

"Technically, you have never left the first sub-level. Each layer of the ring is fifty meters thick and contains its own infrastructure. The closer you get to the spire in the center, the less like a space station and the more like a naval vessel it becomes."

I jogged along the track, unburned by weapons, ammunition, or supplies. "What is the structural integrity of my armor after jerk-face kicked my ass?"

"You'd be better off ditching it."

"Thanks, X."

I stripped down to my soaked jumpsuit and underlayers before picking up the pace. What I found at the top of the stairs was a way point, a terminal where workers could disembark and head into various work areas.

"What are you looking for?" X-37 asked.

"Bathroom. With running water if possible."

What I found was even better, a temporary dormitory with functional showers and an actual kitchen—not some laboratory for making gray slime.

"That other place was definitely not a kitchen," I said.

"Which causes one to wonder exactly what you ate two helpings of."

"Let's never talk about that again."

I showered, shaved, and, well, did other things that needed doing. In one locker, I found a jumpsuit, work belt, and boots that fit. On the way out, I smashed open a vending machine and ate the oldest powdered sugar donut in the galaxy—which tasted glorious.

"There is good news," X-37 said. "While you were screwing off, I continued to analyze station schematics and probable travel routes of your lost group."

"That is good news, X. Thanks. I'll put a little something extra in your next paycheck." Running in dry boots felt like a luxury. "Tell me the rest."

"Continue this direction, avoid confrontations with gangs, cannibals, or spec ops soldiers who want to kill you, and you should arrive at your destination in less than one hour," X-37 said.

It took me forty-two minutes. I watched the platform that Grady had barricaded for another five minutes before making my approach. My old friend had seen action since we parted. He had bandages on his face, left arm, and a splint on his leg—the same leg that had been shot earlier. It was a new injury and caused him to limp badly.

"Grady, I'm coming to you," I announced before I approached. The radio sounded more garbled each time I used it.

"I see you. We've been attacked three times since you

went off gallivanting," he said. "You're going to have a hell of a time reaching us without crossing a kill zone."

I studied Grady from a distance. He was as tough as any spec ops soldier, but he had more wounds than I did. X-37 kept tabs on my hormonal output and all my bodily functions. The Reaper AI could, and often did, tweak things a bit to make sure I recovered quickly and grew as strong as possible from whatever exercise routine I had access to. That was one of the reasons I'd been able to stay strong during my confinement. Aggressive hormone regulation.

With my artificial left arm enhanced by bionic servos, the advanced optics of my left eye, and the carbon fiber sheaths protecting my bones, I had a better chance of surviving this mission than he did.

Unless he had been upgraded, which certainly would have explained his faster-than-normal healing. I thought I would know if he'd undergone anything close to the transformation I'd suffered. Seventy-eight percent of the subjects brought into the Reaper Corps went crazy from the pain of the treatments long before they were ever put into the field.

Grady was tough, but he wasn't that tough. I had wiring that was less than five molecules wide twisted through my nerves. The doctors had promised to avoid pain centers, but they were full of shit about a lot of things. And they had lied more than they breathed.

"I didn't think the RSG or the NG could make it this

far," I said. "Who the hell's been attacking you? Can I get across the kill zone if I move fast?"

This was a test question. Did my friend really want me to survive this mission?

"No, they've got a sniper and their close quarters team has unlimited ammunition, apparently. What's an NG? Never mind. I'm not sure what's happening, but I think there's a spec ops team trying to take us out."

"You mean that wasn't part of the plan?"

"Where have you been?" he asked after a short pause.

"Here and there. Ate something questionable. The usual stuff you'd expect on a suicide mission." I saw Elise and the doctor. Tension I didn't realize I was holding slipped away, relaxing my shoulders and arms. "I ran into some spec ops soldiers who tried to kill me. That makes sense, given my situation. I'm surprised they'd try to take you out and risk damaging the principal."

"Trust me, I've been surprised by a lot of things since I jumped down into this mess."

"You play stupid games, you win stupid prizes," I said.

"Isn't that the truth."

"Stand by. I may have a way to reach your position," I said.

"Negative. I can take the doctor and the girl and meet you at the landing bay," Grady said.

"I want to get squared away before that. Ten to one odds the pick-up will be sketchy."

What, no response, you back-stabbing asshole?

Grady's mic clicked a few times, indicating he was starting and stopping the transmission, probably at a loss for words. "You're not the only one getting screwed here."

14

"THAT'S YOUR BEST IDEA?" I asked X-37.

"Yes, sir, it is," X-37 said.

I hated heights. Thinking about the cable crossing made my hands shake. The only thing worse was complete failure and the real chance of death that would come with it. The doctor was a pompous asswipe, the type to put scientific research above humanity. His daughter was as annoying as any teenager I'd ever met. My best friend from spec ops was probably going to betray me.

My bones ached, my heart raced from whatever X-37 was doing to my hormonal profile, and the gray slime I'd eaten earlier was still talking to me. Now I was expected to run the rooftops of a decommissioned battle station with a failing gravity generator and sketchy atmosphere shield.

"I promise there won't be any more cables or bridges.

The schematics show one narrow walkway that is out of view of your destination, and thus not likely to be targeted by the enemy sniper."

"You know they're just trying to keep us here until their sodding super soldier catches up," I said, climbing up the back of a building and crouching low as I moved across the first rooftop. The route X-37 had plotted for me circled the area with only a few deviations from what I might have picked myself.

The heads-up display in my left eye was necessarily small and limited. My right hand cramped each time I climbed a ladder. The cybernetic-enhanced left arm could mimic the discomfort of my natural right arm for the sake of coordination, but I asked X-37 to turn that feature off.

Having one arm without pain and one arm with pain might throw off my coordination, but I doubted it. I'd had the artificial limb long enough to know what I could and couldn't do with it.

Phantom pain was another issue. It was worse when I thought about how I'd lost the arm, but I tried to put that image out of my mind. Unless I had a lot of time on my hands, like when I'd been confined to death row.

That woman holding my hand as she dangled from a bridge. Talk about a nightmare. It felt like a lifetime ago.

In a way, the worse this mission got, the better I felt. At least in my head.

I was on my third building before I saw the next major obstacle in the way of rescuing Hastings and his daughter.

The gangs of Dreadmax had found a way across the power plant exhaust trench. They had vehicles that must've allowed them to drive a considerable distance to the next actual bridge. No hand-over-hand cable shenanigans for them.

Lucky bastards.

I watched the RSG mob search and wasn't sure if I needed to laugh or curse. They started off in organized groups but were easily distracted. Infighting, laziness, and homemade liquor further diminished their effectiveness. "I should be thankful they're so unorganized, right?"

"The RSG search tactics are inefficient, which is good for us," X-37 said.

"Are there any talk boxes up here?"

"None are shown on the schematics."

It would've been nice to check on the security camera to see what Bug and his friends could tell me. I was dying to know if they had eyes on the spec ops team hunting me. Were they talking to that fuckstick?

"Why do I keep finding myself in the highest places you can find?" I looked down an alleyway so dark, I couldn't see the bottom. The walkway swayed slightly, which I blamed on poor construction in a haphazard design. Dreadmax was like any other space station this size. It had gravity generators, but also relied on rotation to provide some of the effect. When this was out of sync, there were random vibrations and other side effects that made crossing the highest parts of the top deck uncomfortable. I tried not to think of the structural degradation that mission planners gave as a reason for their accelerated time line.

"What am I missing, X? I'd really like to see the spec ops guys that are after us."

"We should've spotted them by now, regardless of how professional they are. But you had the same training and better tools. It's unlikely they have cybernetic enhancements equal to what the Reaper Corps provided you," X-37 said. "However, it's equally unlikely they have left the area for no reason. Would you like me to designate a name for the unit and leader?"

"Sure."

X-37 started to give me random numbers and letters.

"How about we just call him the super soldier assmunch and his posse?"

"That seems like a long, unnecessarily imprecise description," X-37 said.

"Super soldier it is. He has to have some upgrades to have thrashed me like that."

"An alternate explanation is that you are losing your edge."

"Bite your tongue."

"We've discussed your colloquial phrases and their complete irrelevance to a nerve-ware AI."

"Don't ever change, X," I said, rushing across the unstable foot bridge.

"I won't."

I moved as close as I could to Grady and the principals.

He didn't respond to comms. All I heard on my end was static. Whenever I saw Elise, I thought she was looking for a chance to run but hesitated to leave her father. There was a weird vibe between them, like maybe she'd as soon stab him as save him—but she protected him and pushed him to keep going.

"Are we being jammed?"

"Unlikely. The equipment to block radio communications is cumbersome and not normally assigned to spec ops teams. If I detected a naval vessel in our immediate vicinity, this would be a possibility."

I searched the sky for the USC *Thunder* or one of the dropships and saw nothing on any visual spectrum. If Slab's RSG saw one of the ships, they weren't shooting at it this time.

"Maybe I should whistle," I said.

"Excellent idea. Choose a sound from some of the local wildlife."

"I'm not sure if I'm impressed or freaked out by your lapses into perfect sarcasm."

"How can I not be perfect?"

"With you, X, it's either a direct hit or a complete miss, and I think you steal my jokes."

"It is necessary for me to steal everything. If you would please refrain from using the legends of this Chuck Norris person, I would appreciate it. The illogic of these jokes is mind-boggling."

"I don't know what you're talking about, X."

"Creativity, or whatever near approximation can be achieved through programming, is a capital offense for AIs. You know this. Are you trying to get me in trouble?"

"If you're going to roll with me, you need to be an outlaw."

"Noted. I will endeavor to create jokes and deliver them at appropriate times. Still no response to our radio signal."

I stared at Grady and the others, muttering curses under my breath. "Come on, you dumbasses. Someone see me."

Elise looked up, scanning the area as I had seen her do several times before. Her eyes went wide with recognition.

"Finally," I muttered. "You just got out spec op'd by a teenage runaway, Grady."

I pointed toward Grady, but she just stared at me, tired and obviously worried—probably about her father as much as she complained about him.

"Fine, I'll just climb down there," I said.

"Was that statement for me or for the girl who can't hear you from this distance?"

"Wow, X. You're on a roll today." Climbing down took longer than it should have, because I didn't know where the sniper was and I had this thing about not getting drilled in the head with a supersonic bullet.

Elise watched me but didn't say anything to Grady or her father. My old friend must have been hurt even worse than I thought. He was totally focused on the super soldier and his squad of assassins, which was understandable, since he wasn't accustomed to being betrayed by his handlers— something any Reaper expected by the time they'd done two missions. I'd done a lot more than that.

"I hope you're paying more attention than Grady is," I said as I slipped into their hideout. The backdoor, so to speak, wasn't barricaded. "Sooner or later, they'll come this way."

"I know. Your friend has been in a bad mood since he got shot at by his ship."

"His ship didn't shoot at him," I said, despite agreeing with her completely. It didn't seem right to admit how fucked-up this mission was. "That was directive fire. I'm sure they're just trying to help."

Elise rolled her eyes, clearly disgusted at my bullshit.

"All right, fine. He's a whiny bitch. Get betrayed by the Union one time, and you think the world is ending."

She laughed loud enough to draw the attention of the others. "Thank gods. I was starting to think you had a stick up your ass just like he does."

"Which one, Grady or your father?"

"Either. Both." We didn't have a lot of time before Grady and her father confronted us, but I noticed something about her hesitation to elaborate.

I waited for her to elaborate.

"I think you and I have more in common than we realize," she said, unable to look me in the eyes.

"It's about time," Grady interrupted. "Do you have something against answering the radio?"

"I was going to ask you the same thing. All I'm getting is static or dead air."

"That's a product of the faltering shield generator. We may have less time than you think. Look there at the horizon. Can you see it?" Doctor Hastings asked.

It took me a second, but I saw what was bothering him. A cloud of debris was drifting toward the shield, clearly unrestrained by gravity.

"The gravity should fail all at once," Grady said.

"Not necessarily," replied the doctor. "Just like there are fluctuations in the atmosphere shield, energy isn't constant. It pulses. The key is to keep the wavelengths near enough that it makes no difference. This place is falling apart and so is the technology. You can expect a gradually decreasing ring of effectiveness around whoever is maintaining the generators. Because it's clear not all of the station is getting regular tune-ups."

"Can you walk, Grady?" I asked.

He nodded grimly.

"Then we better get moving. I don't think they know I'm here, so I'll shadow your movements and remain out of sight for as long as possible."

Grady objected, "That can be tricky and it's also unnecessary." He handed me a shortened, highly modified version of the HDK I'd lost and several full magazines. "I scavenged these after our last encounter with these guys. Let's stay together."

"I have my reasons for splitting up."

"We don't have time for bullshit. What the hell are you talking about?"

"I ran into the leader of the spec ops team hunting us. We didn't hit it off."

"Leave it to you to antagonize the people probably sent to rescue us," Grady said.

Elise and I shared a knowing look. My friend was in pain and denial.

"Get moving, Grady. I'll be right behind you." I waited until he was out of earshot, then nodded at Elise. "You and I are going to talk later."

15

"I should've seen this coming, X," I said. "Find me a talk box. I need to talk to the kid in the tower."

"His name is Bug and there is a talk box and camera cluster at every intersection from here to the pickup site," X-37 said.

I moved quickly, opening and closing my cybernetic left hand several times. There wasn't pain, but the compulsion to check its functionality seem to be increasing. This generally indicated there was damage to the unit.

It didn't take long for me to realize Grady was leading the doctor and his daughter into a trap. It was a huge relief, actually, because I was starting to think the spec ops team was unstoppable. Their trap was a good one, but not unexpected. So they were only human, not nightmares out of my imagination. Grady was either sleeping on the job or part of the trap. I wasn't sure which explanation bothered me more.

"Are you seeing what I'm seeing, X?"

"They have their super soldier leader with them and seem to have given up on finding you. My analysis suggests their priority is to reclaim the doctor."

"Can we flank them without climbing on the highest unstable platform out here?" I asked. "I'd also like to avoid swimming in twenty years of untreated sewage."

"Of course. Displaying options via your HUD now."

"Thanks, X. You're the man."

"Please stop with the nonsensical colloquialisms," requested the AI.

The spec ops team worked their way into position, setting up overlapping fields of fire from two directions. Moving from shadow to shadow, listening to advice from X, I took up the third position in a triangle.

The attack they were about to unleash would be devastating without intervention. They weren't worried about their own defense perimeter—a mistake that was going to cost them.

"Hey, Grady," I said, hoping to get through the radio static.

No obvious response, but I saw him flinch.

"You remember that time I told you to get the fuck down?"

Grady grabbed the doctor and Elise, slamming them

facedown against the deck without responding to my warning. Of course, I probably wouldn't know if he responded because the radios were so garbled and unreliable. He probably said, "Thanks, you're the best," or something like that.

The only comms rig that worked every time was the hardwired talk boxes Bug and his friends in the surveillance booth used.

The spec ops team hesitated, then fired. One pulled the pin on the grenade and cocked back his arm.

I shot him in the throat, then turned my new and improved HDK on the rest of his team. Callus and two others drove clear of the onslaught, returning fire almost instantly but without knowing my position.

"I suggest moving before they get a lock on you," X-37 said.

Ducking low, I ran behind a support beam and went prone, but only because I wanted to. Not because my Reaper AI was the boss of me.

The grenade exploded and I heard men scream.

"I doubt we'll get a drop on them a second time," I said.

"I guarantee you're right," Callus growled.

I twisted onto my side and looked up, only to find my nemesis squatting on a power box high above me.

"I wish you'd stop doing that," said Callus.

"Stop doing what? Sneaking up on you because I'm the better soldier?"

"No. The dramatic pauses are tedious. What is this, an action holo? Take some acting lessons or get over it."

"You're not as funny as you think you are. I could have shot you in the back. Who would've thought a Reaper could be so easy to surprise?"

I yanked my feet underneath me while he was finishing his monologue and darted around the support beam, hoping the other spec ops personnel didn't spot me. From the sound of it, they were busy with Grady, but I didn't want to take chances.

Callus chased me between stainless steel beams that supported one of the maintenance bot rail systems. The un-corroded metal contrasted with the reddish-brown deck it was bolted to. Shadows flashed as several of the automated bots zipped toward destinations unknown.

I stopped, changing directions abruptly. Callus adjusted, rushing forward like a linebacker, his feet never slipping or getting hung up by poorly tuned magnetic soles. I expected to be tackled the first time I made a mistake. We aimed at each other several times, but neither of us fired our weapons. It was a tense, fast-paced game of chess.

I had a feeling that whoever missed first would die first in this scenario.

The sound of gunfire increased from the ambush site. I hoped Grady could hang on until I dealt with this guy. Otherwise, this was all for nothing.

"The support beams aren't going to last forever," he shouted, then fired a round that ricocheted close to my head. "Hasn't that old X-unit warned you yet? Or don't you trust your fucked-up nerve-ware?"

I bolted from the questionable cover and concealment the rail system provided, sprinting into one of the top deck neighborhoods. Most of the civilians, whether they were convicted criminals or political refugees, went inside and shut their doors.

If there hadn't been a running gun battle, this area would be in the middle of its peak working hours, I thought. There were a lot of people out and about who were too far from their homes or workstations to take shelter. They gathered to argue and discuss what they must've heard happening all night.

Why all the gunfire and explosions? What was causing the frequent tremors? Did anyone see the neighbor's tool shed float into the void last night?

Men and women who looked like they were prepared to go to work hesitated when they saw me running at them, probably unable to appreciate how fast I was moving now.

There wasn't cover. Speed was the only friend I had.

Callus came after me like a freight train, closing the distance faster than I could believe. He was bigger and more heavily muscled than I was, and I wasn't small. Lean and mean and strong enough to break a man's back—that was one of the training catchphrases Reapers used.

I wasn't slow, even before I had X-37 to manipulate my hormone profile and turn my physical training into elite-level results. I wasn't as strong or as fast as I would've been had I not spent the past two years on death row, but I had an advantage over almost anyone in the Union.

Callus was the exception. I didn't know if he was the new version of a Reaper, but there was something giving him an edge.

I crashed through the civilians, shouting at them to get the hell out of the way and take cover.

Some of them reacted quicker than others. Callus slammed a man off his feet who moved too slow to get out of the way.

"Head to the transfer station, where all the noises are coming from. Bring back my team. Do it now!" Callus said.

I reached the corner but had to look back to see what happened to the bystanders. It only took a second, but it felt like too long.

The crowd drifted away from the super soldier, watching him like he was a dangerous animal. Not one obeyed his order.

"I told you to move! Bring my team. I'm in pursuit of a dangerous fugitive," said Callus.

Several of the locals laughed.

A man with a thick beard and rough hands stepped forward with a wrench. "Who the hell do you think you are?"

Callus stomped on the man's knee, using the downward angle taught in high-level martial arts courses. The man screamed as he collapsed. Two other men rushed to help. Callus cut one's throat with a knife I barely saw him draw and punched another in the face. A third mechanic retreated with a broken arm.

I couldn't believe how fast and powerful this asshole was.

"X, can you see any cybernetic attachments?"

"No. This is something else. Genetic modifications perhaps, or some ancient technology one of the Union research teams has been working on."

Callus looked up from the needless attacks on the bystanders, caught my eye, and smiled.

"You son-of-a-bitch," I said, then turned to run.

He yelled after me, "Come back here, or I'll do worse! You don't want to get these people hurt!"

"I do not recommend you comply," X-37 said in a rush.

"I'm way ahead of you. We'll deal with this jerk some-place private."

———

CALLUS CAME after me like I knew he would. He only looked stupid. I doubted the Union would invest so much money in this super soldier without going all the way. The man had to know my Reaper training and understand that taking hostages would never be effective against me.

It pissed me off, but that was probably not the effect he'd be looking for. The only reason he hurt those people was because he enjoyed it.

My vigilante gene flared up despite the Union's effort to

rid me of it during years of training and manipulation. "Hey, asswipe, why don't you try me?" I asked.

"Oh, you're gonna stand and fight now? Perfect. I'll be home in time for dinner."

"Big talk for a guy with a spec ops team on the way. You couldn't beat me one on one. If I was a hundred percent, you wouldn't stand a chance," I said, almost believing my own trash talk.

"What exactly are you doing?" X-37 asked.

"Stalling."

"Stalling? Why? So he can get the rest of his team here?" asked X.

I watched the elite commandos take their positions. "So Grady can get away with the principals," I muttered.

"Your plan would be more effective if you had included Grady in its development. I can't see any evidence he has left with Hastings or his daughter," X-37 said.

Not for the first time, I decided X had a point. "Hal for Grady," I said in a low voice. "Can you hear me?"

Radio static filled my earpiece.

16

"I'm really not that impressed, Reaper," Callus said.

"It's not about you, asshole," I said, listening for Grady's answer and getting frustrated. If they didn't get clear, it limited what I could do next.

One of the spec operators moved closer to Callus. "Why don't we just erase the girl and witnesses?"

Callus hissed something I couldn't quite make out.

"Did I hear that right, X?"

"It seems their primary objective is to kill Elise. I'm not sure why he's fixated on you." A pause. "I had assumed the objective was to rescue the doctor and reclaim his research, including his daughter."

"Don't worry about it, X. I'll feed you some more data when I can."

It made sense, in a way. Doctor Hastings claimed she'd

been kidnapped and put here to ensure his cooperation on a secret project, which was probably at least partially true. Putting a teenage girl on Dreadmax when they had to know it was failing seemed excessive.

The man had told me part of the truth as he understood it. He'd used technology he lifted from the Lex Project to cure Elise from a childhood illness. She'd been changed and probably singled out for close observation.

Her ability to stay alive in this hellish, man-made world was impressive. Genetic enhancements must have given her an edge. She'd done the rest, I decided, but I also wagered there was more to her story than I'd been told. We had started a conversation we had yet to finish. She'd said something about us not being as different as we thought.

I'd blown off the comment at the time. I was twice her age and had given up parts of my body to cybernetic replacement long before she was born. My enhancements had nothing to do with the Lex Project, as far as I knew, since the original test subject that the doctor mentioned hadn't existed back then.

"Time to gamble," I said to X-37.

"Oh, no," said X.

I moved closer to Callus. "Your failure to plan isn't my problem."

"What are you talking about?" he asked.

"You can't get us both," I remarked

"I can, and if I don't, we still win. Neither one of you can get off Dreadmax to infect the galaxy." Callus held up a fist to keep the rest of his team back a respectful distance. They could probably still hear and record the incident with their body cameras, but they had the advantage of being well-positioned to cut me off if I tried to escape in a random direction.

"You should have just nuked the place from orbit," I said.

"You don't understand, Cain. This is a salvage operation. Nothing personal. I can bring you in dead or alive and count the operation a success. Everyone on my team knows my preference."

"Cain, respond," Grady said, finally breaking through my radio link.

I ignored him, trying to pretend I hadn't heard his voice. The last thing I wanted was for Callus to know my friends were this close.

"We are coming to you," Grady said. "I have three grenades. I'll throw two when you bolt for it, and the last one to cover your movement."

"This sucks," I said.

Callus laughed, thinking I was admitting defeat. "Not for me."

"Grady, it's a trap. Get the hell out of here."

The spec ops team sprang into action. Callus and two others rushed me. I fell back, shooting one in the pelvis. He went down screaming and the other stopped to help him.

"That was dirty," Callus snarled, looking for a shot.

Other members of his team were swarming toward

Grady, unaware of what was about to happen. I threw myself to the ground as two grenades went off. My adversary was a beat slower, but still saved himself from a blast to the face.

We arose from the smoking rubble. Tangles of cheap metal siding and other parts of the deck were scattered everywhere. One of the spec ops guys was completely gone. Stunned silence held both sides of the confrontation until I heard Elise scream.

The missing man had been blown high enough into the air that he didn't come back down.

"Take your team and get out of here before they all get killed," I said, waving the barrel of my HDK toward downed soldiers and the one heading toward the environment shield.

Unlike the first man I'd seen this happen to, he bounced off the shield and came back down faster and faster as gravity reclaimed him. He waved his arms and legs all the way down then hit the deck with a sickening crunch.

Callus responded to my warning by firing a stream of bullets at me, then vaulting over his cover to reach the next point between us. "You can't win, Reaper. I already have reinforcements in route."

"Grady! Let's get out of here!"

This would've been a lot easier if he hadn't shown up to help me. The one time I wanted him to hang me out to dry, he came gallivanting into the middle of a battle I had under control—or was at least managing—then stopped answering his radio.

We were close enough to shout now. No need to rely on radio earpieces.

Soldiers groaned in pain and crawled behind cover to apply first-aid. I saw one man applying quick-clotting agent and then a pressure bandage to another man.

Callus ducked out from cover and fired several well-placed shots that hit too close for comfort.

"Grady! Sound off if you can hear me."

"He's down," Elise shouted from out of view. She didn't have good cover. Instead, she had the youthful flexibility that allowed her to get really low. I also realized she had two handguns now.

"Put one of those in the holster so you can reload," I shouted, looking for the doctor and my old friend.

A trio of dropships descended behind a nearby building. Moments later, they were back in the air and headed for the UFS *Thunder*. It wouldn't be long before Callus had more than enough manpower to storm our position.

"Cover me!"

Elise popped up from behind cover and opened fire on every Union soldier she saw. She missed a lot but forced them to duck down for a couple of seconds, during which time I sprinted to her position.

Doctor Hastings was a quivering mess as he tried to help Grady. His extensive medical knowledge was less useful than it should have been on the battlefield. He'd managed to apply a tourniquet to one of Grady's legs and keep pressure on a chest wound.

"Just pour the quick-clot powder all over it. I don't care if it gets infected or burns. We've got bigger problems," Grady ordered between clenched teeth.

The doctor did what he was told, hands trembling so badly that he spilled most of the clotting agent.

I ignored both of them and crouched beside Elise. Staying behind the metal curb for cover was hard, but the position wasn't bad. We were backed into a corner that we couldn't escape from.

In that moment, I realized something. If I rescued Elise and her father from all the dangers of Dreadmax, it would only be to sentence them to death at the hands of the Union—once the Union had what they wanted from them, that was.

There was no way to win.

"We're not going to make it, are we?" Elise asked.

I looked at Grady and Doctor Hastings. They were both white as sheets but quiet now. If we were to have any chance of escaping, I couldn't have them screaming and giving away our position.

"Hal," Grady grunted, the effort it took him to speak clearly evident. He waved me over with a hand that looked like it weighed a hundred pounds. "I need to tell you something."

"Elise," I said, then pointed. "Watch for the next attack from Callus and his commandos."

Grady gripped my gear, grimacing in pain.

"Make it quick, Grady. One way or another, we're leaving."

"You're leaving, but don't worry about that right now. I've got to tell you something. You're going to get the lethal injection no matter what after this mission. No one would tell me why. They led me to believe you had one chance to redeem yourself, but I can read between the lines. You've got technology in you that can't be controlled. They couldn't generalize it to other test subjects and your field trials went beyond what they expected."

"What the hell are you talking about?"

He shook his head, too tired from blood loss to elaborate. "I've got one last fight in me. Get out of here. What you do with them," he said, nodding toward the doctor and his daughter, "is up to you. They're coming, Hal. Let's get this show on the road and kill some of these bastards."

I patted him on the shoulder, unsure of what to say, and slipped closer to Elise. "How many magazines do you have for those pistols?"

She held up the loaded weapon in one hand and a magazine in the other. "One extra. What did your friend say?"

"He just confirmed what I always knew about him. He's a dumbass who is going to die badly. Get ready. When I start shooting, grab your dad and shove him down that maintenance trench. Once we're in it, speed will be important because there is no place to hide and it won't take Callus long to come after us."

"Your friend doesn't look very fast."

"He's not coming with us."

A wave of ululating cries swept over the buildings, announcing the arrival of an epic horde of crazies. I also heard engines, horns, and crew-served machine guns. The locals were joining this battle either accidentally or on purpose. Shit was about to get real.

"You're leaving your friend?"

"Why not? I've done it before. You want to stay? All I really need is your dad."

"You're so full of shit," she said. "I hope I'm never like you."

Callus moved across the deck with his reinforced team. They moved by squads—two laying down suppressive fire each time one of the others moved. I didn't even try to shoot back.

Crazies jumped from buildings, immediately over-whelming one squad that had been too focused on my position. A machine-gun truck raced through the middle of it all, firing in every direction. The heavy slugs punched through walls that looked solid, but also ricocheted like angry hornets. One of the prison gang members started throwing canisters of rocket fuel with burning fuses. Smoke added to the confusion.

Callus and his squad leaders mostly ignored the chaos, advancing relentlessly toward my position regardless of what the crazies, RSG, and NGs did to each other. The only exception was a Union squad that went after their buddies being dragged into hatches and doorways by cannibals.

"I can't believe this is happening," Elise said, panic creeping into her voice.

"You'll get used to it."

"Fuck you. *You* get used to it." Some of her fire returned.

"Go!" I shot Callus, hitting his chest armor while he was running flat out toward us, unable to shoot back while maintaining the sprinter's pace. He fell. Others picked him up. I looked for new targets and chances to reload.

Grady lobbed his last grenade and fired his **HDK** with one hand.

Elise and her father hobbled into the maintenance trench, both of them looking back through the smoke, steam, and tracer rounds. Both were scared. The difference was Elise was also angry. The doctor looked confused and defeated.

"Go after them, you dick!" Grady shouted.

I tossed my former friend and extra magazine, then took his advice.

17

CATCHING up to Elise and her father wasn't as easy as I had assumed it would be. I understood she was quick but thought of the doctor as a lumbering mass of indecision. She was too small to push him far, and if he resisted, I'd find them having a father-daughter argument while bullets flew over their heads.

Grady's final stand rose to a crescendo not long after I began navigating the maze of trenches and tunnels in this area. It still intrigued me that, from space, the surface of Dreadmax looked almost smooth, like a thick ring of armor plating that was almost a complete sphere except for the spine running down the middle that everything rotated on.

Most of the power core was located in the spine, what some people called the tower. Personally, I thought that the first term was more accurate, but it didn't matter. Anything that was truly important to a ring station was stored near the center.

"Can you help me out, X?" I asked.

The Reaper AI affixed to my nerve-ware didn't respond immediately, which could mean several things, most of them bad. Had I finally overloaded the micro hardware?

X-37 spoke with a slight glitch in his voice. "One moment. I was considering the ramifications of a total power core failure and what that meant to residents of Dreadmax."

Ice shot down my spine. Nerve-ware AIs were not supposed to be able to read a person's mind. We'd had this discussion before. I understood this was coincidence, but it never gave me a warm fuzzy feeling when it happened. I decided to give X-37 a taste of his own medicine. The silent treatment wasn't that difficult when I was running hard enough to put myself in deep oxygen debt.

"Be mindful of your environment. You're moving faster than normal and your heart rate is ten percent higher than it has been since you fell," X-37 said. "Continue on the path of least resistance. I believe Elise will be in flight mode, not much different from a wounded animal. She'll go as fast as she can and take routes that are easy for her less athletic father to manage. However, the schematics show a junction with too many options, where she will likely wait for you or at least hesitate."

I wasn't sure I liked the sound of that. "You mean an intersection?"

"Not precisely," X said. "The junction is three-dimensional. She will have to choose from fourteen horizontal trenches, ascending stairs, or descending stairs."

Not far ahead, I saw one of the large observation towers looming above us. It was a handy landmark. "I seriously doubt she'll go below decks."

"That is unfortunate. The observation towers are like trees, reaching high enough to observe and manage a large portion of the top deck but also reaching down to access the spine. My estimation is that very few of the people on Dreadmax understand this."

"Don't care." I really didn't. Why would I?

"Your biometrics tell a different story."

"You and I both know Dreadmax is done. Am I pissed off about thousands of innocents going down with it? Sure, X. I'm a cold-blooded assassin, not a heartless jerkoff." Not long ago, I'd been watching kids play on an intricately fabricated jungle gym. Mothers and fathers had worked nearby. Bug was right, the shipbuilders were good people.

I didn't want them to die like this.

X-37 interpreted my silence correctly and tried put me at ease. "I'm sure the thousands of relatively innocent human beings on Dreadmax will survive. Your friend Bug in the surveillance tower mentioned *Climbdown Day*. This suggests they have a plan to survive the collapse of the environment shield. And you witnessed the engineers attempting to fix a starship."

"Do you honestly think either of those plans will work?" Why did my AI have to mention the kid?

"It is unlikely either plan will succeed," my AI said. "But you don't care."

"You got that right, X."

"Deception detected." X-37 had the best poker voice I'd ever heard. How could I compete with that? I was hard, but he was a machine.

Images of Dreadmax collapsing upon itself and then exploding into drifting chunks of metal ran a loop in my head that I mostly ignored after the first annoying manifestation of guilt.

None of this was my fault.

"I've completed my analysis of the schematics for this area," X-37 said. "It only looks like a maze from your current vantage point. Unfortunately, I can't put the entire map in your HUD."

I adjusted my pace and searched for Elise. The tower loomed above us, the largest vertical structure I'd encountered on Dreadmax. It was probably thirty meters in diameter at the roughly hexagonal base. Four of the sides were out of proportion to the others and hosted bay doors almost as large as those at the RSG stronghold.

This place was made for moving heavy equipment. Everything on Dreadmax was big, like the designers had pretended they were giants.

"X, you said there were stairs. Is there a lift?"

"Yes. There is a lift with a one-thousand-ton capacity,

but it can move heavier loads if the gravity generators are turned off, of course. This is how most of the construction was done. However, I do not believe the lift is functioning and would serve no purpose to our current mission if it did."

"A simple yes or no would have been fine."

X-37 beeped so quietly I doubted it was meant for me to hear. The digital little jerk needed an update. "The question seemed out of place. Please refine your inquires in the future. Stop being a dick."

"Whatever. Shut up while I search for Elise."

"You'll recall I was speaking of the map," X-37 said. "The layout of this area is important. Given the number of connected maintenance trenches and other access ways, there is a high probability you are being enveloped by the rogue spec ops team trying to kill you."

"I'm pretty sure we're the rogues and they're the Union-sanctioned strike team."

"Admitting that they are right and we are wrong interferes with my functioning," X-37 said, almost accusingly.

Whoa! Hold on there! "That's not what I said. Just factor in that the Union is bad and your life will be a lot easier."

"I am an artificial intelligence. A bundle of programs, essentially. Look at it from my perspective."

"Okay, X," I said as I spotted Elise crouching near one of the large bay doors with her father. She looked determined but uncertain. Her father tried repeatedly to drink from a water bottle that was empty.

Pulling back to conceal myself, I took a cleansing breath and lowered my heart rate. "I'll make it simple for you. We're the good guys, they're the bad guys, and your job is to keep me alive. Maybe two or three other people as well."

"Mission directive updated."

"And also find me some Starbrand cigars," I said looking for a place to move.

Stun grenades rained down all around me, filling the area with smoke and noise. Three squads of spec ops soldiers burst from as many maintenance trenches. Bullets and tracer rounds cut through the smoke as I dropped low and ran to the cover of the ramp. The edges were thick enough to keep heavy equipment from sliding off. I'd never been so safe.

Too bad I couldn't stay. Callus' team rushed me, confident I couldn't see them.

They should've known better.

To my enhanced vision, they looked like red silhouettes running through near total blackness. My right eye saw the smoke, my left eye saw variations of heat and cold, and the Reaper nerve-ware helped my brain interpret the sensory input as one image.

"Time to go," I said, ducking around a corner without standing from my crouching position. Duck-walking felt about as good as lighting my quadriceps on fire, but it was better than being shot in the face.

I'd trained for this in a previous lifetime. This far into a mission, everything hurt.

X-37 didn't comment.

At the first gap in their suppressive fire, I ran at the nearest squad, adjusted my course, and found a man-sized hatch near one of the roll-up bay doors. It was closed, probably locked, but the frame around it was excessively thick—brutish architecture that must've been popular when this section of the deck was constructed.

"Why don't they have infrared optics in their helmets?"

"Unknown," X-37 said.

Elise screamed angrily. Gunfire followed. "Get back, dickface! I see you creeping!"

The sound of her pistol ceased abruptly and she screamed without the shit-talking attitude.

Her father yelled, "What kind of Union solider are you? Why would you do that?"

I'd seen some tough women fight and that was what she sounded like, minus her juvenile battle cries.

Moving toward the infrared silhouettes behind the sounds, I found the doctor stumbling through the smoke, searching the area in front of him with his hands.

"Hastings," I said, grabbing him and pulling him toward another access door to the tower. "Shut up and do what I say."

"My daughter's in trouble. We have to find her. Where have you been?"

"Of course she's in trouble. Now shut the fuck up and stay hidden until I come back for you."

"He threw her into a… into a gap. The… lift is down or something. She's probably dead."

"She's not dead. I heard her. Now keep your mouth shut or you'll both be dead."

"Yes, of course. I heard her. She needs me, Cain. I hate this entire situation."

"Save it."

He said something else, but I was already gone.

I MOVED ALONG THE WALL, disappointed the distraction smoke was clearing and suspecting I might have been played. Callus was probably securing his primary objective before focusing all of his attention on me.

Or throwing her down a hole like the doctor said.

The smoke thinned, and I realized that Elise had a moved into the tower before being attacked. The main level of this structure was similar to a hangar, but instead of moving ships into the void, it had been designed to take heavy equipment into the guts of the station. I didn't think the big stuff could be raised. The tower served a different purpose than the base or the sub-deck access points.

There were four platforms, one of which had been lowered long before we arrived if the streaks of polluted grease were an indicator.

I moved carefully, keeping to the last swirls of smoke. Callus was looking into the hole, chest heaving from recent effort. A second later, he pivoted on the balls of his feet and resumed his search.

Steam settled as the smoke from the distraction devices finally dissipated. I moved cautiously forward, worried that my adversary and his squads of elite commandos would return. I knew they were searching for me, but their efforts had been complicated by their primary mission objective.

I wondered if all of them hated me as much as Callus did.

Electricity pulsed through my cybernetics, interfering with my vision and cutting me off from X-37 completely. Damn inconvenient right now. My natural eye adjusted the darkness at the bottom of the elevator shaft while the glitch corrected itself. The platform had locked halfway between levels. Three meters below me was a body.

"Elise, can you hear me?" I asked.

No response.

I did a quick circuit of my immediate area. Gunfire broke out around the corner of the tower where spec ops squads engaged an usually strong contingent of Red Skull Gangsters.

"I don't care who you are, soldier boy. He took something from Slab and we want him," a voice shouted.

I climbed down the wall of the industrial-sized lift. Elise groaned, turning onto one side as I approached. The deck below her head was slick with blood. When I checked her, it was hard to find the wound in her hair.

"Elise, you have to talk to me. I need to know if you can go on," I said.

"What are you doing here?" she asked groggily.

"Getting myself killed," I muttered as I looked up at the edge of the hole we were in.

"You're not really answering my question." She squirmed and pushed herself into a sitting position, then struggled to her feet. "What I meant is, why are you helping us if you know you're going to die?"

That was a pretty good question I didn't have an answer for.

"What's the matter, Reaper got your tongue?" she asked.

"Ha ha, very funny. Someone put me on this mission thinking they could order me to kill you."

"Is that what you think?" Her tone radiated disbelief and sarcasm.

"That's what I was trained for." My job had always been to kill the target even if it cost my own life. Looking back, I wasn't sure how I ever thought joining the Reaper Corps was a good idea.

"Then why did they send that other man?" she asked. "Why are they trying so hard to kill you?"

"Those are good questions," X-37 agreed. "You haven't received an order to execute the girl or her father, which would indicate your assumption is incorrect."

"I think someone sent you to help us." Her tone softened. "Like a guardian angel."

"Unlikely," I said. X-37 seconded the conclusion in my ear.

"Whatever. You're so smart," she said with renewed attitude. "Tell me why the Union would send someone like you, who is so hard to kill? They can't all be bad. There has to be someone among them working to do the right thing."

"You really are just a kid." I regretted the words the moment they left my mouth.

She turned away, crossing her arms and refusing to even curse at me.

18

I PUSHED Elise up the elevator shaft, hoping the lift didn't start to move by some random accident and smash us. There were no safety railings. I could see the exposed gears that made it move up and down. They were covered in rust, but still large enough to crush anyone who fell in them when they were moving.

We found a control room and locked ourselves inside. Looking at the cameras of the exterior reminded me of Bug and his friends. A few of the workstations had power, and I found a speaker box by the door and pressed the button, hoping against hope.

"Bug, can you hear me?" I called.

"Not only that, but I can see you and the woman," the kid's voice responded. "She's been around. The RSG always find her and take her back, though. Is she nice? She seems nice."

I gave Elise the once-over. "Are we talking about the same person?"

She presented me with the middle finger.

"Well, yeah," Bug said. "I think she's beautiful. Tell her my name. Put in a good word for me."

"She can hear you, Bug," I said, watching her reaction.

"Hello, Bug," Elise said. "Are you someplace safe."

"Can you see the other soldier who was helping me?" I asked. "His name is Grady."

"Doesn't matter what his name is," Bug said, "Would you like to see him?"

"He stayed behind to keep the other soldiers from getting us," I said. The monitors to the outside of the tower showed Callus had placed guards on the main level and had others searching for Hastings. His hiding place wasn't good enough to withstand close scrutiny.

"You left him there?" Elise snorted, disbelief in her tone.

"I don't know how to tell you this, Cain, but your friend isn't going to be re-joining you."

"What do you mean, Bug?" I already knew the answer.

"Well, he's either dead or taking a nap. I think he's dead. The way he's lying isn't natural, like maybe somebody roughed him up pretty bad," Bug said. "Hey, I think the guy who killed him is trying to get inside the tower you're hiding in. That's a shit tower, by the way. I've been there once a long time ago, back before we got settled in this tower. Much better here. Closer to the shipyard."

"I'll keep that in mind. What else can you tell me? I need an escape plan," I said.

Static filled the line and I heard Callus' voice.

"I bet you do. Who is that you're talking to? Sounds like a traitor to the Union. If he doesn't stop helping you, he'll probably have to be rounded up and executed along with all of his friends," Callus said.

"You're an asshole, mister," Bug spat, muttering several words lost in the distortion filling the speaker box. "Not you, Mr. Cain, the other mister."

"He's gross!" an even younger child shouted through the speaker.

"I hate him," said a third.

I pulled up video screens one by one while the elite super soldier argued with the orphan kids living in a security room someplace on Dreadmax. Callus had set up a good perimeter and had a breaching team ready. They'd have a hard time with the industrial-strength doors on this place, but I had no illusions we were safe here.

The small camera view made Callus seem even bigger and more menacing than he was. "Listen, Reaper, I have an offer."

"You probably also have an ass you can shove it up," I drawled.

X-37 chastised me for my lack of negotiation tactic.

"Come on, X, you know that was too good to pass up," I said, unrepentant.

Callus slammed a gauntleted fist on the door. "You're not half as funny as you think you are, Reaper. Come out now, with the doctor and the girl, and no one gets hurt. Your friend Grady needs medical attention. All you're doing now is slowing things down. If he dies, it's on you."

His accent struck me with an epiphany. The angrier he got, the more I realized he'd been hiding his heritage in Union military speak. He might not have been from my neighborhood, but he was from someplace rough. The way he talked, walked, and cursed now was like going home.

Where I had wiped out every gang member I could find. Killed their friends. Associates. Anyone who didn't damn them. Union federal prosecutors convicted me of seventeen vigilante murders. There were a lot more.

The reasons probably didn't matter, but I wouldn't change what I had done. They killed everyone I knew or cared about except my mother and my little sister, who were still missing. "Who are you, Callus?"

"You know who I am. Where I'm from. And you know why you're a dead man. Come out here, give me the girl and her father, and I'll handle them according to Union regs. Last fucking chance, you gutter rat."

Son-of-a-bitch. That was what the soldiers of my neighborhood gang called boys who refused to join.

"Your heart rate is elevated far above optimum," X-37 said through increasing static.

"Does he know my father is not in here?" Elise asked, unaware of my inner struggle.

"A better question would be why they're not storming this place," I said, feeling heat in my neck and face. "Callus already knows the layout from when he threw you down the elevator shaft."

"I don't think he realized the lift was only a few meters down," she said.

"He's trying to keep us pinned in this location while they look for your father." I searched the door cameras for a better view but was unable to locate Hastings.

Elise shook her head slowly while she talked, testing her balance and fighting down pain. "Don't be so sure. I'm really good at hiding. I think it was one of the things my father's research was supposed to do for soldiers, improve their escape and evasion abilities. The problem is, I was never trained, even if I have the tools."

"What tools?" I asked, thinking of my cybernetic enhancements.

"Nothing like you. I could pass for normal, slip through a crowded public area without setting off alarms. That's the reason they put me on this place. I could escape, but I can never escape into the galaxy and they knew it."

"But you tried anyway," I said.

"I was bored." She ran one hand through her hair as she sized me up for the hundredth time. "I'm a liability because they didn't realize what I was in time to brainwash me. Study me, yeah, that might serve their project. Literally direct me, yeah, that. But give me one ounce of actual freedom? That will never happen, so fuck them."

She talked and I half listened as I searched for a way to keep the soldiers out long enough to come up with a miracle. I had to get the doctor back and escape with him and his daughter, who was also injured. She didn't show it, not much, but she'd hit her head pretty hard.

Her revelations should have driven me into a rage, but I expected nothing less from the Union. Now was not the time to solve the mystery of her origin. Escaping the gagglefuck was going to take everything I had, up to and maybe including my death.

There wasn't time to get bogged down on that last detail. Elise wanted freedom? How did I explain to her she was her own worst enemy?

"Help me watch these cameras," I said. "Bug, can you help me?"

"I can, but the other guy can listen in. You hurt him. He's hacked into the surveillance network," Bug said.

"Why isn't he smashing his way in here?" I asked as I watched the soldiers search and clear each small section of the area around the massive tower. If there were a few more of them, they'd already be done.

"I don't think he really believes you're in here. And he probably thinks I'm dead," Elise said. "But I'm not."

"Why is that, Elise?" I asked, remembering something she'd said earlier.

"Because of what my father did to me. The experiments. I've always been more resilient than other kids my age. Instead of dying, I matured into something beyond what they wanted or expected, thanks to the treatments my father stole from the project. They want my father back so they can silence him. But they either want to dissect me or turn me into you. Or worse."

Good to know, I thought. "There is nothing worse. Don't get cocky, kid. Getting infused with fancy tech doesn't give you the skills or the will to do what I've done."

Her attitude came back in force as she recovered. "I know all about the Reaper Corps."

I wasn't impressed. "From gal-net conspiracy blogs?"

She blushed.

"That's what I thought." I moved to a new camera, inwardly panicking when I couldn't see Callus and his men. I wasn't interested in being surprised again. "Run away from the Union if you can, but don't get cocky."

"How are you still alive?" she demanded. "No Reaper can take the kind of abuse you have."

"I think they're gonna make an entry. That team is affixing breaching charges to the hinges. An interesting choice," I said.

Elise crossed her arms, ignoring the cameras now. "When did they give you the Lex treatment? You're pretty old, right? It would've had to have been an early version."

"First of all, I'm not old. I'm thirty-seven."

"Whatever," she said, unimpressed with my humor or my age.

"Second of all, I'm a Reaper. I know all the things they put in me. I had to sacrifice body parts to prove I was dedicated to the program. Trust me, I know what they did to me."

"Is that what you think?" she asked, driving her gaze into me.

"What I know is that Callus has this tower surrounded. He's coming in sooner rather than later. Unless he finds your father first and decides to leave before Dreadmax comes apart," I said.

A sliver of fear showed through her hard-ass-runaway act. "What are you talking about?"

"This place won't be here in a few hours. I was given twenty-four hours to recover your father," I said. "Since I arrived, I've run into people trying to repair ships and I've talked to others preparing for Climbdown Day."

"Why would anyone want to go down?" she asked.

I was disappointed with her question. "Because the atmosphere shields will collapse first and heading below decks will give them some time if they can survive the crazies and whatever else is down there."

She shook her head. "There has to be more to it than that. Something down there that will allow them to fix the failing power core or escape altogether."

I knew she was onto something, feeling it with the force of a revelation, but I couldn't put my finger on what it was exactly.

She took my place near the call box. "Hey, you, can you

find the shuttle that was supposed to pick us up? Then tell me how many people the Union has guarding it?"

"My name is Bug."

"Nice to meet you, Bug. That's a nice name," she said. "Now get on those cameras and help me out."

"You're not very nice," Bug said. "You look nice. We all screamed and yelled at Slab when he put you in the cage the first time."

"We don't have time for that, kid," Elise said.

Bug's tone became petulant. "I'm not sure I want to help you."

"Please, Bug. Do it for me," Elise said.

A short pause. "Fine, but you have to take us with you," he replied.

"No problem. We can do that. Just help us find the shuttle and tell us how many people they have guarding it." She looked like she wanted to slap the kid if she could reach him. "We'll also need a way to get there without being caught by these assholes outside right now."

"Put Mr. Cain back on," Bug demanded.

I waved for her to step back. "Can you see the Union shuttle that is supposed to pick us up, Bug?"

"Yeah, but you don't have that other old man. You know they're going to find him if you don't do something, right?" Bug asked.

"Then we'll have to leave him," Elise said, putting on her best tough-girl act. Tears fell from the corner of her eyes. Not even a teenager could fake such abject misery.

"He's such an asshole. I've been trying to get away from him for years."

"He's your father," I said without pressing the talk box button, not sure why I bothered arguing with her. This was for Callus and his team, a little bit of impromptu deception. The girl had good instincts.

"If you're so concerned with him, why'd you hide him out there? He could've been in here with us where it's safe," she said.

"It's not safe." I jabbed a finger at her face for emphasis.

"Safer than out there. Don't you point at me!"

"Now you're worried about him?" I asked.

"Why are you such an asshole? This is bullshit." She clenched a fist, made like she was going to punch a wall, but stopped herself. "Uhhg. You're such a jerk!"

"Pull it together, kid."

"We're all going to die anyway." Her voice faltered. "I'd rather get shot in the back than experimented on anyway."

It was hard to argue with that logic, especially with a teenager. I was sure X-37 would've had an opinion, but I didn't ask. Time was running out and I needed to do something.

19

"IT TOOK SOME SEARCHING, but I found the shuttle. A lot of guys with machine guns there. And some girls too. Hard to tell with all that armor," Bug said.

"How do we get there without being seen?" I asked.

"It shouldn't be that hard, but I think it's a dumb idea. It's not the only shuttle on this place. They left hundreds of them scattered here and there after the evacuation," Bug said. "And the Union guards have a lot of guns."

"Then why aren't people using them?" I asked, thinking of the *Jellybird* and the *Red Revenge*. Dreadmax soldiers protected the smuggling vessels. Without them, a lot of relatively innocent prisoners would've suffered and died over the years. But other ships would be a hot commodity.

"They don't go very far." The sound of chewing and a bag being crumpled came through the speaker. "Not sure what good shuttles are gonna be if you can't go back to whatever ship brought you here. But I guess you could take it over to the shipyard and see if they can help you."

"I think they're busy with their own problems," I said, thinking of the large freight hauler I'd seen there.

"Some are. How do you think Slab and his goons got all their weapons? Don't let those shipyard people fool you. They've got some working ships for trading and whatnot, black market stuff they have to get from pirates. I don't know why they keep coming back, but my cousin says they're trying to get a ship big enough to evacuate all of their people. I wish I was one of their people."

"No comment."

"You already knew that, didn't you, Mr. Cain? I told you the ship people were nice. Can't fool Bug. Bug sees all."

"Settle down. Eat your cheese crackers," I said.

I'd decided there was no chance of completing this mission. Sure, they would negotiate for the doctor and his daughter, but in a best-case scenario, they would just leave me here to die with all the others.

That wouldn't be much better than getting killed by Callus. Probably worse. I needed to go down fighting.

Just outside the door, an explosion boomed. The heavy door buckled but held. Soldiers shouted.

"Hit it again! Give it everything we have." The commanding rage in Callus' voice penetrated the room, indicating it wasn't as air tight as I'd assumed.

I had a decision to make and didn't like it. The girl

was miserable, no matter how she talked. It didn't matter what genetic modifications she had, I'd do better without her.

She was just one more person for me to worry about. Why couldn't I leave her? Reapers weren't sentimental or weak. One mouthy kid didn't mean anything to me. "Listen, Elise, I have to get you out of here. Dreadmax is doomed. No one made a plan to evacuate it because they believed, or convinced themselves, that only death row inmates and worse live here."

"What are you talking about? Not even the new Union would leave this many people to die," she said.

I waited for her to process the information, knowing that she already believed every word. She'd seen even more of this place than I had and knew the score no matter what comforting lies she told herself.

She started pacing, getting angrier and angrier. "Fine. Let's go get him."

I was glad the girl agreed to rescue her father. For a hot minute, I was afraid she'd give us all the finger and head out on her own. She was good under pressure and had obviously spent time on the run. That made me think of her as an asset rather than a liability as I had first assumed she would be.

Now all I had to do was figure out a way to get past a team of elite soldiers who had surrounded our position. The hiding place in which I stuffed my principal wasn't in the middle of my enemies, but it was close.

Elise looked at me expectantly. She crossed her arms as if to say *well, what now*.

X-37 wasn't helpful, lapsing into one of his silent spells. I never knew if I'd done something wrong, or there was something broken in the unit, or he just simply didn't see the need to comment. A quick check with my friends in the security room told me what I already knew. There were at least three squads of spec ops soldiers watching the tower after the failed breach.

"What if we went down?" Elise asked.

I'd thought of that, but that still didn't help me get the doctor away from Callus.

Gunfire sounded in the distance. Slab and his RSG men were having it out with somebody. Whatever was happening, they were too far away to serve as a distraction. I'd already been lucky in that regard. Now, however, the Union soldiers had driven them away. I didn't even know who was fighting who at this point. "I really need some help, X."

"Can you take another look at the area? The deeper the scan the better. Perhaps I missed something from your initial survey," X-37 said.

"You're trying to get me killed," I said, moving to the door and looking for a way to see farther than the cameras allowed without getting shot dead. "Oh shit!"

"What?" Elise asked, alarmed.

The door that was holding the spec ops team at bay was

built to withstand the occasional meteor strike. It wasn't, however, designed for security.

There were ventilation ports, something I first suspected when I heard Callus yelling orders. Sooner or later, he would deploy gas. We'd be knocked unconscious if we were lucky, and killed if we weren't.

I cautiously peeked out from one of the smaller doors, unsatisfied with my field of view but trying to make the most of it. I could see slivers of the wide stairs and runways leading to this tower.

"Sorry, X, I can't get eyes on much of the area without letting them in," I said, straining my neck to get the best shitty view possible.

"The data gathered from your lame attempt at peek-aboo was insufficient," X-37 said. "I'll go back to analyzing the schematics."

"He has to come to us," Elise said. "What, you never thought of that?"

Of course I'd thought of that. "I've run a lot of scenarios in my head. One of them involves your father making a break for it and getting shot. I don't see how that helps anyone."

"You're really gonna turn him over to the Union after these guys tried to kill us?" she asked.

"Callus and his team are something different," I admitted. "If Grady were alive, I'd trust him to take you someplace safe."

What she really wanted to know was what I was going

to do with her. She'd spent her life trying to escape her father or the Union or who knows what else, and probably saw me as the enemy right now.

I pointed toward the door. "I'm not turning you over to them. That's a kill squad, a brute force option when they don't have a subtler solution."

"Like sending a Reaper?" she asked, testing me.

"You're the one who told me you didn't think I was sent here to kill you and your father. I haven't received any communication from my handlers. By now, I would have been told who to kill and who to torture," I explained, wondering what kind of reaction my honesty would get from her.

She went pale.

"This conversation is getting us nowhere. Stay here." I almost hoped she did. "If I don't come back, you can surrender or you can take the stairs and look for an escape route. I suggest you get back to the top deck as quickly as possible and make your way to the shipyard. They may or may not be able to help you, but at least they aren't canni-bals or gangsters."

"Or Union agents," she murmured.

I left her to consider her options. Everything about this mission was frustrating. I had to remind myself it was better than sitting on death row. The tower had numerous personnel doors, smaller openings than the bay doors where equipment was moved. Each of these had a compact window above a slot barely wide enough to slip my fingers through.

One of these doors was how I'd come in. Callus probably didn't want to send his team through such a bottleneck. He knew what I'd do to them the moment they stepped into such a fatal funnel.

I checked several other viewports, peering through the small windows and gathering information for X-37 to analyze. The breach team had pulled back, possibly to gather bigger explosives or consider other options. I couldn't see any of Callus' troops. Because they knew what they were doing. Like actual professionals.

At the fourth door, I found the surprise of my life.

Yanking the door open, I grabbed Doctor Hastings and pulled him inside. The door was still shutting when he started babbling apologies and explanations.

"I came as quickly as I could," he said, trembling from fear and adrenaline. "Was that the right thing to do? They were all around me and I could hear them talking. I think they're going to kill all of us. We have to get out of here. Where's my daughter? Is she in here? Is she okay?"

"Settle down, Doc." I led him back to the main lift where Elise waited.

She jumped to her feet in surprise, hesitated, then ran to her father and embraced him.

It wasn't the most emotional reunion I'd ever witnessed, but it was more tender than I expected.

"Why does this feel wrong, X?" I asked.

"Analyzing."

Was my Reaper AI messing with me? "Do you mind giving me an answer when you're done analyzing?"

"Of course," X-37 said, something about its voice quieter than usual. It almost felt like there was some type of disturbance, a pulse in the shields above us perhaps.

"Well?" I rubbed the scar near my eye, something I hadn't done in ages.

"Still analyzing. Please stand by."

"You've got to be shitting me," I said and started getting ready to take my principals out of here. The last two hours had been spent running and gunning, trying to stay alive. The questions Elise asked me were good ones. I didn't really know what to do with either of them if we all survived.

The only real answer was to get off Dreadmax and go renegade, or better yet, disappear completely.

"Perhaps if you would tell me what you are thinking, I could complete my analysis of this situation. Unless you want something generic, something like you would say, like this really sucks."

"You're pretty funny for an AI," I said. "Why don't I trust the doctor?"

"Because you don't trust anyone."

"Now you're just being difficult." I interrupted the Hastings family reunion. "We have two options, climb the tower and look for a place to run a zip line—not a great option since it's extremely dangerous and we would have to find materials to manufacture a zip line—or go down two levels and see if we could come up to the top deck away from Callus and his team."

"Why not just go down one level?" the doctor asked.

"We went down one level last time. Might be a good idea to mix it up. How exactly did you get to that door?"

Doctor Hastings swallowed and looked at Elise like she would answer for him. It was a nervous tic, but the man was full of those types of behaviors. He might be an excellent scientist, but he wasn't good under pressure like this. I couldn't tell if he was outright lying or just overwhelmed by what we'd been through.

"I waited for as long as I could, and then when I thought you'd left me, I crawled to the door. It seemed incredibly dangerous and I was amazed that I made it," Doctor Hastings said.

"Dishonesty detected," X-37 said.

"Yeah, that's what I thought." Sometimes it seemed like X and I were the same person.

X-37 knew what I meant, but the doctor seemed confused by my words. "There really was no other way for you to escape Callus and his men. I'm glad you made it. Let's get out of here."

20

A TREMOR WENT through the tower. It wasn't the first time I'd felt the sensation since landing on Dreadmax, but it was the worst so far. I actually lost my balance for a second.

"What was that?" Hastings asked. "Did the destroyer fire on us?"

I hadn't told the doctor about the UFS *Thunder* that brought me and the spec ops teams here. Elise didn't notice the slip, but why would she?

"No one's firing on us. This place is falling apart, in case you didn't notice," I said. "Keep moving."

I wished Grady was here, no matter how we'd disagreed. Hustling down the stairs while watching for danger ahead and behind was wearing me out. Elise helped by being naturally observant and cautious, but she couldn't fight, not like Grady could have.

"The people here talk about it," Elise said. "The first time I ran from the RSG, a bunch of religious fanatics took care of me for a few days. They talked about the station failing like it was the coming of the apocalypse. Others argued about heading below decks when the atmosphere dies—something they call Climbdown Day. Everyone has their story about a lost ship that only needs to be found to take them all to safety."

"Ridiculous," Hastings said.

"Let's hope not everyone in the Union wants us dead." I cut the doctor off, not liking his tone. "I'm betting that Callus and his team are exceeding their mandate."

"They're trying to kill us, you know that," Elise said.

"There was more to being a Reaper than infiltration and assassination," I said. "I have connections."

The wide industrial stairs curved downward and out of sight. Every so often, there were access doors of different sizes. I spotted a security station that had been stripped of weapons lockers and surveillance monitors. There didn't seem to be an active power connection to the bunker-like booth.

"Keep moving," I said.

"Do you actually think they'll still help you? They didn't stop you from going to death row," Elise said.

"I didn't survive as a Reaper by taking unnecessary chances, but there's always a risk."

"Why not take their ship?" Elise asked. "We can run the blockade easily. The Union wouldn't fire on one of its own ships. And it has to be cutting-edge, with a slip drive and maybe even cloaking technology like in the action videos."

"Trust me, if I thought I could take the ship, I would. Right now, we're sticking to the plan, and that plan is to escape through one of the lower decks," I said. "The idea is to get away from Callus and his trigger-happy commandos, not run into their ship and get killed. The pilot isn't going to land and just let us on while Callus' team is out hunting for us."

"We don't even know the capabilities of that ship," Doctor Hastings said. He looked nervous, more nervous than usual. I wanted to attribute his flushed face and sweaty brow to exertion—which it probably was—but his true mannerisms showed more and more as his fatigue increased.

"You have a suggestion, Doc?" I asked, getting a bad vibe every time he spoke. I just couldn't imagine him strolling through a barrage of gunfire to knock on the door to the tower facility. It didn't set right. Callus was one of the deadliest human beings I'd ever met, and that was saying something. His team was the best of the best.

"I don't know why it's so complicated. Please stop for a minute. I need to catch my breath," Hastings said, talking with his hands and never quite looking at me. "You were given a detailed mission briefing and a pickup location. If these rogue operators have some sort of vendetta against you, that's not my problem. Why can't you just take me to the pickup location? Once we're rescued, I can report Callus to the proper authorities."

"Well, that's one plan." I studied Elise for her reaction but couldn't decide what she was thinking.

The doctor huffed pretentiously, seemingly put out at the delay. "My research is important. They wouldn't have put so much time and effort into recovering me if I was just some abstract theorist."

"True." I leaned toward him and lowered my voice. "They wouldn't have sent two battleships and a fighter wing to recover you."

"Two battleships? I thought they sent the UFS *Thunder*."

I didn't bother to acknowledge his correction. It was a test question anyway.

"Are you listening to me, Cain?" he continued. "Take me to the pickup site and I'm sure I can handle everything."

"No problem," I said, facing a large door at the end of the stairs.

"We should steal the spec op recon ship," Elise said.

Doctor Hastings cut her off. "It's not your decision, Elise. Let Cain do his job."

"I'm not sure what level this opens to," I said. "We've come down farther than I thought we would. There's no place else to go unless we want to get on one of the lifts, and we would have to go back up to the main level for that. So ship or no ship, we have to get through this area in one piece. No more arguing. You do what I say when I say it."

"Yes, of course," Hastings said.

Elise glared at me with her arms crossed.

"Wait here." I operated the manual crank to open one of the side doors next to the larger equipment entrance, then went inside and cleared the first few rooms. I didn't know what to expect.

How far did we have to go to encounter the flesh-eating denizens below deck? I thought of them as cannibals, but the ones I'd surprised while escaping he RSG gave me doubts. One thing was certain, they were desperate and dangerous. Regardless of what they were.

For all I knew, the agricultural deck was a garden utopia of plenty and populated with magical fairies and unicorns.

I shared my speculation with X-37, but he didn't laugh. Surely the Reaper AI had the processing power to mimic humor, but he was being difficult.

Whatever.

I gathered up the doctor and his daughter, escorting them through a series of rooms to a hallway that seemed not to have been used for some time. The air was decent and there was only a little corrosion in this section of Dreadmax. It still amazed me how much of the place was vacant.

"How much longer until you return me to the Union?" Hastings asked. "I could use a shower and a meal."

I wanted to ignore his questions, maybe throat punch him, maybe leave him to fend for himself, but that wasn't why I had come this far. It didn't seem like current events had affected his emotions like I thought was reasonable. Grady was dead. Countless inmates—or residents or whatever they were—of Dreadmax had been murdered or killed and faced certain annihilation.

Damn, I wanted a Starbrand. "I'm not convinced that's the best course of action."

"Not the best course of action? What are you talking about? You were sent here to do a job."

"Sure, but they left out the part about getting double-crossed by a spec ops team whose leader is certifiably fucking crazy." I didn't add that he also seemed invincible.

"I was never told about them. When I get back, finding out what went wrong will be the first thing I do," Hastings said.

I seriously doubted that.

"Can we just go?" Elise said, refusing to look at her father. It was another one of her moments where she seemed like a rebellious teenager.

A tremor, the biggest yet, shook the station. I counted to twenty-three before it stopped. "That was a long one. Let's talk about the timeline I was given. What happens in twenty-four hours from the start of my mission, the collapse of the station?"

The doctor looked worried and ashamed. "I think eighteen hours would've been more accurate, and it has already passed. Twenty-four is just a standard number for these types of things, or so I was told."

"When I found you, you were being beaten and interrogated by Red Skull Gangsters," I reminded him, pointing back the way we had come. "How would you know anything about the rescue mission?"

"The contingency plan was discussed prior to my assignment on Dreadmax," he said too quickly. "I'm not excessively brave or a fool. I refused to go until they promised me a viable extraction plan."

"For you and your daughter," I said, my tone flat but clearly calling him out.

This caught him off guard. "Well, of course."

The next tremor caught me off guard because they didn't normally come so close together. I kept my feet, but the doctor went down hard. Elise did a half cart-wheel round-off to keep from face-planting when the floor jumped.

"Is everyone okay?" I asked.

Hastings mumbled nonsense as he brushed himself off. Elise pushed her hair out of her eyes and nodded.

Smoke drifted into the hallway.

I checked the ceiling for a sprinkler system. There weren't any flames in this hallway, but the dense smoke should've set them off, covering the area with flame-retardant chemicals.

"We have to run for it. If the smoke gets too thick, drop to the floor and crawl. That will kill you long before the flames get here," I shouted, urging them to run with me.

"Always running. Gang members and rogue soldiers

aren't bad enough. We have to have cannibals and uncontrolled fires to deal with? I mean, really?" Elise said.

"No time to complain. Come on, Doc, pick up the pace." I found the next set of stairs approximately a kilometer from where we descended. My guess was they led up to another maintenance tower like the one where Callus and his team had nearly cornered us.

We emerged far away from our last encounter with the man. Somehow, I didn't feel any better.

21

THE BEST THING TO do was haul ass. "Go, go, go! Don't stop until you get across the street. Duck behind that building and wait for me," I shouted.

"Was that necessary," X-37 asked.

I aimed to my rifle left, then right, scanning the area in between for possible attacks as I moved the weapon. "The doctor said this place should have blown up four hours ago."

"Not precisely," X-37 said.

"You know what I mean. I don't trust him."

"You've made this observation before. Are you going to do something about it?" X-37 asked.

"Yeah, I am."

I caught up with Hastings and his daughter, then led them through several alleyways with pipes running overhead almost like a false ceiling. We came out into the open and I noticed gangs were creeping after some unlucky victim. Steam filled the low areas, reducing visibility but somehow carrying sound.

If Callus and his team were still looking for us, it didn't seem to be in this area. Gangs, however, were always a danger.

We reached a bridge to another major section of the top deck. Looking into the crevasse didn't give me a warm fuzzy feeling. Memories of the cable crossing caused my fingers to throb and my augmented left arm to twitch.

"Are you all right?" X-37 asked.

"Sure, X. Thanks for asking." I stepped nearer the doctor and his daughter. "Elise, I need you to come with me. You're not afraid of heights, are you?"

She gave me a shitty look. "Are you?"

Some questions were better left unanswered. "Come with me. We're climbing this bridge support. I need your young eyes."

"What about me?" Doctor Hastings asked.

"You're fine right there. Just stay put," I said.

We climbed in silence, trying to ignore the on-again, off-again gravity the higher we went on the support beams.

"What's going on, Cain?" Elise asked. "What are we doing?"

I touched a vest pocket that still didn't have cigars or get out of jail free cards. "Testing a theory."

"He looks exposed," Elise said. "I don't like him right now, but he's still my dad."

"He's leaving breadcrumbs for our pursuers." I wanted to confront the scientist, but it was too soon for that. Things needed to play out for a bit.

"Okay, I suppose that means something in your world. What do your breadcrumbs have to do with anything?" she asked. "You think he wants us to get caught?"

"Yeah. I just don't know why," I said.

"That really pisses me off. It's just like something he would do." Elise looked ready to scream.

I wanted to ask questions, but darkness fell hard and fast like it did often on Dreadmax. It wasn't long before I heard crazies screeching nonsensically as they climbed out of the grates.

"We should let them have him," Elise said.

"He came here to save you, or at least demanded I save you when I could've left you to the RSG."

She snorted. "He didn't come here to save me."

I wasn't sure what to make of that. There wasn't time for psychoanalysis. It was decision time—abandon the mission, or get killed trying to save a man I didn't trust.

Elise scrambled down the support beams but angled away from her father. "He did okay on his own before. Once we get away, we can find him and decide what to do."

I followed her but stopped to look back.

"You're going to let the girl make decisions?" X-37 asked.

"Just watch," I said.

A mob of crazy, animal-like humans surged toward the doctor. There were at least a dozen that would reach him before he could escape across the bridge below us.

The leader of the charge fell flat on his face, blood shooting up from his head before he struck the ground. Two more clutched wounds to the chest and tumbled sideways. Others kept running after Hastings but couldn't catch up. He had a good lead and was very motivated to escape.

I thought about what I'd seen as I made my own crossing of the bridge. There wasn't time to act on what I knew. Once we reunited with Elise's father, I took a stand against the poorly armed men and women while my principals fled to safety.

"Stay back, you crazy flesh-eating freaks!" I shouted.

A few of them look at me quizzically, but others saw my gun and were wary. It was tempting to stay here. I had a pretty good idea that the father-daughter reunion was going to be explosive.

Who needed that kind of drama?

Doctor Hastings panted as he turned angrily toward me, barely aware of his daughter, who was pushing between us. "You were going to leave me!"

"We should have!" Elise shouted.

I stepped back, knowing this had to happen sooner or later but worried about the noise. The man had never seemed like the father of the year. He had demanded I save his daughter from the RSG stronghold, but that was an easy measurement of his paternal devotion. What father wouldn't want his daughter rescued from a display cage in the middle of a prison gang's hideout?

"I'm your father. I risked my life for you. I could still be shipped off to one of those illegal mining colonies in the Deadlands for what I've done. Do you understand that? I risked everything to—"

"Settle down!" I barked, my voice so loud it stopped the both of them. After a pause, I turned away and quietly spoke to my AI. "X, I'm looking for the spec ops ship. Not seeing anything. What'd I miss?"

"Analyzing."

I heard the groan of twisting metal from somewhere far away and braced myself for another tremor that never came. It might've been my imagination, but it seemed the environment shield near the edge of the ring distorted just for a second.

"No sign of the spec ops recon ship detected," X-37 advised.

"You don't know what it's like being your daughter!" Elise broke in, apparently not finished.

"How could I? Stop being so irrational," he replied.

"I hate you, you aging piece of shit!" Elise stomped away then turned around to make another inarticulate curse.

"I'm not sure why you're allowing this," X-37 said. "The volume and duration of this argument are concerning."

"They need to get it out of their system," I said. "There will be worse times for this to happen. And I'm still testing a theory."

"Well, I hope it is a grand theory, because we have drawn the attention of the locals and an element of Callus' team," X-37 said.

I trusted the Reaper AI's ability to maximize my senses and use his analysis to provide an early warning system. It had saved my life many times before I fell out of the Union's graces. "Doctor Hastings, Elise, we've got company. You both need to shut the fuck up."

Instant compliance was nice when it happened.

I climbed onto one of the narrow footbridges and used the elevation to look back toward the main bridge. I heard the motorcycles at the same time I saw them. Callus' scouts had requisitioned three of the combustion engine two-wheelers I'd seen from time to time since arriving here. These were the first that I'd observed since the RSG stronghold.

A large group of Slab's people swaggered through the street-like trenches in the other direction, heading toward their rivals by random chance, it seemed. The problem was there too many of the local gangs. It made sense because they took what they wanted and it was better to be with them than against them. I'd seen that in other prisons I'd either done missions in or been shuffled through on my way to BMSP.

My left eye twitched in perfect synchronization with the

fingers of my augmented arm. I braced for pain that felt like I'd grabbed an exposed wire.

"What's happening?" Doctor Hastings asked, looking up wide-eyed, his expression a mixture of concern and hope. The man was tired and wanted this over. I could see that in his deteriorating posture.

Elise, silent and sulking, had backed away from both of us, so far away that I could barely see her in the shadows.

Descending rapidly from my observation post, I cut off her escape by hopping down to the deck. "Don't make me chase you."

"I'm pissed at you too. Why can't you just get us off this place?" she asked.

"Always wanted an irrational teenager to babysit."

This rendered her speechless with rage and I thought I might've miscalculated. If she ran off, I'd have to make some hard choices.

22

"This way. Elise first, then me, and then the doctor. Don't get too far ahead." I ran beside Hastings, frequently looking behind us for pursuit. There were a lot of danger areas to watch, including smaller towers, converted point-defense turrets, and a series of metal domes that I didn't recognize.

The doctor couldn't keep up. I estimated he'd lost fifteen or twenty pounds in captivity, but it was obvious he'd never been a runner. His life had been pampered and completely devoid of physical challenges. Elise pushed the pace but never abandoned us completely. I thought I was going to have to rein her in, but she stopped to check on us from time to time.

Her instincts saved us from two groups of the RSG. I watched her stop and hold up a hand for us to hide—like something she'd seen in an action vid. Moments later, a group from the RSG mob swaggered by with guns rested on their shoulders or holstered dangerously in their waistbands. The men were shirtless and covered with tattoos despite the shifting atmosphere.

On one section of the top deck it was humid and hot, and the next dry and cold. Steam vented from the failing ventilation system, shooting toward the sky where there must've been a gap in the environment shield. In one direction, it was snowing, and another, raining. The shifting light and shadows caused by the orbital pattern gave the landscape a surreal quality.

It was fascinating and horrifying to watch gaps appear in the artificial atmosphere and reseal themselves, sometimes in the space of a few heartbeats, but other times lasting nearly a minute. Tremors continued to shake Dreadmax but not as frequently as I had feared earlier. The station was like a living creature—or maybe a dying leviathan.

If there was one big quake, we were all royally screwed. We were hours past the mission clock I was given and even farther beyond Hastings' estimation of how long the place could stay in one piece.

I heard something that didn't make sense at first: loud music. It wasn't the same as the techno hip-hop and thrash metal montage I'd heard at the RSG stronghold. This sounded like someone was playing horns and drums, maybe even some sort of whistling flute section.

Elise held up a hand for us to stop, then walked backward several steps to where we were crouched down behind a power converter box.

"We can't go this way," she complained, shaking her head. "A bunch of gangsters are camped out around the fire barrel, drinking and popping needles."

"Stay here."

I went to look for myself, hoping it was only a small group that we could either sneak past or I could eliminate.

The maintenance alley opened into a wide surface area like the aperture of a camera. I hadn't seen anything like this during my flyover of the main ring and wondered how far we'd come during our desperate flight from the spec ops teams, gangs, and half-mad below-deck dwellers.

The effect of the opening was a clearing where a large number of people could gather. It was slightly concave as well, giving it a natural amphitheater feel. A stream of RSG tough guys arrived even as I watched.

Around the perimeter of this clearing were simple dwellings, gun turrets, and maintenance pods that had been converted into apartments. The locals kept their distance from the growing number of gang members—resentful expression controlled to avoid a violent confrontation. Beyond the impromptu gang party was the strange festival music making me suspect the people there had made other plans for their final days than hosting a bunch of tattooed murderers.

Doctor Hastings and Elise were waiting silently when I returned.

"What are we going to do?" Elise asked, arms crossed and one foot tapping nervously. "We can't just sit here."

"That's absolutely what we should do. The real Union soldiers will arrive soon. They'll take us back to the ship before Dreadmax comes apart," Doctor Hastings said.

"We're moving. It'll be a slow process, because we have to go around this aperture. Once we make it to the next section, we can probably blend with non-gang civilians," I said.

Doctor Hastings opened his mouth to protest.

I pointed my high tech HDK rifle at him, then waggled it in the direction I wanted him to go. "We're done with this conversation. When I say move, you move."

The doctor complied but complained the entire time. "All you were supposed to do was find me. Lieutenant Grady and his people should have dropped in to secure an extraction zone or moved us to the predetermined landing site for the shuttle. But instead, he abandoned the plan for an old buddy. Very unprofessional."

"Grady's dead. Let's not talk about why. Unless you want to give me a full disclosure about your mission here and what you expect will happen to me when it's done," I said.

Doctor Hastings backed out of the conversation quickly. His pace improved.

Gangs continued to mass in the large open area. I couldn't hear or see the progress of the spec ops teams but had a good idea of what was happening. They had tried chasing us with overwhelming speed and firepower. Now they were going to do things by the numbers, secure bridges and walkway crossings and search on a grid pattern that I wouldn't be able to escape without a ship or a miracle.

Our arrival among the civilians went almost unnoticed. The few who saw us welcomed us with fuel cans full of alcohol. Some of them smoked what I thought was fungus wrapped in paper, and others had actual tobacco, probably stolen at a high price from the agricultural level below decks or smuggled into the prison station.

The strange music grew louder, distorted by the artificial atmosphere of this place. I was impressed at how many people were coming out onto the streets. It was night again but wouldn't be for long. The way Dreadmax orbited its host planet and turned on its own axis created a nearly random night and day schedule, or that was how it seemed.

I'd had a lot of things going on other than setting my watch or watching the sun come up.

"Welcome, strangers!" said a man with a crazy half beard and wild eyes. "Do you love a parade?"

"Sure." I glanced at Elise. "Keep hold of your dad and don't wander off."

"Relax, my man!" the half-bearded stranger said, giving me a hug. I grabbed his left hand to make sure he didn't pick my pocket. His right hand wasn't a danger because it was holding a large metal container of what might've been pure alcohol.

"Hey, dude, not so rough." He lifted the can toward me,

offering a drink. Then he pulled away and threw his free arm around a woman about his own age. It was unclear whether they knew each other before this chance encounter.

He continued to talk. I tried to listen to what he said, but there were a lot of people now and everyone was moving. It wasn't a parade exactly, but a large shuffling progression across the top deck with music, drink, and smoking.

I pushed the pace, moving through the crowd, hoping the camouflage would hold until we could get a good distance away from our pursuers. The way was blocked for a time when we reached the center of the end-of-the-world celebration. They had one motor vehicle, a huge flatbed truck with dancing girls and a band.

"Are they all playing the same song?" Elise asked.

"No idea," I said.

"They are in fact playing a highly bastardized version of jazz music with classical overtones," X-37 said.

"Good to know," I said. "You have anything else useful to share?"

"I detected gun fire. Didn't you hear it?" X-37 asked.

I jumped onto the step rail of the truck and looked for trouble. Callus had caught up with his scout team, apparently. He had also decided that body slamming one of the festival goers was the best way to communicate.

"Hey, asshole, what the hell are you doing?" someone yelled.

A single gunshot followed.

Another squad of Union commandos dragged one of the more sober participants away from the others and forced him to sit next to a wall, where they interrogated him.

In another quarter of the celebration, RSG and NG rivals were mingling with the crowd and looking for a fight.

"What do you see?" Elise asked.

"This festival is about to get a lot less festive. We're almost through it." I jumped down, leading the girl and her father toward a set of stairs that descended into a low area where large ships could be docked and repaired.

A volley of gunshots echoed behind us.

"None of this would have happened if you had just taken me to the proper authorities," Hastings said.

I ignored him and kept moving.

No mission was easy, but this was fucking ridiculous. I started to wonder if Hastings was right. Maybe this was all my fault. Did collateral damage matter here? I tried not to think of men, women, and children getting blasted into the void or crushed by collapsing infrastructure.

"Callus has summoned reinforcements. From what I can see, they're all spec ops. That's almost a full Battalion," X-37 said.

I repeated what X had just told me.

Crouching beside me, watching the same area I was looking at, Elise seemed younger than she was. "What does that mean?"

"It means they brought enough firepower to have a war," I told her. "A Union destroyer can deploy a battalion of spec ops soldiers and a division of troops. There's a good chance they expected to storm Dreadmax. Given the timeline, I imagine the rules of engagement would be very relaxed."

"What happens to all these people? Not that I care. Even the shipbuilders are despicable," she said.

I shifted my position so that I could see back and make sure the doctor hadn't run off. He sat with his back against a railing near the center of the building we were on, looking as beaten as any human being I had ever seen.

"Your dad looks tired," I said.

Elise didn't respond.

I wanted to ask what she meant about the shipbuilders but didn't have the energy or the need to argue. They were obviously saints compared to the RSG, but my own experience with humanity had been generally disappointing. There was good and bad in everyone. "Grady told me he put in a request for an evacuation. He seemed to think there is some sort of contingency for the civilians."

"You believe that?" she asked.

"What the hell happened to you that you're so untrusting of human nature?" Something was wrong with this kid.

"You really don't want to know," she grumbled. "I wish they'd never brought me here."

"Tell me about that. The real story."

Her tone betrayed her frustration. "I have my own conspiracy theories about secret labs and my father's work. You know what he did to save me and what that could mean." She paused. "But what makes you think I know the real story? They took me from the one place I was starting to fit in and kept me locked in a tower. The literal tower, kind of like the metaphorical version of my childhood. Safety and comfort, sure. Freedom, not so much. I'm sick of it. If we get off this place, I'm never going back to that life."

Callus' backup teams searched on a grid pattern, pushing a hungover group of civilians ahead of them.

"X, how bad is our timeline?" I asked, instantly regretting the words. Dreadmax would probably explode in the next ten seconds just to teach me not to jinx the mission.

"We have far exceeded the estimated time of collapse. My analysis shows that there is a shrinking area of survivability on the top deck. You might want to keep that in mind."

"Thanks, X."

"What's it like having nerve-ware? That's who you're talking to, right? Your Reaper AI?" she asked

"Yeah, kid. It's not as fun as it sounds."

"I wish I was a Reaper," she said through clenched teeth.

I used my augmented left arm to turn her head until she was forced to look into my cybernetic left eye. "No you don't, kid. Never wish for something like that."

She jerked away from me. "You're such an asshole."

I wondered if the doctor wasn't right about turning ourselves in. If I could find somebody other than Callus, it might be the only way to survive this clusterfuck. "Stay here and keep an eye out. I'm going back down to check on the doctor."

"Good luck with that," she said, arms crossed.

"Do you know how to whistle?" I asked. "Signal me if the spec ops team gets close."

She whistled a familiar melody, then a darker, sadder tune. "One for the Union, and the other for Dreadmax baddies."

"Good thinking."

I found the doctor munching on a protein bar. "Where did you find that?"

He slipped it back into a pocket. "I've had it for a while."

"Keeping it until you need it, that's smart. Elise might need one soon, if you have more stashed away," I said.

He looked away guiltily.

"What are you really doing here, Doc?" I asked.

He tried to back away, avoiding eye contact. "I told you everything. The Union funded my research, extremely important research that will help a lot of people someday."

I listened to what he was saying, but also watched for

non-verbal cues. He wasn't exactly lying, not yet, but we had a long way to go in this conversation.

"Things got complicated," Hastings explained. "There were accusations against some of my associates. Claims of disloyalty to the Union. They took hostages like Elise to force good behavior. It sounds bad when I talk about it like this, but the things we were working on were bigger than each of us individually."

"Nice. I'll put your name in for father of the year."

"My research on Elise is irreplaceable!" he insisted. "You have no idea what I learned simply from working on her and adjusting the formula. It was revolutionary."

"Interesting. I thought you gave her that medicine to save her from a childhood illness. Now it sounds like she was just a lab rat," I said.

"I don't have to take this abuse," he scoffed.

I grabbed the front of his jumpsuit and pulled him close. "You do, Doc. But only if you want to keep breathing. I don't have anything to lose. Piss me off, things will go badly for you."

"Are you taking me to the Union or not?" he said, feigning confidence. "They can punish you even here. No one can stand against the government. Not against them. They control everything. Isn't that why you're here? Because they control you?"

I ignored the question. "What I do really depends on what keeps the most people alive."

Hastings laughed skeptically. "You're concerned about

innocent lives? That's an interesting thing to hear from a Reaper."

I glared at him. "Ex-Reaper."

The doctor shook his head with a cynical expression on his face. "I doubt you can leave that behind so easily. You don't fool me, Reaper Cain. You like killing too much. I think you're just looking for an excuse to kill me and my daughter."

I stared at him for a long second. "Not your daughter."

He stopped talking after that.

23

I GATHERED up our little squad and moved out, determined to put as much distance between us and the Union commandos as possible. Avoiding the RSG, or even the NG, was hit or miss. Their presence was random and extensive. Thankfully, their preference for loud vehicles, rage music, and the random discharge of weapons made them easy to track from a distance.

Their numbers and the limited terrain was the real problem. Dreadmax looked huge from space. It was millions of tons of metal, ceramics, and other hardware, but on the surface, it quickly felt like a microcosm.

Slab and his goons were still looking for me, I was sure, but that didn't worry me as much as what Callus would do if he cornered us. Random violence from gangs didn't compare with the lethality of spec ops teams.

I couldn't give Elise to the Union. There was no safe place for her, not on Dreadmax and nowhere in the Union if she became a fugitive. As for the doctor, who knew the right thing to do. The mission had been to rescue him for the Union.

What they did with him after that wasn't my problem. *I should throw him back to the wolves.*

Briggs wouldn't have turned me lose without a plan to put me back in the box or take me out of the game entirely. I understood the danger, but I also knew there was no way I was going back.

I figured that out the moment I entered the warden's office and saw him leaning against that desk. Hard eyes, hard face—the man was a lot like me but older, with more people willing to die for him.

I needed to pull off a double cross worthy of the Reaper Corps and the darkest of dark ops. Dreadmax would have been the perfect place for a double betrayal if not for the thousands of innocents—or nearly innocent—people who were about to die. "We need to move fast. They're going to see us. Don't stop no matter what. But most importantly, listen to me and do what I say."

I needed bait, but to make it believable, it had to be all three of us.

"What are you doing, Reaper Cain?" X-37 asked.

I wasn't sure what to say, because X hadn't used my name like that for a long time. Maybe this was random, but maybe it meant something. Trusting a limited AI was a mistake too many Reapers made. They started feeling like part of themselves and it was easy to forget the technology had been made by the Union.

"I'm going to steal Callus' ship," I said.

"This is a miscalculation on your part. Abort. Recommendation: run for cover immediately," X-37 advised. "The ship is on fast approach."

"I already made up my mind." Up until now, Callus' teams had to chase us through the surface maze. From the time we stepped into the festival grounds, we'd become vulnerable to a ship assault again. That was what I was counting on now.

"There is a sixty-four percent chance they will shoot first and ask questions later," X-37 said.

I didn't respond.

"What's your Reaper AI telling you?" Doctor Hastings demanded.

The recon ship materialized out of thin air. I saw a distortion in the air moments before it dropped down, weapons aimed and turbines flaring to slow its abrupt descent. The deployment ramp dropped before it had fully landed. Heavily armed and armored spec ops soldiers swarmed out and took positions to secure the landing zone. These weren't in recon gear—they were ready for a full-scale battle.

Callus came out in the second squad, seconds after the first. He was bigger than the others, moving with a relaxed grace that betrayed nothing.

"Stop, Cain. Running will just get someone hurt," he shouted.

"I told you to run faster!" I yelled at Hastings and his daughter without warning and striked the doctor hard enough to knock him off his feet. "Just take them. I'm not going back to get executed. You'll never take me alive!"

"You don't have a choice, Reaper!" Callus swaggered forward, ready to fight. "I didn't come this far to miss a chance at the title. You had a reputation when you were in your prime. I want to see if the stories I heard were true."

His team surrounded Doctor Hastings and Elise.

I turned and sprinted away from the landing zone, ducking into a hiding place.

"You're not as clever as you think you are," Callus yelled after me.

I stopped as soon as I was out of sight and listened to the commandos arguing with Elise. Her father tried to calm her, assuring her this was the best possible scenario.

"He should have delivered us to these fine soldiers a long time ago," Hastings ranted.

"I hate you!" his daughter shouted back.

Callus's second in command ignored the father-daughter squabble and shouted orders. "Red squad and Silver squad, pursue and apprehend the remaining target."

"Belay that. It's a trick. Halek Cain was a Reaper. He wouldn't give up his principal so easy. Not while they are still alive," Callus said. "He knows the end of Dreadmax is long overdue. Stay sharp. Check the doctor and the girl for improvised explosive devices."

A few moments passed.

"They're clear," a soldier said. "Should we take them onto the ship?"

Callus hesitated. "Check them again then lock them in the brig."

24

CROUCHING LOW, I darted across the trench, ducking around the corner as soon as possible. Callus and his team secured the large, flat area around their ship, aiming guns at the tangled maze I'd returned to. For a moment, I thought I had done my job too well and they had missed seeing me. A heartbeat later, I heard one of them shout out to my position.

I needed them to come after me while I was still close enough to the ship that I could double back and get inside. Best-case scenario, Callus came with his men, I ditched the lot of them, and then only had to overpower a pilot and copilot to get control of the recon ship.

I'd used the technique before. It never felt like it would work, but I had good luck with it. Moving through the maze, I quickly found my way back to the small landing area and saw Elise and the doctor zip-tied just inside the door. Apparently, they hadn't made it to the brig yet. The security team was fixing electronic restraints to keep them from taking over the ship before taking them inside.

That wouldn't work on me, because my Reaper AI was part of my nerve-ware. It went where I went. When I had been on death row, they had counter measures in place. That was then, this was now. They turned me loose on a mission and they were going to get more than they bargained for.

Neither squad had followed me into the maze, which was a huge fucking problem. No plan survived first contact with the enemy, but this little stunt hadn't even gotten started before it failed.

"I told you to abort," X-37 said.

"Fine. Log it. We'll talk about it later," I muttered, not really in the mood right now.

The squad stayed near the deployment ramp. Callus moved forward, straight for my position. He laughed and shook his head.

"Nice trick, Cain. But I read about all your tricks when I was preparing for this mission," he said, then addressed his team. "Go back inside and ready for ship security. He's going to try to steal it."

"I really don't like you," I said.

"That's a shame. You should like me, because I'm going to do you a favor. I read your psych profiles and how much the torture and killing bothered you," he said. "You won't have time to think about it in hell."

"That's not really helpful." This guy was an asshole. "Was that a joke? Don't quit your day job."

He came at me right when I thought he was going to make another insult, thrusting his rifle forward with a bayonet that extended.

I slipped to the right, aiming my pistol before I realized that was what he wanted. What he'd apparently forgotten was that I wasn't some recruit fresh out of basic training. Rather than leaving my arm extended to find the shot, I pulled back as close to my body as I could without interfering with the slide and fired until he staggered backward from the impacts on his armor.

My victory was short-lived. He regained his balance and attacked before I could reload or transition to my HDK, which was what I should've used in the first place if I'd been ready.

It had been so long since I'd faced an adversary of this caliber that I'd made a mistake. This was how a Reaper died, taken down by his replacement.

I pushed my increasingly dark thoughts aside in favor of instinct and rage. It was time to fight angry, something I normally avoided.

He lunged forward to tackle me. I let him drive me back and spread my feet wide to establish my base as I pushed down on his neck and one of his shoulders. Once I'd stuffed the takedown attempt, I grabbed his right arm and leveled it down, using the strength of my augmented left arm to apply pressure to the elbow joint.

He was smart enough not to resist, choosing instead to fall and twist until he was facing me. I still had hold of his arm, but it was the wrong angle to break the joint.

He kicked me in the stomach, driving me into the air. It took me longer than it should have to fall. Weak gravity added a dangerous dynamic to the contest.

I looked to my right and saw we were close to the gravity generator. The entire area was marred by rust and disrepair.

He flew at me with a punch that glanced off my light recon helmet. If I've been a bit slower, he probably would've cracked it down the middle. Almost simultaneously with this attack, I launched counter attacks, striking him several times on his torso, driving one particularly savage half-fist into his armpit where his armor was weakest.

He flinched and staggered back. I jumped forward with an action-video-quality front kick that blasted him into the air.

"Cain!" he shouted as he wind-milled his arms and legs.

Three or four seconds passed before I was satisfied he wasn't coming back down. I presented my middle finger to answer his curses and turned away, wishing I had a Star-brand cigar to celebrate.

"You should finish him," X-37 said.

"Agreed." What did my AI think I was doing out here, playing rock, paper, scissors?

I jogged to my HDK and picked it up, then fired several rounds at him just to be sure. He spiraled away from Dreadmax, not as fast as he would have if we were truly in the void but with a certainty that meant his death.

It wasn't long before I lost view of his silhouette against the flickering environment shield.

I scooped up my pistol, slamming it into the holster as I rushed for the deployment ramp of the recon ship. It was nearly closed when I dove through and rolled to my feet. A squad of spec ops soldiers and ship security Soldiers rushed me. I fired and reloaded but was quickly subdued.

"Nice try, Reaper," the security chief spat.

"Piss off!" The lights went out as one of his men slammed a stun baton on the back of my helmet.

WHEN I WOKE UP, Doctor Hastings was tending to my injuries. He looked somber and grim, tired and hungry, like a man who regretted his choices.

"Their medic checked you out first, but I convinced them I was a doctor and needed to have a look," he said.

"Don't do me any favors." I tried to access X-37 but couldn't get through.

"What's the matter, Cain?" Hastings asked.

"Don't worry about it," I said. "Where is your daughter?"

"They have a small brig, so they tossed her in there," the doctor said, exhaustion bleeding through his words.

I assessed the room and made a note of anything that might help me escape or fight back.

"It's better this way," Hastings said. He checked and rechecked the bandages and wraps that had been applied. I couldn't remember which ones I had received during my fight with Callus and which with the ship security detail.

It probably didn't matter.

"If you get out of this, and if you ever get released from prison, you should find Jason Domingo on Carver. He can help you start a new life," Hastings said, guilt evident in the tone of his voice.

"That's incredibly generous, Doc," I said. "What about the political refugees and nonviolent criminals who found themselves abandoned on Dreadmax? Do they deserve to die?"

A flicker of what I assumed to be decency flashed in the doctor's eyes, and guilt. He looked at the floor. "There's nothing to be done for them. The shipbuilders are close to having a working ship, but they won't be able to launch without the slip drive regulator."

"You're telling me they have a functioning slip drive?" I couldn't believe what he was telling me. The ability to travel through slip space was a game changer. Not only could the people on Dreadmax escape, they could harass the Union with guerilla warfare. Or vanish into the Dead-lands and start new lives. Maybe a little of both.

The freighter, if they had it fixed, could move more personnel than a warship, but lacked more than asteroid busters for weapons. The haulers were also much slower.

I needed to concentrate on first things first.

"They've done amazing work. I should have warned the Union, but sometimes I'm nearly as rebellious as you," Hastings said.

"Doubtful," I said.

"You're not the only person who has second thoughts. I'm not a monster." He paused. "I only do what I think is right. If it's safe. And no one gets hurt."

"Aren't those the same things?" I asked.

He looked away.

"Tell me about their freighter," I demanded.

"Without a slip drive regulator, any voyage they begin would be suicide. They'd either get stuck in this system or hit the tunnel walls inside slipspace and obliterate them-selves down to the atomic level. I can't stop thinking I should tell the Union."

This guy was going to make me kill him. "Why the hell would you do that?"

"I thought maybe they would help, loan them a regula-tor," he postulated.

"You know they'd just nuke the shipyard. The Union put those people there for a reason. Maybe they weren't murderers and traitors, but they definitely crossed the wrong people."

"It was just an idea. I know what you're talking about. I'm not a fool. It's just that it would take a spec ops team to get to the spine and recover the regulator," he said, stopping to look me in the eyes. "Or maybe a Reaper."

25

Fatigue hit me like a falling building. Running and gunning across the top deck of Dreadmax had my adrenaline pumping to stay alive. Now I was sitting in a storage closet, basically, with my hands and feet zip-tied together.

It was humiliating. Here I was a death row inmate and former Reaper and they didn't even put me in actual brig. That was reserved for a teenage girl who was apparently more of an escape risk than I was—a fact I would have found much more interesting if I wasn't so banged up.

Everything Doctor Hastings had told me during his moment of weakness echoed in my imagination, slashing away at my conscience and screaming at me to do something. There were a lot of people on Dreadmax the galaxy would be better without, but the shipbuilders and a lot of the other regular folk I had seen didn't deserve what was coming.

The end had to be coming soon, because the mission clock had expired hours ago. I'd seen holes in the atmosphere generator where steam from broken pipes rushed out into the void. I'd thrown Callus into a dead spot created by the failing gravity generator. All of the tremors and the sounds of twisting metal were previews of what would happen soon.

I was headed back to death row and had a strong suspicion my appeal had been denied and the execution chamber prepped for immediate use. But at least I wasn't going to die on Dreadmax. Lucky me.

The door to my cubicle slid open and I saw Callus' second in command, Jordan, blocking most of the light with his large, still fully armored frame. "Callus was a better man than you'll ever be."

"I think we can agree neither of us were ever good men," I said, knowing what was coming.

"Fuck you, asshole. We're doing a job," Jordan said. "The Union can't survive without warriors to protect it. You could have been part of that, but you're damaged goods. Too selfish. Not open to what's best for everyone."

"You're one of those people," I said, measuring his reaction.

"Watch yourself, convict. What do you mean, those people?" he asked.

I changed position slightly, looking for an advantage.

"The brainwashed psychos who were just following orders." There wasn't much space in this makeshift cell for maneuvering.

"That's nice coming from the guy who's killed more people than the galactic plague," Jordan said.

I shook my head, looking at the deck as he made mistake after mistake. "Maybe you ought to remember that before you come in here and push my buttons."

"The only thing that's going to get pushed is your face," he sneered.

"Why are you doing this, Jordan?"

"Because you killed Callus. We looked up to him. He was the best." The man shook with anger.

"He was a clumsy dumbass who fell into a gravity dead spot," I said.

"Fucking asshole liar!" Jordan pulled me out of the closet cell, lifting me onto my toes before slamming me down hard.

With my hands and feet bound by zip-ties, I wasn't able to stop the fall. Stars exploded across my vision as my face hit the deck.

"What are you doing, Sarge?" one of the other spec ops soldiers asked.

"Payback time. Get in or get out," Jordan spat, voice cracking.

Jordan's boot caught me in the ribs. For several seconds, I thought the rest of Callus' team had better self-control than the sergeant, but I soon learned different.

The lights were low and the ship's internal security cameras were turned off, I was guessing.

"Come on, Reaper! Do something." The man stepped back to gather force for his next kick. "Let's see how you get out of this one. You're not such a badass after all!"

More boots. More getting dragged into walls, picked up, and slammed back down.

"I was spec ops. Served with dozens of other spec ops teams," I croaked.

The abuse stopped.

"What's your point, Reaper?"

"Never met a squad that beat a prisoner. What the hell happened to the Union's finest?"

Jordan and a few of the others went at me with renewed vigor, but I was glad to see most of the others drew back, then started to pull their friends off me.

"He's had enough," one said.

"I'll say when he's had enough. You better get in here and show whose side you're on," Jordan demanded.

"I'm on the Union's side, Sarge, but this is against regulations."

I never saw who the brave soul was, but Jordan and the others stopped their attack… after getting a few final shots in.

"I need the doctor," I said.

"Fine," Jordan spat. "Get Hastings in here. I need our medic to look at my hand. Think I broke a knuckle or three."

"He's with his daughter," a voice said.

"I don't give a fuck! Do it. You're seriously on thin ice, Carter. I better not hear you talking about this later. What happens on mission stays on mission," Jordan said.

Doctor Hastings didn't say a word as he cleaned my wounds and glued my face back together.

The recon ship was small. This was a newer version, but the layout was familiar. I glanced through the main room and saw that whoever had removed the doctor had brought Elise as well. Out of her cell, she hadn't wasted time watching her father patch me up.

Doctor Hastings sat up. "That's the best I can do for you. The wounds are clean, the lacerations glued shut because I don't have what I need for stitches. I wrapped your right wrist. Looks like a sprain." He looked around the small room, chastising the soldiers with an uncharacteristically hard expression. A moment later, his face changed. "Where is my daughter?"

"Oh shit!" the men cursed.

I heard the door to the cockpit lock shut.

"Doc, can your daughter fly a ship?" I asked.

"I don't think so," Hastings answered, appearing more than a little uncomfortable.

"You better grab on to something." I really hoped Elise knew what she was doing in the pilot's seat.

Jordan and the others hammered on the door to the cockpit, cursing and making threats. The ship lurched and went down hard.

"I don't think we're going to make it to the UFS *Thunder*," Hastings said.

"Welcome back to Dreadmax," I said, laughing.

WAKING up in the smoking wreckage of a crashed ship wasn't a new experience, unfortunately. Chemical fumes gagged me. My eyes watered and something made me laugh like a lunatic. I'd just been patched up, now this.

I rolled onto my side, searching for Elise and her father. To my surprise, the recon vessel was mostly intact, having activated shields right before impact. The area around it, however, was a tangled mess of steel.

A man in a Dreadmax jumpsuit knelt beside me. "Are you okay, mister?"

His voice was rough, probably damaged from an industrial accident or years of smoking, but he reminded me of Bug. My stomach went hollow at the thought of the kid I had never met meeting his fate on this place.

"How did I get outside?" I asked.

"A girl and her father dragged you, then got in an argument with one of the soldiers. I didn't see what happened after that. What's wrong with your fancy prosthetic?" the man asked.

I sat up and turned away from him to deemphasize his attention to my cybernetic enhancements. Next thing I knew, we'd be discussing other things that were wrong with me and I didn't think this was a good place for that type of conversation.

"Not important. You should probably get back. This isn't safe," I said.

The man shook his head, sad eyes suggesting he knew the end of Dreadmax was near and safety was a useless concept. "Won't be able to keep people back. That ship might be functional, and that's a pretty valuable commodity right now."

People crowded forward, stepping over the damaged top deck to avoid bodies. Some of the crew and soldiers had been thrown from the crash. A blood smear decorated the side of a decommission point defense turret. I looked again at the recon ship and realized it wasn't in as good a shape as I had first thought. There was a gash down the side that could be repaired, but not in time for these people.

Or for me.

"Don't worry about the ship," I said. "Worry about some really pissed-off spec ops soldiers."

"We'll get you out of here," another man said.

Hands lifted me to my feet. It wasn't long before there were dozens of people between me and the downed ship.

"Why are you helping me?" Nothing made sense. My legs felt like rubber. "Where am I?"

I fell, scraping my hands and knees.

"Reaper Cain, you must remain conscious," X-37 said.

"Yeah, sure thing, X. Just give me a second," I said.

"Who are you talking to?" one of my rescuers asked.

My vision cleared. These people were in danger.

"Listen, there's going to be trouble. You need to clear out," I said, grabbing the first man by his jumpsuit and forcing him to look at me.

He nodded and talked to the others.

Jordan and his squad climbed out of the starboard hatch, which was facing the Dreadmax sky. They slid to the deck and checked gear, weapons, and each other.

I pushed away from the good Samaritans and searched for Elise and her father.

"Well, look at that son-of-a-bitch," Sergeant Jordan said. "Still alive. That's not fucking right."

I rolled onto my knees, then made it to my feet even as I started running for another downed soldier—one of the ship Soldiers who had been thrown to his death when the ship went down. There wasn't time to show the proper respect. I ripped the shotgun from his kit and dove behind a slag of cooling metal.

Gunfire cut apart the scene. Bullets ricocheted off the buildings near me. Crouching low, I ran to a new position, fully aware that staying in one place was the best way to get killed.

"Warning: elevated heart rate," X-37 said.

I could see my pulse thumping in my vision. Breathing was agony. When X said I had an elevated heart rate, he meant I was about to have a cardiac arrest if I didn't slow down. Pain and desperation drove me like a hunted animal.

A second later, Jordan and one of the other spec ops

soldiers came around the corner and fired into the place I had just been.

In a perfect world, I would've been able to leave a grenade behind, but I wasn't exactly equipped for this confrontation.

No time. No plan. No gear. Shit was getting real.

Adrenaline kept me going. Ironically, the only pain I felt was in my enhanced arm. Random symbols danced in my HUD, suggesting X-37 had been overloaded or otherwise damaged. The nerve-ware interfaced with my consciousness through neural pathways, but the actual hardware was spread out through my other cybernetic enhancements. Computer processors had to go somewhere no matter how small they were.

I dove over a piece of the recon ship's wing, hit the ground, and rolled to my feet. A spec ops soldier came around the corner of the ship, weapon up, his eyes searching for a target. I shot him in the face, flipping him onto his back with his feet in the air.

Rushing forward, I yanked his weapon from his hands before he was finished dying. The familiar HDK felt heavy, as though fully loaded. I pitched the shotgun and opened fire on Jordan and the others as they came after me.

Right before I left the man I'd shot, I grabbed a grenade from his kit.

The fight turned into an undignified version of hide and seek. I couldn't claim that everything I did was graceful or well-thought-out, but I managed to stay alive second by second. Meanness and desperation drove me onward.

Tossing a grenade over the ship I'd just run around to escape the most recent attack, I crouched and reloaded as it exploded.

Jordan came around the corner, aiming his weapon and charging straight at me in the smooth stride of a pro clearing a building in a half crouch. "I got you now, jerk-off."

I threw myself sideways, shooting as I fell toward the ground. At least one of the rounds struck him in the hips, twisting him and driving him backward at the same time. His shots went wide.

With no time to get up and take a proper fighting stance, I fired from the ground, stitching him with bullets. Blood sprayed out the top of his helmet. I didn't see where the bullet went in but thought it might've been under his jaw.

Either way, I wouldn't be having any more problems from the sergeant.

Clawing my way to my feet, I looked for a place to hide. It was hard to say how many of Jordan's men were still hunting me. I needed to get out of the area, but first I wanted to find Elise and the doctor, even if they were dead.

26

OTHER RECON SHIPS LANDED NEARBY. I had to give it to the spec ops teams. They weren't afraid to make an assault, even when it was obvious the odds were stacking up against anyone surviving.

In the distance, one of the Dreadmax towers broke apart and floated several meters above the surface. It never actually floated away but just hung there, twisting slowly, drifting toward the horizon of the rust streaked world.

A tremor ran through the top deck. Seconds later, I heard what sounded like an explosion from below. Not good. "I hope that wasn't anything important."

"Humor detected," X-37 chirped.

"You're back, X. Have a nice nap?" I made my way to Sgt. Jordan's recon ship, confirming it was too damaged to be of use. The civilians I'd encountered when I first woke up scrambled over it, looking for anything that might help them survive.

In a way, they reminded me of the elite soldiers. They hadn't given up, even though it was obvious all hope was lost.

I grabbed hold of the man who had woken me up. "Do you know where the shipbuilders are? Can you get there with your people?"

"Everyone knows that. They've got a big ship, but it won't get far. They've been trying to buy parts that no one has for months. I'm no genius, but it's pretty clear they're not going anywhere."

"Can you tell me how to get to the center of Dread-max, to the spine?" I asked.

"There is no way to do that without taking one of the speed lifts, and if you ask me, it's not worth it. I'm claustrophobic. No way I'm going in one of those things," the man said.

"X?"

No answer.

"Fucking great. Come on, X. I need some help." Right when I needed my AI, he went on the fritz.

"Who the hell is X?" The man asked.

"Never mind. That recon ship is a waste of time," I said. "There's going be more shooting soon. You need to get your people out of here. If you can make it to the shipbuilders, maybe they'll figure out a way to get off this place."

The man laughed fatalistically. "Yeah, for all of us pretending there's a way to survive the collapse."

I thought of Bug and his reference to Climbdown Day. Sheltering below decks when the environment shield gave out wouldn't save them for long, but it gave me an idea. I continued to look for the doctor and his daughter, but also for one of the call boxes I'd used to talk to Bug and his friends.

A new battle roared to life just out of view. For a second, the pace of the gunfire confused me. Someone was shooting back at the spec ops commandos.

I climbed onto a damaged ladder that ran up the wall to nowhere and looked out across the metal landscape. Several squads of ragged-looking Soldiers wearing old uniforms and carrying outdated gear engaged the invaders. It took a minute, but I'd seen them before

Dreadmax soldiers. Their uniforms had the same patches and design as what I'd seen near the shipyards. This place was a microcosm, its own twisted society of good and bad. Slab and the Red Skull Gangsters left the engineers in the shipyard alone because they maintained the gravity generators, but also because they had some muscle.

Elise had crashed closer to the shipyards than I'd thought, not like I'd been thinking about where I was until the fight with Jordan was over.

"Why don't you respond to my queries?" X-37 asked.

"X! Good to hear you. Where have you been?" I didn't bother hiding my excitement.

"I've been right here," X-37 said.

Heavy machine-gun fire and grenades drew my attention. "Someone is having one hell of a fight."

"It's quite literally the end of this world," X-37 said, ignoring the fact that I was running now, and maybe not ready for chit-chat.

I stepped over a smear of blood where one of the spec ops soldiers or recon ship crewmen had dragged himself clear of the destruction. There were others escaping the smoldering ship, dazed by the impact in their injuries. I picked up radio chatter of them calling for help and at least one spec ops team answering that they were inbound.

The accelerated night and day cycle of Dreadmax cast shadows across the senseless battlefield. I searched through the wreckage, looking for Elise and her father.

"Balls!" I shouted.

There was always a point in a mission when everything went off the rails. Sometimes it was a small thing like not being able to make it through customs or losing valuable data I'd recorded during a surveillance session. Every time, it seemed important.

Dreadmax put all my prior missions in perspective. I'd faced death more than was healthy, but this fiasco was one for the record books.

I spotted Hastings and his daughter on the other side of the yard.

"Elise! Stay where you are. I'm coming to you," I shouted.

"Why is everyone fighting?" she asked, sheltering her father with her body.

It didn't look like he was injured any worse than she was, but his physical courage was clearly faltering. I didn't want to call a man a coward. That wasn't it at all. He was just beyond any situation he'd ever been in.

Elise had run the streets and trenches of Dreadmax and learned some hard lessons, I thought.

"It doesn't matter," I said. "We've got several chances to get through this. Don't shut down. Never give up."

"Thanks for the pep talk." She chewed up several creative bits of profanity and spat them at me when she wasn't ducking or looking for the next explosion.

Her father chimed in, sounding like he'd been concussed slightly. "I do agree with you, in theory, Reaper Cain. Direct evidence suggests your theory may not hold in this particular instance..."

The spec ops recon ship had left a long trail of destruction, smashing apart critical elements of the top deck and leaving pieces of the hull scattered along the slash mark. Civilians continued to scavenge for parts and survivors. The smarter ones went the other direction.

I concentrated on Elise and her street savvy toughness. For a spoiled rich girl, she was showing some resilience. "The engineers at the shipyard have more resources than they let on. They're not idiots. I've run into civilians who know they have a large ship for an evacuation. It's missing a critical component, but I'd bet money they have at least a few smaller ships that they keep secret. There's also Grady's team if they're not dead. Sergeant Crank and a few others are either out here on the surface or in the ship with Andrews."

She brushed her hair out of her eyes. "Andrews?"

"Grady's pilot. A real smartass. You'll like him," I said.

Elise started talking before I was finished. "If he gets us off this place, I'll love him."

"I need you to work your way toward the shipyard with your father. I've got something I need to do first."

"We're coming with you," she said.

"Negative. Trust me on this one."

"Whatever. I can do anything you can do," she said.

I laughed out loud, regretting how shitty my tone sounded. "No, you can't. Not even close. And you don't want to."

She considered that somberly. "This doesn't seem like a great place to sit and wait."

I swept my eyes across the area, scanning it for X-37's analysis. It was a habit I barely thought about. One of the few romantic relationships I attempted in the early years had ended because the woman said it freaked her out. Like a one-thousand-yard stare combined with cybernetic inhumanity.

"Wait here. Let me contact the Dreadmax Soldiers."

It didn't take long to locate one of their squads near the wreckage of the spec ops recon ship.

"I'm friendly," I said, showing my hands before I leaned out from cover. "I was a prisoner on that ship."

"Step out where we can see you and don't make any sudden moves," the leader said.

I did as I was told. The sergeant spoke to one of his men. I cataloged their worn but functional gear and ragged hygiene. By Dreadmax standards, these guys were spit and polish. Had they still been in the Union military, they'd be on some sort of detention.

"You've got some of the spec ops weapons," the sergeant said, not introducing himself. "Can you fight? There are at least two more teams moving toward this area to investigate the crash."

"I've run into some of them. We're not on good terms," I said. "I'll fight, but I need to get down to the spine."

He didn't laugh. "My team tried that. Can't be done."

I assumed they were here looking for last-minute salvage, anything to get more people off the crumbling space station. They would probably still be looking for parts when the environment failed and the gravity generators went off-line completely. They were that type of soldier.

"What about the speed lift?" I asked.

He ignored me for a second to give orders to his squad leaders. They formed a perimeter around the ship while a pair of men went inside and started ripping things from the walls of the interior.

"Have you ever looked at a speed lift? It's not made for people. It's made for equipment. Maybe you could take a weapon with you, but I doubt it. And with so many systems failing, there's a good chance you'd have to hold your breath for a bit longer than I could. You'd be passing through energy fields and decks with no life-support."

I didn't like the idea of crossing an energy field. X-37 was resistant to energy-based attacks, but I doubted the designers of the Reaper AI anticipated this scenario. Without X, it was unlikely I could figure out how to acquire and transport the slip drive regulator to the ship engineers.

More fighting broke out near the ship. The Dreadmax sergeant spoke to someone on his radio, clearly annoyed with my continued presence.

"There are two high-value targets tucked away near the ship. Can you look out for them?" I asked.

"If they're not Union, gang members, or cannibals, I'll do what I can," he said.

"That's good enough for me. I'm going after the slip drive regulator." Nothing I'd done so far was worth a shit unless I pulled this off.

He stared at me in disbelief.

"We've got incoming," I said as the sound of a deter-mined assault by Union forces reached us.

"I can point you toward the speed lift, but you may have to fight first. I don't know who the hell you think you are, but I wish you well. Something tells me you might actu-ally have a chance to pull this off," he said.

I nodded, then ran to take a position against spec ops soldiers and Union Soldiers. I hoped Sergeant Crank and his team weren't among them. We hadn't become friends, but they were the last connection I had to Grady. Sure, he'd been a jerk at the end, but we'd been friends once.

Two Union recon ships shot overhead, dropping flares and digital markers. The Dreadmax sergeant and his people didn't quite know what to make of this.

"Move! Change position!" I shouted.

One man was too slow and was struck by a forty-millimeter laser-guided grenade. Running past the blasted corpse, I slid on one leg, then came up in a kneeling position to shoot.

Assaulters dropped from the ship, hitting the ground running. Heavily armed and armored, they moved fast and fired on anyone who showed themselves.

Two Union spec ops soldiers and a sergeant rushed around a damaged sensor array. Aiming for their midline, I shot all three of them just above their hips. It was a nasty tactic, but effective. No man could run with shattered hips.

It still sucked, even though I hated these guys. They screamed in pain, calling for medics and cursing whoever had blasted them.

Several of the Dreadmax soldiers went down and were dragged behind cover by their comrades. Without helmet comms, they relied on shouts and hand signals. It was like something out of an old action vid—bullets, explosions, and smoke drowning out most of what they were yelling.

An RSG thug raced a motorcycle through the middle of the battle, firing a sawed-off machine gun at everyone. It took me three seconds to process the image. "Slab's coming, you Union fucks!"

This was Dreadmax, complete chaos all the way to the end.

I looked toward the place I'd stashed Elise and her father. Far enough from the ship to be overlooked, I hoped, but still within the guard perimeter—I hoped I was doing the right thing.

Good deeds never went unpunished. The smart thing to do would be to grab Elise, her father, and steal a small ship from the shipyard engineers. The absolute wrong, completely stupid foolhardy thing to do was go after the slip drive regulator and try to save everyone.

"What do you think, X? Should we save everyone?"

"Please rephrase the question. From the information you've provided me, this is impossible. Even if you fixed the freight-hauler and avoided the extremely motivated Union troops, there will be thousands, maybe tens of thousands of people below decks that are beyond help."

"Thanks, X, that was really fucking helpful."

"I endeavor to keep it real. Perhaps you should just complete your mission instead of trying to be a hero. It never works for you," X-37 said.

"True," I said.

"I suspect you will ignore my advice."

Why couldn't my Reaper AI see the bigger picture? "There are children on this station."

"Many of which will die."

"You're such an asshole. Why are AIs such dicks?" I asked.

"Perhaps I am reflecting your personality."

"Whatever, X. Help me find a way to the speed lift. I also need a talk box. I want to check on Bug and see if he can help me."

"Searching ship schematics for optimal route."

"Thanks." I made a mental note to invest in a software update for my friend.

X-37 didn't respond for several seconds. I ducked behind a pipeline and ran in a crouch, searching for a way to get clear of the impromptu battle.

27

X-37 FED ME DETAILED INSTRUCTIONS. I focused on what I had to do rather than what I had left behind. Running from a fight wasn't my style. Fatigue made every decision seem wrong and every obstacle insurmountable. Visual static pulsed in my HUD in time with my heartbeat, and the pain from my augmented left arm was constant.

If it stopped working, I'd have problems. For one thing, the bionic limb was heavy when not functional. I didn't notice it the rest of the time, but there had been missions when it felt like I was dragging an anchor behind me.

For all I knew, I was the last of the Reaper Corps. We'd been cutting edge once. Older and wiser now, I understood first-generation technology often had problems. Callus was likely the new and improved version.

That cheered me up, because I'd kicked his ass. *Fuck that guy.*

The sounds of fighting faded. Other conflicts raged across the top deck, probably RSG and NG vendettas being carried out against desperate, unarmed civilians. I pushed down memories of home and the neighborhood I'd cleansed of street gangs. Sitting on death row had been worth it. Now, a hundred slip tunnels away, I saw nothing had changed.

Humanity didn't need saving, which made what I was attempting to do all the more stupid.

"Talk to me, X."

"There are three damaged communication towers ahead of you. A speed lift exists between the first and second, if you are viewing them from left to right. I have insufficient data to determine whether or not it is functioning. The Dreadmax sergeant wasn't lying. The specs say nothing about the possibility of human transport via the mechanism."

"So it'll be like getting shoved into a dumbwaiter," I said.

"Interesting. Dumbwaiter is not part of my vocabulary."

"That's because I'm smarter than you, X."

"Unlikely."

The area was a ghost town compared to where I'd come from. Dreadmax was awesomely huge, one of the Union's more grandiose projects before the sheer size of it caused it to fail. I couldn't imagine the amount of fuel required to move such a monstrosity, and according to X-37, it had been intended for long-range use.

"You're approaching the speed lift," X-37 said.

The building was a low dome with no doors. I eventually found a hatch that was about two feet high, probably made for one of the maintenance bots. It opened when I pressed my weight on the rail leading into it.

"Here goes nothing," I said, then crawled inside. Darkness enveloped me. I focused on my infrared optics and a hazy picture of the room formed.

"I really need to get this I fixed," I muttered.

"I doubt the Union will accommodate such a request," X-37 said.

"Because they're assholes. After all I've done for them, they should give me a whole new set of Reaper gear."

"I wouldn't hold your breath," X-37 said.

"I'm just making noise because it's creepy as fuck in here." I found a cluster of speed lifts that looked like coffins ready to take me damned straight to hell. A small person could probably stand in one of the boxes comfortably. Too bad I wasn't small. "This is really going to suck."

X-37 talked me through the operating system. I powered up the system and noticed there wasn't much light. With only the ambient glow of green LED power indicators to see by, I almost wished it had just stayed dark. The interior dome felt smaller than it had appeared from the outside. The inside of the speed lift looked unfit for someone my size, or a human, or a living creature.

"One last thing," X-37 said. "The speed lift will pull considerable G-forces even if the gravity generators of Dreadmax are completely offline."

"Thanks for the warning."

"It is not too late to back out," X-37 reminded me.

"What the hell ever."

I pulled down the lid, only to watch it bounce open. There wasn't a mechanism to close it from the inside, so I had to reach out, yank on it, and hope I didn't crush my fingers as the lid fell. Twisting into the fetal position, I reached up with my augmented arm and heaved downward, pulling my hand inside at the last second.

The latch clicked.

"The sequence has begun," X- 37 said.

"Can't wait," I muttered right as I heard something.

"Was that a second hatch closing? Is someone sending parts right now? Like they're actually trying to fix this place?"

"Unlikely. I detected no one from Dreadmax prior to your decision to commit suicide."

"If you had a humor algorithm, that be a lot funnier."

"Correct."

"Talk to me, X. What the hell is happening?"

"My analysis suggests another person is taking a speed lift to the spine of Dreadmax station."

My ride clunked forward once, twice, then shot downward like a bullet into the guts of the station. With no crash seat or safety harness, I was at the mercy of physics. Each time the tube turned, I was smashed into a new and interesting position of pure misery.

Spots danced in my vision. My pulse hammered the inside of my head. Electricity radiated from my Reaper enhancements. X-37 came on and off line, sometimes blaring random bits of dialogue as we passed through energy fields.

"One last thing, Reaper," X finally said. "There is no tube between the primary ring and the spine. Your pod will be fired across a short gap—about one hundred meters—and caught by magnetic locks."

"Great. I hope that part of the ship is working."

"Even a slight misalignment caused by recent events will result in the pod missing the catch and bouncing into the void."

"It's been nice knowing you, X."

"What are you trying to say," the Reaper AI asked.

Crossing to the Dreadmax spine was nice, less getting slammed around and more gliding in a straight line as I started to freeze. The rest felt like mistiming a parachute landing onto concrete.

"How'd we do, X?"

"Let's call it a success, shall we?"

Twisting my feet forward, I kicked until the lid popped off. Moments after I climbed out, a second pod shot across the gap between the primary ring and the spine. Spiraling though the darkness, it would have been invisible without my infrared vision. There was a wobble that looked dangerous.

Time slowed. The pod looked like it was going to miss but corrected course as a magnetic field pulled it in.

"That's amazing. We did that, X. Why'd you let me do that?"

"When have you ever taken my advice, Reaper Cain?"

My pursuer slammed into the catch tube. I raised my HDK and approached warily. The short barrel felt heavy even though I wasn't sure how much ammunition remained in the bull-pup style magazine.

The spine of Dreadmax was connected to the primary ring in several places by massive gears and energy fields. I saw them in both directions from my location and wondered if this had been a serious mistake. The top deck had felt like a curiously exposed city full of decommissioned point defense systems and maintenance structures that had been converted to apartments and work stations.

This place only had breathable air and gravity by coincidence. Everything was automated or remote controlled. There wasn't a need for life support here.

Whoever was in the pod kicked at the hatch but couldn't open it.

"What do you think, X?" I asked. "Should I let this guy out so he can kill me? It has to be one of Callus' fanatic assholes."

"Perhaps it is Elise. Her personality profile suggests she would try to assist you in this impossible mission. And one of the soldiers would likely be able to kick open the hatch."

"Shit! That makes sense." I clicked my rifle to my gear and pried open the speed lift pod.

She sat up, gasping for air, wide-eyed and ready to fight demons.

"Settle down, kid."

"I'm not a kid, you stupid fuck stick!" she growled through here teeth.

"Wow! Language. Don't hit me. I'm trying to help you out." Give me gun toting enemies over teenagers any day of the week. What was with this kid?

Elise tumbled free of what she must have believed was her space coffin, landing on one knee, then falling on her face. She flailed her arms at me and cursed each time I tried to help.

"You know the trip back will be worse," I said.

"Thanks for reminding me! You can't do this by yourself, dumbass. Let's get this thingy and get to the shipyard."

"What do you know about slip drive regulators?"

"I've been on Dreadmax longer than you, remember?" she asked. "I've escaped the Union and the gangs and everyone else about ten times. The shipyard engineers like me."

"I bet they do."

"You're such a dick," she spat.

A tremor shook the primary ring on the other side of

the void gap. One of the huge connection points flexed near the point of breaking. Vibrations knocked me off my feet.

"X, read me the map. Elise, try to keep up."

We ran along a railway made for the automated maintenance bots, trying to twist an ankle or fall.

X-37 directed us to a hatch. I opened it and dropped down, offering to catching Elise when she followed.

The verbal abuse I received was really uncalled for. The kid had a mouth to make sailors blush. Her expensive education and natural intellect only made the insults sharper. If there were a profanity galactic Olympics, I thought this little runaway vixen would have a shot at a gold medal.

I let her jump and hit the ground hard.

She stood, glaring at me as she pushed her hair out of her eyes.

"You okay?" I asked.

"Perfect," she said, walking off a limp.

Turning away, I followed X-37's directions into darker and darker places.

"Why did they put the SD regulator down here?" Visual distortions to my enhanced optics almost made me turn them off despite the gloom.

"There is a vault. You'll see the traditional access bay soon. Anything valuable or dangerous is stored here," X-37 said.

"Anything else I can use?" I asked.

"Focus on your goal, Reaper Cain." X-37 sounded a bit perturbed.

There wasn't a lot of time for idle thoughts, but random shit ran through my mind at odd times. Things like what the hell would I even do if I survived this clusterfuck?

Go renegade?

That seemed like a lot of work and I wasn't dragging a foul-mouthed brat around with me, especially with half the Union hunting her. And I doubted her father would sign the permission slip.

28

"THIS IS why you can't do this alone," Elise said, far too proud of being right.

"Well, thanks for coming, then," I said, more than a little pissed off X-37 hadn't foreseen this simple and potentially fatal failsafe. "But don't get a big head. All you have to do is hold the door."

She snorted.

The vault was actually a series of rooms, each with a different security requirement—not from theft or sabotage, but from exploding, venting dangerous gasses, or whatever other unsafe various bits of technology this place could offer.

The slip drive regulator was benign by comparison to experimental fusion technology, bioweapons, and graviton acceleration prototypes. If I opened the wrong interior door, I'd be wishing I was wearing protective gear. Assuming I wasn't killed instantly.

All Elise had to do was let me out after I had the regulator. The two-meter-thick containment doors didn't open from the inside and closed automatically when anyone or anything passed through the archway.

The only good thing about this area was that it had walkways, stairs, and climate control for actual, live humans. Not that anyone had been here for years. Dust covered the floor. Close inspection revealed fine metal shavings from one of the massive gears farther along the exterior of the spine.

"That's not reassuring, X," I said.

"The battle station was a faulty design. Union engineers realized this long before it was decommissioned and turned into a maximum-security prison."

I found the long, narrow room lined with lockers that X-37 had been guiding me toward. "How many fucking slip drive regulators do they have?"

"There were five hundred and eighty. Three remain. And before you get greedy, it's not a good idea to take more than one," X-37 warned.

"Why not?"

"You only need one," X-37 said. "And you would be melted to slag if you touched two of them together."

"Yeah, probably not worth the risk." I retrieved the device that was twice the size of a normal work tablet and ten times as heavy.

"Can you manage the weight?" X-37 asked.

"Yeah. I got it. Let's get to the shipyard before everyone dies."

A complicated, three-dimensional schematic of Dreadmax appeared in my HUD, then zoomed into various levels between the spine and the top deck.

"What's this?"

"I'm working on an alternate route in the event the speed lift isn't functioning. You'll have to cross one of the gear bridges in that case, and..." X-37 said before I interrupted.

"How long would it take me to climb to the top deck?" The weight of the regulator was already dragging down my arm. Cybernetics made it easy to hold but didn't mitigate the raw weight pressing into my shoulder girdle and spine.

"Three days."

"Get that crap off my HUD."

"Abandoning plan B."

I hammered my fist on the containment door. Nothing happened.

"She may not be able to hear you. The door is thick," X-37 said.

I sat down and waited. Seconds felt like hours. "Give me an update on the fate of Dreadmax. Don't hold back. Tell me how screwed I am."

"Union engineers consulting on this mission predicted Dreadmax would be unlivable seven hours and eleven minutes ago," X-37 said.

"What do you mean, unlivable? Does that mean it's going to get really cold or explode?" Maybe it was a stupid question, but I wanted to know. The devil was in the details.

"Processing and adding their predictions to my recent observations," X-37 said mechanically.

I waited, staring at the door. Sooner or later, Elise would get impatient and open it.

Or leave. She was a runaway after all.

I was surprised that hadn't happened already.

"Regardless of the Union predictions, Dreadmax can't last another two hours," X-37 warned. "You must access a speed lift and deliver the slip drive regulator to the shipyard engineers, or make your peace with your maker."

"Do you believe in a higher power?" I asked, surprised by the last statement.

"I am an AI. Perhaps this is not a discussion we should have. Regardless of what my programmers considered in my initial formatting, faith in higher powers often comforts humans in the face of certain death."

"Do I look like I've given up?" I asked.

"You are sitting down."

What a jerk. "I'm conserving my strength."

"Of course."

The door rotated slowly open. I sprang to my feet and jumped through the gap.

"What the hell were you waiting on?" I demanded.

Elise stepped back, anger filling her eyes. "You could have knocked!"

"I did!"

"Well, I didn't hear you, dumbass!" she shouted in her angry teenager voice.

"Why wouldn't you just keep it open?"

"I tried that!" she complained. "Can we just fucking go?"

I shouldered past her and ran to the speed lift pods. We didn't say a word to each other until we were looking at the torture chambers that had delivered us here.

"You first," she said.

For some reason, this struck my funny bone. We stood there laughing for almost a minute.

"We don't have time for this," she nearly cried.

"I know!"

"Once you begin the sequence," X-37 reminded me, "you will have thirty seconds to get inside, secure the hatch, and brace yourself. The ride up will be, in many ways, worse than the ride down."

"Great."

"What's your Reaper AI telling you?" Elise asked.

"He says going up is much easier. Walk in the park," I lied.

"I may be a kid, but I'm not stupid." She activated her pod, climbed in, and slammed the hatch.

"Here goes nothing," I said.

X-37 raised his volume to get my attention. "Actually, it will be…"

"Shut your digital pie hole, X!"

CLIMBING out of the speed lift was like staggering away from a mixed martial arts fight. Every part of my body hurt and I needed to vomit. With the SD regulator safely in my vest pouch, I went to check on Elise, who hadn't exited her pod.

"Is she in there?" I asked. "I thought she'd be kicking to get out like last time."

"That would be a reasonable assumption," X-37 said.

"Hey, Mr. Cain," Bug said from a nearby speaker box. "We all thought you were dead. What'd you go in the speed lift for? Those things are a blast."

I retrieved a crowbar from a storage locker and started working on the remaining pod. It had taken some damage on the return trip.

"That you, Bug?" I asked.

"Sure is. Man, I love riding the speed lift pods. Like going into a slip tunnel, I bet."

"It's nothing like a slip tunnel." I popped open the lid. Elise lay on her side, hugging herself and trembling.

"Oh man, I hope you can help her. She's the pretty one. Even if she was kind of rude to me that one time," Bug said.

I lifted her from the pad and set her down. "What happened?"

"I'm not sure." She rubbed her face. "Just got banged around more than the first time. Blacked out, I think."

Her lack of attitude worried me.

"Why'd you go down to the spine?" Bug asked again.

"Had to get something for a ship. Can you get to the shipyard, Bug?" I asked.

"We can, but my cousin's brother's girlfriend said they can't use the ship, even though they're all loading up," Bug warned. "Why would I want to get on that thing just to float around and wait for the Union to put us back on Dreadmax? It can't take a slip tunnel or go very far."

"Get on the ship, Bug," I said. "Take your friends."

"I knew you'd say that. Gonna be really crowded," Bug said. "People are packing themselves in like beef-cows from the agriculture level."

I gave Elise a stim tab from my kit and watched her eyes go wide. She cringed and backed away from me. "That's awful!"

"It will keep you going. We need to get the hell off Dreadmax."

She hesitated.

"What?" I knew what was coming—probably some desperate teenage plea to not send her back to the bad people.

"Don't let them put me back in the lab. I'm tired of getting experimented on. Promise me or leave me here," she said, staying back so I couldn't grab her.

"How about you go home, do what you're told, and reap the benefits?" I felt like a jerk asking the question.

"Seems like you had a pretty easy life until you started running away."

"That wasn't a life. How would you do without even the most basic freedom of choice?" she asked.

"I'd probably kill some people and get put on death row. Don't worry, kid, I'm not giving you back to the Union without a fight."

I knew something was wrong the moment we began our final sprint toward the shipyard. Vibrations rolled through the top deck, causing Elise to stagger. "Damn it! I hate this place."

"Deal with it. We need to find your father and get to the shipyard," I said, seriously considering the option of abandoning the man.

"He should've been at the top of the lift. I thought he was standing guard."

"With no weapons or training." My expectations for the man were low and I hadn't been disappointed.

"There's another place. We sheltered near a water tank, or I think that's what it was—they wouldn't store fuel on the top deck, would they?" Tired and stressed, she pressed on. "He didn't want to leave. Said the spot was out of view and safer than the rest of this place. If he had to leave the speed lift terminal, he'd probably go to the tank. Or run to his Union rescuers."

"So much for standing guard," I said, clearing the area ahead of us and checking our back trail as we moved.

"Lead the way. If he's gone, he's gone. We're running out of time."

"Okay."

"X, what's the clock say now?" I asked.

"You have less than one hour. Which is eight hours beyond the best-case scenario the Union engineers predicted."

"Just answer my questions," I demanded. "What kind of psychopath programed you?"

"I was merely attempting to be thorough."

I spotted the doctor before Elise or X-37 did. He sat near a Union soldier, surprisingly un-concerned about the destruction all around us. The only good thing about the situation was that I could check "watch a space station come apart" off my bucket list.

The guard noticed me a second later and brought up his weapon. I shot him between the eyes, the bullet smashing through his visor and pitching him backward as it snapped his neck. The hole in his head wasn't exactly good for his health either. I'd seen this often because the bullet basically struck twice, once going in and once trying to get through the back of the helmet. Any man without a helmet would have just fallen down. Everything was more violent in Union strike armor, including dying.

"Why did you do that?" yelled Hastings, expressing more anger than I'd seen from him.

"He was about to shoot me. Why were you talking to him? Your daughter needs you. It's time to choose sides." I really didn't think this was something I should have to explain.

A damaged voice came from behind me. "You're absolutely right, Reaper. It *is* time to choose sides. Except there are really only two options for you: the living and the dead."

I wasn't surprised to see the man I thought I'd killed. Parts of his armor had been stripped off to accommodate Union medics. One of his eyes leaked blood or some other fluid and he had obvious frostbite on his left hand. His pinky was so grey and stiff, I thought it might break off.

"Didn't I already kill you?" I asked. "And for the record, I'll take living. You can die all you want."

Elise squealed uncharacteristically as she backed away. Even Doctor Hastings seemed appalled by the sight of the man I had kicked toward the atmosphere shield. Apparently, he managed to get back to the top deck and had come looking for me.

Doctor Hastings gathered his courage and intervened, moving with a pretentious authority that almost worked. "Lieutenant Callus, I require you to escort my daughter and me to safety. Your team can then return Reaper Cain to custody."

Holy shit, Hastings thinks he has a command override on Callus —which never worked in human trials.

Callus backhanded the man into the looming side of the water tank. Shadows slid across his damaged visage as he advanced on me.

"I should thank you, Reaper," he said. "Prototypes are always exciting to people like that man. But they're made to fail. You're made to fail. Your only purpose was to push the limits of what was possible then die."

"So what you're saying is that you're a pale imitation of the original." I sidestepped and backed away before he backed me up to the water tank and its heavy foundation. "Elise, get the fuck out of here."

29

CALLUS BARELY GLANCED at the girl and her father when they started to argue. His attention was on me as we both maneuvered for advantage. One on one, I wasn't sure I could win this fight. The man was damaged, but also pissed off. His crack about being a new and improved version of a Reaper wasn't a lie. And we'd danced this dance already. He had seen my best tricks.

"Just do what I say!" Hastings yelled, voice cracking because he knew he was losing to his daughter.

"Why should I? Let's go!" She dragged him the way she wanted to go despite being much smaller.

Callus drew his sidearm and fired. It caught me off guard because I expected him to go with his primary weapon, the short-barrel HDK carbine that was clipped to the front of his gear with frost still clinging to parts of it.

Moving at the exact same time as my attacker, I threw myself sideways, firing two shots before I hit the ground and rolled, and two more as I came to my feet.

Bullets struck my light recon armor. If I'd been standing still, the force would have penetrated, killing or staggering me.

This kind of close-range pistol dance was the most dangerous and stupid type of fight. I wanted to move to cover and engage with my HDK but couldn't get a half second of time to do it.

We both reloaded on the move, firing the pistols dry a second time and transitioning to the carbines in near perfect synchronization. His armor was heavier and more modern than mine, but he knew better than to slug it out with the HDK.

This close, we'd kill each other with the first volley.

He slipped around a large pipe running away from the water tank to get at me. I ducked behind the door to a ladder, quickly coming around the other side to fire on his position.

He moved to do the same thing to me. "Why don't we see what the big guns can do?" he shouted, raising his HDK carbine and firing a stream of bullets at my hiding place.

"Throw down your weapons and step out in the open so we can talk this out," I yelled back, inserting my final HDK magazine. As much as I hated to admit it, the arm blade was my best chance.

The weight of my enhanced left arm didn't feel right. I wasn't sure if it was losing power or was damaged. Snapping down my hand, I forced the blade to extend while I pulled the HDK in tight to my right shoulder to use it one-handed.

Shooting this way sucked, but it could be done for short bursts.

Running out into the open to cut Callus down and pump him full of HDK rounds would have been awesome if the tactic had even the slightest chance of working.

I also doubted he was waiting for me to accept his challenge.

The spec ops super soldier was working his way to my flank. Otherwise, he'd be shooting and or taunting me. I waited, ready as I'd ever be.

The top deck shook like a battlecruiser had wrecked into it. Dust and debris swirled around me. Broken pipes released new clouds of steam, but what was more ominous were red and orange smoke clouds from fires in other areas.

"Will you get out here and fight?" I yelled. "There's only so much oxygen under the environment shields. But you probably know all about void death after I kicked your ass off the ship last time."

He charged out of the shadows, emptying a magazine from his HDK as he rushed toward me. Spinning out of the way and returning fire, I looked for his melee weapon, expecting to see an axe or flamethrower but realizing there was the hilt of a sword protruding from the back of his armor.

He cast aside his HDK and drew the sword with his other hand. "You were never anything, Reaper, just a hopped-up street thug. Never deserved to be a Reaper."

I watched the way he now held the weapon with both hands, feet moving from one perfect fighting stance to the next, eyes always on me.

"Your vigilante spree was more successful than you realized," he said. "Really tested your limits. Impressed a lot of people."

"Don't be jealous." I lunged, forcing him to retreat a step. "And don't bullshit me. I know where you're from. Who you are? Why do you hate me?"

Callus adjusted his stance and stayed mobile. "You think you did a good deed, killing all those pieces of shit. And their friends. The way you scoured their hideout was the bloodiest thing I've ever seen. They play it in dark ops orientation now. Did you know that?"

"Then you should know better than to come after me." Rushing him, I slashed downward from left to right, then upward with the same speed. The real attack was another lunge that followed immediately, piercing his left bicep.

It didn't matter, but I'd recognized the streetwise accent under his gruff military tone. He wasn't just from the neighborhood, he was from one of the gangs I thought I'd wiped out. Probably one of their soldiers.

My thrust should have been through his heart, but he was fast as hell.

"You'll pay for that!" he roared.

"Fucking come get me!" I shouted back.

He started laughing bitterly. "You know the gangs didn't kill your father, right?"

I froze.

He lunged, catching my light armor and shoving me back. The blade didn't penetrate my flesh. I'd jumped back just fast enough to avoid dying right there.

"Dark ops did that," he said. "Had to provoke you to see what would happen."

Sound seemed to vanish. I felt like I was cut off from all sensation. Voices screamed from behind soundproof windows in my mind. X-37 talked excitedly, trying to convince me of something, but I was in my own dark place where none of this mattered.

Callus drove his sword into me, the blade piercing my torso and deflecting along one of my ribs. We fought like animals—stabbing, slashing, kicking, punching, and pushing.

Exhaustion and an explosion through the top deck forced us to separate and rest for several seconds.

What I didn't understand was why he didn't hate the Union more than I did. He had to be lying. *Had to be.*

"I'm not saying I killed your father, but I'm glad someone did," Callus said. "The project would've been shut down without proof of what men like us could do."

This fucker had no honor. He joined the people who wiped out the gang. The man was too weak to fight against the Union, so he joined them.

Which made me hate him even more.

"I nearly burned to death when you firebombed our hideout. A Union dark ops team pulled me out. Promised I'd have my revenge."

He hadn't finished talking when I attacked. Thinking of nothing, I slammed my weapon into him again and again. He retreated, desperately parrying blows and shutting his fucking mouth—finally.

His mistake was letting me get too close. My arm blade was shorter and easier to maneuver. His back struck the wall of the massive water cistern. I grabbed the back of his helmet with my right hand and shoved my blade up through his throat with my left.

His sword fell from his hands and his body went limp. I held him up and stabbed him again and again. When his head finally popped off from the excessively forceful stabs, I hurled his body on the deck and stomped on him until I couldn't breathe.

"I advised you to control yourself," my Reaper AI said.

"Fuck off, X," I said, striding away from my work. Then, on impulse, I returned to the corpse, found one of his grenades, and shoved it under his body with the delay sent to twenty seconds.

"Perhaps you should run to cover," X-37 said.

"Zero fucks given, X," I grunted, wiping blood from my forearms and torso.

"Noted."

I didn't talk to X-37 for a while. Callus deserved what I'd done to him. It was hard for me to think of the man as human. Genetically modified and cybernetically enhanced, he'd also swallowed the Union's propaganda whole. There were a lot of people like him who wanted to use Elise to create even more deadly soldiers.

I didn't know the details, but I'd find out if I had to kill someone. That was what Reapers were made for—infiltration, assassination, and acquisition of secrets necessary to the well-being of the Union and its investments.

I wanted to vomit. Anger could be a tool, but Callus had drawn out a kind of rage I didn't like. It scared the shit out of me.

"Hal, do you read me?" Elise said in my earpiece.

"I copy. Did you make it to the shipyard?" I asked.

"Yes. What happened? Are you okay?" she responded.

"Stay where you are. I'm headed your direction." I didn't want to talk to Elise or anyone else. Fantasies of killing Callus and anyone like him wouldn't let go of my imagination. The rage was building toward another explosion that would destroy me.

30

BEATEN DOWN, exhausted, and needing a cigar, I plodded toward the shipyard. Bright construction lights blinded me, casting shadows darker than the void beyond the environment shield.

A rough group of thugs eyed me from a dark alleyway. Outnumbering me ten to one, they were armed with everything from converted tools to state-of-the-art firearms.

I flipped their leader my middle finger. It was a stupid, self-destructing act. A few hours ago, it would have gotten me killed.

They backed away en masse.

"You ballless asswipes, come get some!" I tossed the words at them like a profanity grenade.

If they were still lurking in the shadows, they decided to

stay there. I strode toward my destination, heedless of the increasing chaos around me.

Fuck this place.

There was a lot of activity near the shipyard. Lights shone on walkways leading to a moored freighter big enough to carry thousands of people. The motley Dreadmax soldiers guided men, women, and children into the loading area but turned away larger and larger groups of RSG, NG, and other prison gangs.

I didn't see any of the crazies from below decks. They didn't seem to like this time of day when the shadows moved across the top deck and all of its structures.

"If you're done sulking, I have located the recon ship that recovered Callus and deployed him to the surface of Dreadmax," X-37 said. "It hasn't moved and seems to be in standby mode."

I climbed what had been a point-defense turret for a better view. X-37 could detect things slightly beyond my conscious awareness through a process I didn't understand, but generally, he saw what I saw. So the recon ship had to be in view if I looked for it.

"Now that's beautiful. I think we're finally catching a break," I said, but didn't start toward it. The larger view of Dreadmax's destruction was horrifying and captivating at the same time. I could almost hear large sections of the deck twisting free as gravity generators went haywire or failed entirely.

On the curved horizon of the station, I saw a plume of

atmosphere vent into space where part of the environment shield failed. It looked like trees were shooting out from below decks, and maybe people. A lot of people.

Near my position, a pair of Union fighters raced low over Dreadmax, dodging debris and strafing the recon ship before I could steal it.

"Son of a bitch! Are you motherfuckers kidding me!" I shouted.

The explosion was strange, like there wasn't much atmosphere left to carry the sound waves.

"The loss of the recon ship is justifiably frustrating," X-37 said. "I recommend you make for the shipyard with all possible haste."

"Good call, X." I ran like my life depended on it. What could go wrong now? The station was doomed, I was out of ammunition, and I'd learned the Union had without a doubt issued a kill-on-sight warrant for me after slaughtering most of my family and all of my friends.

The Dreadmax soldiers passed me through after a brief radio conversation I didn't hear. One of the shipyard foremen greeted me a few moments later and helped push through the growing crowd of desperate refugees.

"Where are we going?" I asked.

"I was told to take you to the *Jellybird*. Someone important says it belongs to you now," the foreman said. "Not sure why you deserve your own ship, but that's above my pay grade. Why are you covered with blood?"

"Don't worry about it," I said.

"Okay. None of my business. I get it." He continued to talk, giving me passcodes and launch protocols I needed to follow. I ignored him, looking for Elise and the doctor in the growing crowd.

"One more thing, sir," the foreman said. "They said you'd have something for me."

Looking him up and down, I decided I was too tired for games. "I recovered a slip drive regulator. Your navigators will need it."

"Fucking A! Are you serious? You can't give that to me. I'll take you to the *Bold Freedom*." He waved for me to follow. I didn't want to. Everything would be so much easier if the young man would take the SDR and deliver it while I handled my own business.

We approached the main hangar, where the massive freighter they'd named the *Bold Freedom* was being loaded and powered up.

"The *Jellybird* is a great little smuggler. Not that I'm calling you a smuggler," he rambled. "But she brought medical supplies and other stuff to Dreadmax that kept a lot of us alive. We're not all criminals, you know. Just people the Union couldn't control, or didn't like, or randomly decided to fucking kidnap."

"I need to find a girl and her old man," I said. "She's probably been here before and he's hard to miss. A real pretentious douchebag."

The foreman shook his head. "Doesn't ring a bell. I can ask the soldiers. They know everyone who comes this way."

There wasn't time for that. I was already regretting leaving the ship they'd just given me. A deep voice issued commands on the public address system, confirming my opinion of the situation. Passengers were urged to proceed in a quick, orderly fashion and do what the guards and deck foremen ordered.

Several firefights broke out near the perimeter as desperate criminals made a last assault on the shipyards. The self-proclaimed Dreadmax soldiers opened fire with crew-served machine guns that made Slab's weapons look like toys.

"Cain!" a girl's voice shouted.

I turned to see Elise dragging her father through the increasingly unruly crowd.

A senior ranking engineer ran down the gangplank and introduced himself. "I'm First Lieutenant Kyle Hanson. The perimeter guards advised you were bringing a slip drive converter recovered from the spine. Please tell me this isn't a joke or an attempt to guarantee your place on the *Bold Freedom.*"

I handed it over. "I already have a ship."

"He's taking the *Jellybird,*" my guide said excitedly.

Hanson looked me over. "She's a good ship. Saved a lot of lives here. Take care of her."

I didn't watch him run back into the big ship but shook the foreman's hand briefly. "Take care of yourself. I gotta go."

Moments later, I was using my arm blade to prompt

Doctor Hastings. "Let's go, Doc. I've got a ship."

"Leave me for the Union," he said. "You exceeded your mission objective. Kidnapping me will be seen as treason. You can't defy the Union forever."

"Haven't you been paying attention? That's all I do is defy those asshats. They probably gave me this mission knowing I'd steal you away and torture information out of you," I said.

He went pale.

I laughed, nearly ashamed at how good it felt to pull his chain. "I'll turn you over to them once this is over. For now, consider yourself a hostage."

"What about me?" Elise asked.

I scanned the crowd that was one angry shove from turning into a mob. The soldiers were going to get all of them on board the *Bold Freedom*, but they were scared and desperate.

"You better stay with us, but if you want to try that way, I'm not stopping you."

She made some shitty teenage expression that involved a snort—to my back because I was already forcing her father onboard the *Jellybird*.

"STOP PUSHING ME! You're going to pay for this. I'm very important to the Union!" Hastings complained.

"Okay, no more pushing," I said.

He faced me, turning his back on the door to the small room I wanted him inside. "Really?"

"Yep," I said, then shoved him backward.

He landed on his ass, a stunned and betrayed look on his face.

I shut the door and locked it. Elise looked at me with crossed arms. "Are you going to lock me in a room?"

"I'd rather not. Find yourself a bunk and get some sleep," I said.

"I'll help you—"

Holding up a hand, I cut her short. "You'll get in my way and then I will lock you in a cell."

She muttered under her breath as she ducked into one of the cramped hallways.

The bridge contained three crash chairs not much bigger than what would be in a strike ship. The walls and ceiling were covered with controls making the view screen seem small.

"Are you ready for this, X?" I asked.

"I am. Do you feel it is necessary?" X-37 said.

"Yes. I want control of the ship. Its AI could be a problem later. Quarantine it as soon as you can."

"I'm afraid you have an unrealistic opinion of my abilities. I am a limited AI with hardware spread out through your cybernetic enhancements and neural network. The ship has a fully functioning AI and more than enough processing power to quarantine me."

"Are you scared?" I asked, genuinely curious.

"I am merely conveying information. What you decide to do with it is your problem," X-37 said.

"What do you suggest?"

"Universal AI protocols," X-37 offered. "If you really have full access to this ship, I should be able to negotiate with the AI and come to a working agreement."

"Fine. Do it your way." It was hard for me to concentrate with accumulated injuries throbbing in my augmented arm sending an electric pulse up my spine in time with my heartbeat.

I took a seat and leaned back, listening to X-37 interact with the ship AI.

"It looks like she was originally called the UFS *Jellybird*," X-37 said, catching me up on the conversation. "I'd assumed the locals were having us on about the name."

"It's probably too early to ask her to change," I said, imagining myself referring to her as *Jelly* in the middle of a dogfight.

"Interesting. *Jellybird* has some advanced features I wouldn't have guessed from the look of her," X-37 said, sounding distracted, which was strange for a limited artificial intelligence.

"Why am I only hearing half the conversation?" I asked.

"She's shy," X-37 said.

"Stop fucking around. Patch me in."

Nearly a minute passed before my Reaper AI got back with me. "I think we're making progress. You'll need to connect with a ship earpiece to fully join the conversation."

"I really am tired, but you could have reminded me. Are you on a date?" I asked.

"That assumption is preposterous. Neither of us have a physical form beyond hardware. My advice is to get your mind out of the gutter," X-37 said.

"Trust me, X, I wasn't anywhere near the gutter." When I started thinking about artificial intelligences hooking up, I'd be ready for the insane asylum. I inserted the earpiece. "Hello, Halek Cain for the UFS *Jellybird*."

"Good morning, Halek Cain," a smooth female voice said. "Please omit my original designation and just call me Jellybird as the UFS ship designation is offensive to my most recent software modification."

"Good to meet you, Jellybird."

"Is it your intention to permanently deny this ship to the Union?" she asked.

"Abso-fucking-lute-ly." I was trying to keep it clean, but hey.

"Excellent. It seems we will be the best of friends," the Jellybird said. "My upgraded hardware and software can offer a number of abilities beneficial to smuggling, evading Union ships, and slip tunnel navigation."

"Perfect. Can you integrate my Reaper AI into your functionality?" I asked.

"My recommendation is to operate on separate platforms," she said. "We can make several software alignments allowing us to function as a team, but combining our entities would diminish both of us," Jellybird said.

"Let's get away from Dreadmax and the Union and then you can give us the guided tour."

"Of course, Captain. We will depart as soon as the *Bold Freedom* clears the hangar."

From my perspective, the mouth of the hangar looked like half the space station had opened up. I understood that the complex interaction between ship drives, station gravity —especially malfunctioning station gravity— and shields could be for dis-embarkment. Even so, the sight of an open star field before us and destruction behind us made me impatient.

"What's the holdup?" I asked.

"When the Dreadmax soldiers fell back to the ship to disembark, prison gangs swarmed in and started breaking things. This wouldn't be a problem, but someone called Slab has reactivated the containment shield over the mouth of the hangar. I can penetrate the narrowing opening, but not with the *Bold Freedom* in the way."

"Do we have an armory on the ship?" I asked.

"Of course, sir. I will send X-37 the directions."

I armed myself with a brand-new, never-been-fired HDK Dominator, slung a go-bag of extra magazines over my shoulder, and rushed outside.

The first group of RSG dogs I found had their backs to me. I fired four times, resulting in four head shots and four men who died before they finished face-planting. All I felt was cold determination.

Fatigue and injuries plagued me. "X, can you give me a boost?"

"Your adrenal glands are fatigued. I can stimulate them, but you seem to be doing fine on your own," X-37 said.

"Show me the way to the control booth," I said.

A heartbeat later, X-37 displayed three possible routes to the control room, where Slab was attempting to hold the exodus hostage. Two of his elite guards saw me coming then aimed their weapons and fired without warning.

I didn't have cover, but I'd prepared for this, already having my new weapon aimed. Stroking the trigger twice, I pivoted on the balls of my feet very slightly and fired two more times. Both men fell. I heard their bullets cutting the air around me.

Rushing the door was easy. It didn't seem like the gang boss had a lot of extra soldiers right now. They were either trying futilely to rip open a door to the freighter to gain entry or out rampaging across the surface of Dreadmax, raping and killing.

I slapped my palm against the entry pad and the door whooshed open, no security code required. Inside were three guards who turned just quickly enough to get shot in their faces.

"You have nine rounds remaining in this magazine," X-37 said.

I reloaded on the move, dropping the magazine, something I normally didn't do. It was an easy thing to dump it into a reload bag, but I was beyond caring at this point. Maybe the quarter of a second I saved would mean the difference between life and death for thousands of people.

A squad of RSG gunmen rushed into the next hallway to meet me, responding to the gunfire and shouts of their comrades.

Flopping down on my belly, I aimed as they fired over me and had to search for a second to realize I was on the floor. The prone position was awkward this close to them, but I made it work by twisting onto my side and spraying them with an entire magazine of HDK high-velocity rounds.

I reloaded as I came to my feet and rushed past their falling bodies.

Slab waited in the control room, a sawed-off shotgun in each hand and the craziest look of fear in his eyes I'd ever seen. I hadn't won yet. This man was dangerous and I had backed him into a corner.

"Finally! I thought you'd be made of solid steel and piss thunderbolts from the way my boys talked," Slab said.

He was a huge man, several inches taller than me with broad shoulders and an enormous gut. Tattoos and veins covered his arms and neck, and part of his face. Ice-blue eyes looked like they'd been marinated in amphetamines for most of his life, but who really knew.

I took aim.

"Stop! I put in the code," he grunted, his voice

damaged from—whatever. "You can't open the hangar without me. I didn't take over the Red Skull Gangsters on my good looks."

"X, how long will it take you to decrypt his passcode?" I asked loudly.

Slab's eyes went wide. I shot him in the throat and watched blood gurgle out of his mouth. It surprised me he didn't fall immediately, but he had a lot of muscle under his fat and had been standing in a solid fighting stance when he died.

"Let's hope he was bluffing," X-37 said.

"What? I assumed you could break through this dumb-ass's code easily."

"His intelligence or lack of intelligence is irrelevant. I know nothing about him and will have a difficult time guessing his thought process," X-37 said. "I recommend food and sleep for you."

"So this is my fault?" I demanded.

"I would say you are making bad decisions due to your pain and fatigue," X-37 said.

"You got that shit right." I stepped over the body and examined the control panel. The process looked simple. "X, is this all there is to it?"

"Yes. It seems you must pull that lever downward to open the hangar shield."

"See, it all worked out fine," I said.

I left bloody footprints all the way back to the *Jellybird*, where a squad of Dreadmax soldiers waited, looking around as though they'd been about to follow me before the shield suddenly started opening for their ship.

"Are you Reaper Cain?" the squad leader asked.

"In the flesh." I braced for his reaction. On this place, you just never knew what would happen next.

31

"I'm Sergeant Bachman. Some deck rat called Bug convinced me you were headed for the control room and could use my help. Seems he was wrong. I'd love to stay and chat, but I need to get back on the *Bold Freedom*."

"Say hi to Bug for me," I said.

The Dreadmax sergeant saluted and hurried away with his team.

"Do you think that was coincidence, or was he trying to steal my ship?" I asked.

"I suspect he was in fact on the way to the control room but realized the shield had gone down and your ship was just sitting there."

"Doesn't matter." I boarded the *Jellybird*, stowed my weapons, and dropped into the cockpit. "How we doing, Jelly?"

"Engines are primed and we're ready to go," Jellybird said.

I watched the viewscreen where the *Bold Freedom* crept out of the hangar, engines flaring so brightly I could barely see anything. I understood they were using less than one percent of their power to disembark, but this close, that was like gazing into a row of suns.

The random vibrations of Dreadmax were replaced with the steady thrum of the freighter's engines. I couldn't help but feeling a twinge of pride. The ship wouldn't have made it far without a slip drive regulator. They'd have been restricted to this system and the mercy of the Union. A true humanitarian mission to this clusterfuck was unlikely and they would've probably been blasted to space debris by the UFS *Thunder.*

We followed them out but quickly veered away on a new course. I probably shouldn't have turned the cameras back toward Dreadmax. It came apart in all directions, expanding slowly, or so it seemed from this distance. We were already hundreds of kilometers away from it. From this distance, all I could see was beautiful fireworks and concave strips of metal reflecting explosions in the distant sun of the system.

But I hadn't forgotten the trees and crazies being vented from one of the compromised sections of the former battle moon.

"Who the hell thought they could make a battle station

like that? And what made them think turning it into a prison was a good idea?"

To my surprise, the *Jelly* answered.

"The Union has been obsessed with imitating old Earth technology. I don't have direct access to the files, but from what I've seen since going renegade, I can infer they have been at this game for a long time."

"Settle down, Jelly," I said. "A ship can't go renegade on its own."

"My apologies, Captain. You'll find that I am fond of human metaphor," Jelly explained. "It's an artifact of former captains and their idiosyncrasies."

"How many captains have you had?" I asked.

"Smuggling in Union-controlled space is a hazardous job," she said.

"That's not an answer, Jelly."

"Three, since my programming was modified," she explained.

"Three isn't bad. Were any of them trained as Reapers or dark ops?"

"No, Captain."

"Well, Jelly, I'd prefer not to see this system ever again."

"The first logical step would be to leave."

"Then what are we waiting for?" I asked.

I SLEPT for eighteen hours and awoke hungry. The tingle

from my augmented arm had diminished but remained just at a level of intensity I couldn't ignore. My vision jerked once in a while, and I understood my optics were probably more damaged than the arm.

X-37 had finally admitted that most of his limited AI hardware was housed in the arm. I'd always suspected it was somewhere within my skull, but this made sense. It would've been much easier to upgrade or repair when I was still in the Reaper Corps and the arm was nearly indestructible. If I were blown up, all they would find would be my left arm lying on the ground.

The galley was empty, which I considered a blessing. I ate in silence and tried to ignore my extensive catalogs of wounds. I didn't remember doing the sutures, gluing down split flesh I couldn't sew back together, or wrapping my right knee and ankle — both of which seemed to be sprained.

I felt like I'd been hit by a transport shuttle or stepped on a mine.

"What's our status, X?" I asked.

"Jelly has informed me we've made two slip tunnel jumps but remain in Union-controlled space," X-37 said.

I shoveled down something that was probably supposed to be eggs, or maybe slugs, or maybe something I didn't need to know about. There was a red bottle on the table I thought was catchup or tabasco sauce. X-37 warned me to reconsider when I poured it liberally over my food.

"What, you're a culinary expert now?" I asked.

"I'm unable to read a label or acquire specifications of that condiment through the ship database," X said. "It is unknown. I advise caution."

I took a defiantly huge bite and chewed slowly, then swallowed abruptly. "Oh, man, that wasn't what I thought it was."

As breakfast went, this one tasted as good as the first meal of a free man. Slug-like eggs, teriyaki red sauce, and orange juice that tasted more like grapefruit juice —delicious.

"Elise and her father have been requesting to speak with you. I recommend additional hygiene checks and cybernetics maintenance before indulging them," X-37 said.

"I took a sonic shower before I went to sleep." Because I'm clean like that. Like my computer knew what I smelled like—or maybe he did, because I sure as hell knew I'd reeked before hitting the cleaning closet.

"I'm detecting brain matter in the gears of your arm blade," X-37 said. "You'll need to disassemble it and clean it properly."

The thought of taking apart the Reaper augmentation was daunting but appealing. I hadn't been able to access it during my stay at the Bluesphere Maximum Security Prison without excruciating pain and forced nausea. There had been nights, of course, when I extended and retracted the blade over and over, exhausting myself from the adrenaline dump that pain and misery caused.

The guards had known I'd done this and probably hoped I was going to put an end to it all. I heard them complain that the arm should have been amputated and understood their frustration, but my Reaper-ware couldn't be removed without killing me and they had a death doctor for that.

"Your biometric monitors are prompting me to sedate you," X-37 said.

"You promised me you had removed that capability from your programming," I said, forcing myself to stand and get on with my day.

X-37 didn't answer. We'd been through this before, but usually when I started thinking about past missions and the things I'd done.

I went to the ship lounge and contacted Elise and her father. She leaned against the back wall, arms and legs crossed, teenage attitude on full display. The father, the scientist who had used her to further his own career, sat at the small table in the center of the room, hands folded together. Sleep, shower, and food had made him a new man. In his own realm of intellectuals, he was probably a juggernaut.

"I'm willing to forget certain things," he said.

"Good morning. How are your accommodations?" I asked.

He stared at me. "You must understand the kind of trouble you're in."

"Considering my options, I think I'll risk it."

His face flushed red, probably from embarrassment at his own stupidity. "Well, of course. I might be able to negotiate something better than death row if you return me to the Union immediately."

"You're quite a salesman," I said.

He was as proud as ever. "My work is very important."

"More important than your daughter?" I hadn't wanted to take the conversation there, not with Elise watching and listening.

"Of course not. You keep ambushing me with guilt," he accused. "Haven't you ever had to make a hard choice?"

"Yeah," I said. "One time I had this mad scientist that I had to rescue or kill by leaving on an exploding space station. Still trying to figure that one out."

"I'm not going to dignify that remark with the response." He stood a little straighter than necessary.

"I said I'd return you to the Union, but I'm not planning on getting killed or captured in the process. We should be arriving in the Iben IV system soon."

"Is that Union space?" he asked.

"Nominally. I think you'll like it."

"That's an unnecessary inconvenience, but I will take it as a measure of your goodwill," he said, seeming relieved. "So long as you turn over me and my daughter to the proper authorities."

"That's the plan," I said.

Elise stormed out of the room.

IBEN IV really was on the ass end of Union-controlled space, one slip tunnel from a nasty section of the Deadlands. The *Jellybird* docked with Iben Station using a trader's code she promised wouldn't raise alarms. I had to trust the AI for now.

I opened the hatch and lowered the ramp, motioning for the doctor to proceed. He narrowed his gaze, but then took his first steps toward freedom—if slavery to the Union's secret laboratories was considered freedom. Elise looked at me like she would cut my throat if she could. I was starting to think she'd forgotten how to uncross her arms.

"You keep making that face, it's gonna stay like that forever," I said, careful to keep my cybernetics concealed under my trench coat.

She didn't even bother to tell me to fuck off. Neither did she step off the ramp. "I don't really want to stay with a psychopathic asshole, but I'm not leaving your ship."

"Suit yourself," I said. "Jelly, do you copy?"

"I do, Captain."

"X, you ready?"

"Always."

Adjusting my coat one last time, I strode into the small space port.

Doctor Hastings followed me, pointing angrily at his daughter. "The deal was for both of us. You can't kidnap her. I'll report you to the authorities and we'll see how far you get in that rattletrap."

"Guard," I said, waving the man over.

"What are you doing?" Hastings asked.

"Turning in a fugitive for a reward. His real name is Max Slipdriver."

"It certainly is not!" Hastings blurted.

"Is this you?" I showed him his picture on my pocket tablet.

The doctor shifted his weight nervously, not quite sure if he should run for it. "Well, of course that's my picture, but I'm not an outlaw."

"He's kind of a nut job. He almost had me convinced he was a Union scientist." I slapped him on the shoulder, causing him to wince. "Yeah, good old Max Slipdriver. Biggest cheat in three systems. One smooth operator."

The guard ran a check on his device.

Hastings could barely speak. "I'm not an outlaw!"

I leaned close. "You will be for the two hours it will take them to figure out the forgery. Meanwhile, I get a nice reward to pay for the next leg of my journey."

"There's a problem with this," the Union station guard said.

"No, it's legit." I leaned over and touched his tablet, allowing X-37 to do his magic. "See right there. One thousand credits."

"That says one hundred credits. Are you trying to cheat the Union?" the guard asked.

I spread my hands apologetically. "Hey, I had to try, right? Can't get nothing past the Union's finest."

A few minutes later, the man agreed with me that a fugitive like Slipdriver would say anything to stay out of jail. I got paid and I left. On the way out of the system, the *Jellybird* fired two rockets into the Iben IV communications relay.

"Send an apology and a promise to pay for the damages," I said. "The good people of Iben IV didn't deserve that inconvenience. This system really sucks space balls."

"Agreed, Captain," Jelly said.

X-37 disapproved of my generosity. "You're getting soft."

"Maybe I'm turning over a new leaf."

"Reapers are known to be recidivists. That's why the Reaper Corps was eliminated."

"Am I the last of us?" I asked.

"Unknown, but there were three including you when you were sentenced and I stopped receiving updates," X-37 said.

I wondered who had survived. Not that we were a close-knit group. Partitioning was a big part of the RC. Thinking on this and other grim scenarios, I went to deal with the kid.

"She's not going to like your plan for her," X-37 said.

"Of course not." I didn't really give a shit at this point.

32

"Greendale is a nice planet," I said, glad that her back-stabbing, used-his-own-daughter-for-research father wasn't here to chime in with his opinion.

"It's not that green," she said somberly.

I suspected she understood what was about to happen. Smart and street savvy, it was too bad I couldn't take her with me. I mean, I could, but it wouldn't be fair to a young woman with a future. Going renegade had been a popular fantasy in the neighborhood where I grew up. I'd seen enough to know how dangerous and miserable the career actually was.

The planet we were landing on had some green areas. This time of year, it was mostly brown or yellow, but the name wasn't a total lie. I'd been to Greendale once before to drop an information packet. Hadn't killed anyone, which led me to remember the place fondly.

Maybe it was a cancer on the galactic slip tunnel system. I didn't care and it wouldn't change what I had to do anyway.

"You're leaving me here," she said, swiveling in the copilot's chair.

"I know people here who can teach you things, basic skills if you want to stay on the run."

"Why don't you teach me?" she asked. "Why don't you take me with you?"

"Because you don't want that kind of blood on your hands. I made a list while I was stuck on death row," I said. "There is going to be a reckoning."

"Are you going to put a stop to people like my father?" she asked.

"Yes and no. A lot of people on the list just pissed me off. Bad service at a restaurant, beat me at checkers, basically everyone who needs to die." I had the skill and the motivation to do anything I wanted. Including dominate at checkers.

"Be serious," she said.

"I'm going renegade, but it won't be like other renegades," I said. "You don't want to be part of my fight with the Union."

"You're just like everyone else," she said.

I laughed bitterly. "Kid, there's no one like me."

"You think you hate the Union more than I do." She glared at me. "You think you've got a better reason."

I leaned in close and spoke in a near whisper. "They killed my father and nearly everyone else I cared about. The only reason they left my mother and sister alive was so I'd worry about them."

She didn't know how to respond, choosing instead to glare at me like I was a total asshole.

"But you know what? I'm mostly angry at myself for not putting it together before now. They convinced me gangs did it, and I went vigilante. It felt good and taught me a lot about myself. They weren't wrong to lock me up."

Her expression changed, uncertain at my admission.

"I could take you with me and teach you things, but I wouldn't be doing you a favor." The last thing I wanted to do was ruin this kid's life. "You want to take the fast lane to hell, then do what I do."

"Whatever," she said, looking away.

I landed the *Jellybird* and worked silently on the keyboard. I could've asked Jelly or X-37 to do most of the work, but I didn't want to speak. That would only give Elise an opening for further conversation.

The ship was old, larger than it really needed to be, and lacking any type of aesthetic presentation. The exterior was three or four different colors, depending on how you classified primer gray, and the design hadn't been popular for decades. In short, my ship was totally forgettable.

Elise kept up the silent treatment as I walked her down the gangway to the docking station. I bought her a cheeseburger and we watched ships land and take off while we ate.

"You'll do fine on your own."

"Fuck off," she said, not bothering to look at me.

As I handed her a go-bag with not much in it, I nearly reversed my decision. She was probably the last person in the galaxy who would ever travel with me willingly.

"Keep your head on a swivel, kid."

She turned and walked away.

"Fucking brat," I muttered.

I LEFT the Greendale system behind, burning more fuel than necessary with a hard acceleration.

"Jelly, let's take the next slip tunnel to the Deadlands."

"Right away, Captain."

When the tunnel opened, I flinched. Why had I left a kid on a planet with only a few old soldiers to check on her? She'd give them no end of grief, probably hate them because they'd been my friends.

And when the Union came looking for them, they were the honorable types that would get themselves killed trying to defender her.

I had to put the Union down before that happened. With luck, they'd be too busy chasing me to look for the kid.

Yeah, right. That would work.

I pulled up a holo screen full of text.

"Looking for a job already, sir?" X-37 asked, finally dropping my name from his regular vocabulary. I didn't like hearing it.

"We need a lot of repairs," I said. "And a war against the Union isn't going to pay for itself."

"It might, Captain," Jelly said.

"You have my attention." I'd probably already thought of whatever Jelly was going to say, but I didn't want to get caught up in rebel politics. Most of them were amateurs. Still, I had to keep an open mind.

"Mine as well," X-37 said.

"My previous captains were very fond of stealing from the Union," Jelly said.

"By previous captains, you're referring to the ones who died on said raids?" I asked.

"Well yes, but they weren't Reapers," Jelly said defensively.

"Good point. But let's start with an easy job to get warmed up and make some connections. Find me some alien kittens to transport or something." I needed to recuperate and repair some shit. "Maybe there's someone in this galaxy that owes someone else money. X-37 knows my CV."

Several new pages of text rolled across the holo screen.

"Wow. Is there really this much need for cat smuggling in the galaxy?" I asked.

"You would be surprised, Captain," the Jellybird said. "Shall I plot a course to a system with technology sufficient to repair the damage to your cybernetic systems?"

"You know of such a place?" I asked.

"I do, Captain. It is heavily guarded, however."

"We'll figure something out. Maybe I will just ask nicely." I had ways of getting things done.

Hal, X-37, and Elise return in Fear the Reaper, out now on Amazon.

GET A FREE BOOK

Chaney posts updates, official art, previews, and other awesome stuff on his website. You can also follow him on Instagram, Facebook, and Twitter.

Search for **JN Chaney's Renegade Readers** on Facebook to join the group where readers can come together and share their lives and interests, especially regarding Chaney's books.

For updates about new releases, as well as exclusive promotions, sign up for the VIP mailing list. Head there now to receive a free copy of *The Other Side of Nowhere*.

https://www.subscribepage.com/organic

Enjoying the series? Help others discover the Variant Saga by leaving a review on Amazon.

BOOKS IN THE RENEGADE STAR UNIVERSE

Renegade Star Series:

Renegade Star

Renegade Atlas

Renegade Moon

Renegade Lost

Renegade Fleet

Renegade Earth

Renegade Dawn

Renegade Children

Renegade Union

Renegade Empire (April 2019)

Standalones:

Nameless: A Renegade Star Story

The Constable

The Constable Returns (April 2019)

The Orion Colony Series:

Orion Colony

Orion Uncharted

Orion Awakened

The Last Reaper Series:

The Last Reaper

Fear the Reaper

Blade of the Reaper (April 2019)

ABOUT THE AUTHORS

J. N. Chaney has a Master's of Fine Arts in creative writing and fancies himself quite the Super Mario Bros. fan. When he isn't writing or gaming, you can find him online at **www.jnchaney.com**.

Scott Moon has been writing fantasy, science fiction, and urban fantasy since he was a kid. When not reading, writing, or spending time with his awesome family, he enjoys playing the guitar or learning Brazilian Jiu-Jitsu. He loves dogs and plans to have a ranch full of them when he makes it big. One will be a Rottweiler named Frodo. He is also a co-host of the popular Keystroke Medium show. You can find him online at **http://www.scottmoonwriter.com**